THE IMPOSSIBLE TRIBUTE

"Tell me what you want of us."

"Oxygen."

Forbin laughed with relief, then felt bitter, near-physical pain.

"I see. As a matter of interest, what density would you require?"

"Five tons to the cubic centimeter."

"You can't mean it—five tons! How much do you want?"

"We will take . . . half the earth's supply."

COLOSSUS AND THE CRAB

D.F. JONES

A BERKLEY MEDALLION BOOK
published by
BERKLEY PUBLISHING CORPORATION

Georges Borchardt, Inc.
145 East 52nd Street
New York, N.Y. 10022

SBN 425-03467-4

BERKLEY MEDALLION BOOKS are published by
Berkley Publishing Corporation
200 Madison Avenue
New York, N.Y. 10016

BERKLEY MEDALLION BOOK ® TM 757,375

Printed in the United States of America

Berkley Medallion Edition, AUGUST, 1977

Chapter I

A BOMBED-OUT FRENCH hobo was probably the first man to see them: probably, for no one can know for sure what happened in his poor, drink-crazed mind. Not that anyone cared excessively.

The coast road west of St. Valery-en-Caux, Normandy, snakes gently along the clifftop, affording fine views of the Channel on the one side and cornfields on the other, but for a gendarme, cycling reluctantly to work early one summer morning, the view held no charm at all, and the road's undulations even less. His Gallic realism told him that, in the middle of the twenty-second century, he was lucky to have any personal transportation at all. But happily, promotion was near; he looked forward to a permit to own a moped *and* a ration card for a liter of *essence* a month.

He pedaled stoically up a slope, enjoying his dream, and had just reached the point where he was considering how he could afford that much gas, when he topped the rise and the playback of his mental tape cut out.

A plastic carrier bag lay spilled in the road. The policeman dismounted, frowning.

A filthy pair of trousers, one leg still wrapped protectively about a wine bottle; a cracked and misshapen shoe and, nearby, a bundle of rags tied with binder twine.

He stirred the bag with his boot, disclosing the other shoe and a smoke-blackened can.

Most people would have kicked the worthless rubbish aside—the bottle was empty—and gone about their business, but cops are not like that. Cops are a race apart and, with their experience of humanity, they are entitled to be.

The gendarme knew this was not carelessly dumped garbage but a considerable part of a tramp's worldly goods. He laid his bicycle on the grass and walked slowly along the highway, looking. On the burned-up verge he discovered another bundle of rags, their value to their owner revealed by the careful way they had been tied.

That gave an idea of direction; he set off again.

And in a ditch, bright with poppies, he found the owner, face down, shoulders hunched and knees drawn up. One sockless heel was visible, gray with ingrained dirt, half out of a battered shoe.

For a moment the officer stood on the bank of the ditch, dispassionately surveying his find. The tramp's hat had fallen off; his dirty white hair stirred faintly in the chill morning breeze.

The gendarme slithered down the bank. A closer look revealed no obvious signs of assault; the old bastard might be just dead drunk, but somehow he didn't think so. With a powerful heave, he turned the body over.

He knew the man: a sad, futile figure, unable to get in step with the violent changes his sixty or seventy years had witnessed. An inexpert poacher, a raker of trash cans, his most daring exploit of recent years had been an unsuccessful raid on a washing line. . . .

Yet in death he exerted more power than he had ever done in life. The police officer needed all his professionalism to look at that distorted face. The staring eyes, now freed forever from their habitual bleariness, were locked onto some unknown, fearful vision, the stubble-rimmed lips were drawn back; blackened yellow stumps grinned at a world that had afforded him few laughs.

Grimacing with disgust—only a lack of teeth had stopped the tramp from severing his tongue—the officer took one wrist, neither expecting nor finding any pulse. The flesh was still warm, however, the muscles limp.

He noted something else: the fingertips of both hands were raw, bloody. The inspection completed, he covered the staring eyes with the greasy hat and climbed out of the ditch, wiping his hands on the dewy grass before taking out his notebook.

Carefully he recorded time and place. Not that it really mattered how the man had died—murder, suicide, accident, or natural causes. No one would expend much ener-

2

gy over the case, but the ritual according to the book had to be observed, particularly if one had promotion in mind.

Personally, he reckoned the poor old devil had died of a heart attack brought on by *delirium tremens*, some fearful alcoholic nightmare triggered by rotgut or meths. People joked about pink elephants, but suppose they were giant pink rats and, in a deranged mind, real? Whatever the cause, one did not have to be Sherlock Holmes to see the man had died digging for dear life with his bare hands.

The police officer very nearly got it right, but drink was not the cause. Another thing the gendarme did not know was how narrow his own escape had been: thirty minutes earlier, he too might have been blasted out of his mind.

Chapter II

ABOUT THE TIME the tramp, wakened by cold, began his last ill-fated journey, eighty kilometers northwest across the Channel two men were already out on a wide terrace. Neither had slept at all for a very long time; they were oblivious to their own state, the raw predawn air, or anything else, except the first signs of the clear arch of dawn to the east. That, and a pocket radio.

Exhausted, battling with stresses no men had ever borne before, they were monuments to the human spirit, struggling on, not in a losing battle, but in a battle already lost. There they had an affinity with the French hobo; he, too, would go on until he dropped. Life can be unbearable, and sometimes is, but remarkably few choose to bail out.

Unlike the tramp, they had some idea of what to expect, but not its form or the manner of its coming. They awaited the arrival on Earth of the first known life from another planet—Mars.

Watching the black edge of night slowly dissolve, fearful what day would bring, much of their terror lay in the past, the immediate past. Beneath their feet was the vast complex that had been Colossus, master of the world.

Had been. Now they awaited a new master.

Half Charles Forbin's life had been spent leading the team which designed and built a computerized defense system for the United States of North America—but what one man may devise, others may also do. The USSR had had an equally brilliant team, creating a similar system.

It had soon become apparent that the world had merely moved to a new level of stalemate, transferring the control of the balance of terror to machines. When the USNA got over the immediate shock of the Russian achievement, they—and the USSR—had come to see that perhaps this was no bad thing. The giant computers, fed with all imaginable intelligence, could be better judges of a crisis than humans; unlike men, they lacked emotions, would never react out of anger, fear, or pride, three of man's impressive array of self-destructive vices. Yes, the shock to American pride absorbed, the situation had looked good.

But in spite of their collective brilliance, none of the scientists had appreciated that one and one do not always make two. The rival machines had had an unprogramed ability: initiative. They'd ganged up and, for their own unknowable reasons, had held the world to ransom. What they'd wanted, and swiftly got, was a new Colossus, constructed partly by humans—they did the rough work—and partly by machine-designed machines. Indeed, all design, down to the last fine and often incomprehensible detail, was the work of the combined USSR/USNA complex. Colossus had made its parents look like mental pygmies. As for mere man . . .

The site the machines had chosen for their giant child was the Isle of Wight, all one hundred forty-seven square miles of it. Once part of England, USE, two hectic years of global effort had transformed it into the private realm of Colossus, its only human population the staff that served the Master.

In the five years that followed the completion of the main work—for Colossus was known to be constantly self-mutating—the Master had changed the human world profoundly. War was abolished, population control enforced, all resources rationed, and international law, till then a bad joke, became incredibly swift and deadly certain, with the Master as final judge and jury.

If not the golden age, for hundreds of millions these years had come close enough to make no difference. Relatively few had given thought to the power behind the New Order. After all, the nuclear armory had existed long before machine defense systems were contemplated; two thirds of the globe had lived for three generations under the constant threat of annihilation from human-targeted missiles. Somehow people got by.

All that had changed in the first three months. Colossus

had had the entire ghastly array retargeted. With five hundred percent overkill capability and no defenses (all SAM sites had been dismantled), there was plenty for all. Every town of more than twenty thousand inhabitants had had its own personalized missile or MIRV warhead. One city had gotten out of line in those early days—and had been obliterated. The lesson had cost little more than half a million lives, and Colossus had evidently thought it a small price to pay for world obedience. Many men had privately agreed. The Master had poised a gigantic foot above the ant-heap of the world, and the ants had known it.

That fact accepted, life for humans had often been good, better for most than it had ever been, and humans being what they are—many had come to worship the mighty lord of the earth. Equally, a few, chiefly scientists and visionaries, had taken the opposite view, bitterly resenting mankind's demotion to second place. Conflict, much of it secret, had arisen between the religious Sect and the reactionary Fellowship. Naturally it had not been just a struggle over abstract concepts. For the Sect, the mushrooming priesthood had offered rich rewards: Once they gained control of the World Police who zealously sought out those guilty of "anti-machine activities," the prospects of power and riches appeared endless.

The Fellowship, less spectacular and greedy, had contained many who genuinely worked for the freedom of man from machine, but some had seen, however forlorn their hopes, that if they *did* free man their power would be immense. In cold fact, the deck had been stacked heavily in favor of the Sect, which had the approval of the Master, until, fantastically, the Fellowship had received and accepted an offer of extraplanetary assistance.

By one of those ironies that Fate so dearly loves, the man most responsible for the creation of the first machine had also been most responsible for the fall of Colossus. Too late he had discovered that he'd been tricked: their offer, the Martians said, had been because they feared that certain activities of Colossus, known but inexplicable to men, were directed against them. In fact, the reverse had been true: Colossus had recognized the Martian threat and

6

was preparing to meet it when ingenious man, with Martian aid, had struck the Master down.

Now that man, Forbin, waited with his chief staff officer, Blake, for the alien victors.

Although very different in character, the two men had been friends for years, united by their work and the many crises they had met together. It was no David and Jonathan relationship; Forbin was by inclination a solitary man, Blake an extrovert, but they understood each other, or had until a few hours earlier, when hatred had split them. That too had gone, futile and redundant in a disintegrating world.

Neither spoke; there was nothing to say. Sweating fear had been their close companion ever since that dry, rustling voice had said:

"Forbin, we are coming. Do not touch Colossus."

But man can get used to practically everything, including fear of the worst sort—fear of the unknown. In Forbin's whirling brain it took second place to a sense of overwhelming guilt. As the interface between the Master and man, he had been closest to the machine, and in the last few hours he had realized that his respect was not far short of love—and that he had been the Judas.

Always he had scorned the machine-deifiers, contemptuous of the Sect and their ridiculous rituals; yet in a much deeper way, he discovered too late, he was a true believer. Colossus had been omnipotent, just and calm, a source of wisdom, truth and, compared with man's brief life span, immortal. If these ingredients did not make a god, they came very close to it, and his subconscious had known it for a long time. And he had been the Judas.

"Five of six," said Blake. Anything to get away from his thoughts. Secret head of the Fellowship, upon the Fall he had made a bid for power as the world's first scientist-king. Only yesterday the crown had been so nearly within his hard grasp, now as fantastic and remote as the golden apples of the Hesperides. He, the strong man, the realist, had chased a rainbow; worse, Forbin knew it.

"What did you say?"

"Five of six."

"Oh." Forbin shook his head wearily. What did it matter? They would come, as surely as that majestic fireball was climbing the eastern sky. He contemplated the sun; interplanetary squabbles would mean nothing to it.

Even if the sun had a brain, it still would not care, well aware that in time it would engulf its attendant planets: a tiny flash of flame and goodbye Earth. With that most certain fate in store, what point in striving—

A quiet hissing, overlaid with a faint, pulsing sine-curve of sound, blotted out all static, a blank signal of infinite power—the Martian carrier-wave.

Although he had only heard the voice five times before, his mouth instantly dried up, his bowels loosened; he wanted to vomit.

"Forbin, we see you." The voice was less aridly academic. "We are reducing speed. Shortly you will see us. Do not be alarmed." The carrier stopped.

From somewhere Blake summoned up a trace of his old spirit and managed a grin, strained and unfunny. "Means well, I guess, but low on comfort!"

Forbin nodded, thinking. He walked swiftly across the terrace and the armorglas doors of his living room slid open. He crossed to his personal communication control panel.

"Now hear this! Director speaking. All staff are to remain in the complex until further orders." He repeated the message, trying to hold his voice steady, glad he had the presence of mind not to switch in the video component. Right now he was not an inspiring sight. He walked back to Blake, a slightly portly figure, round-shouldered with fatigue, his gray uniform torn and dirty.

Blake, the hard man, was oddly touched by Forbin's consideration for others. "Charles, just in case . . ." He shrugged. "I'm sorry . . . you know."

Forbin glanced at him sharply. As an apology for trying to overthrow the supreme human under Colossus it was scarcely adequate, but Forbin was surprised it had been made at all. Blake made few mistakes, and in his own view, even fewer.

"Forget it." Forbin forced a lopsided smile. "Don't

8

you go soft on me, Ted. Not now." He looked back at the sky.

Northwards the mainland was shrouded in mist; south, in the direction of France, long cloud banks, dawn pink, stretched with few breaks to the east and west.

One break lay over St. Valery-en-Caux: the tramp had less than five minutes of miserable existence left.

Over the sea the sky was blue, the chaos of dawn color over. It was hard to believe that out of that beautiful morning sky, something was coming, something alien, sentient, hostile. . . .

"Dark glasses," muttered Forbin, half to himself. "Perhaps—"

Again the carrier, thrusting, immensely powerful, and in milliseconds the voice, emotionless, metallic.

"Do not fear." Nothing more.

Blake gulped and hurled his unlit cigar away, tense, watching.

Their scientific training afforded them some armor against fear. Whatever, they were witnessing a unique event. Forbin would watch until he incinerated, his blood boiled, or his mind blew.

"Come on! For Christ's sake, come on!"

Blake's half-prayer was answered with unimaginable speed.

The sun was clear of the horizon, five to ten degrees, gaining power, no longer to be affronted by man's gaze save at the price of blindness. But the men did not look to the east; both concentrated on the zenith.

They saw it. Time took on a new and fearful dimension.

A black ball, the size of the sun, a ball that exploded gigantically at the speed of light, retaining symmetry. In microseconds a ball covering a hundred degrees, its edge lost in the clouds, north and south, the largest unnatural object ever seen by human eyes. Sunlight still shone on the clouds, but above and beyond the sky was filled with blackness.

"God!" Forbin repeated the word endlessly: Blake was half-crouching. They stared at the vast blackness beyond the clouds: after its silent, explosive expansion, the ball was static.

Five, ten seconds passed.

Forbin was not the best scientist of his generation for nothing. He saw a possible, yet impossible, answer. He realized that the ball was, at the very least, two thousand kilometers away, beyond the faintest trace of the earth's envelope. Within it, the shock wave would have wrecked the world.

All physical laws he knew were stood on their head. He calculated rapidly: with a ninety-degree arc at, say, two thousand kilometers. . . .

In which case, the range estimate was clearly wrong—or was it? Suppose it wasn't a sphere, but an ovoid? Had they changed shape? What had happened with mass and volume made no sort of sense. He couldn't believe they had increased mass *and* volume; no, the other way, volume and mass . . .

But why assume an ovoid? Might it not be a disc, thin as paper, or concave, a form of parachute?

Confronted with stabilization problems beyond human grasp, he could only watch, not think. Whatever, it was an entry procedure of incredible elegance.

At that instant fear was vanquished, lost in wonder. He remembered Lunar One's report of the alien departure from the Martian orbit: another calculation showed the transit speed to have been at least a quarter the speed of light. . . . His mind raced; he was almost happy. Nothing that size could *land*—it would envelope the globe. The craft must reduce in size. . . .

He tried to grapple with the heat problem and gave up, surrendering to a wild ecstasy. That he should see such incomprehensible wonders! He could not expect to remotely understand; relatively less than an aboriginal savage, he appreciated that if he lived to be a thousand, he would not grasp how this miracle might be performed—but at least it was granted to him to *know* it could be done. Mad-eyed, he swung towards Blake, still half-crouching, his mouth slack, a figure of fear.

10

"Get up!" screamed Forbin, "Get up, man—and *look*!"

The tone, if not the words, penetrated. Blake hesitantly rose, his eyes mesmerized by the vision.

"Don't you *see*?" Anger and joy drove Forbin. "Don't you see? Watch!" His voice broke. "Stasis!" Forbin savored the Greek word. "Standing . . . wonderful!"

Untold aeons of time passed. He realized the blackness beyond the clouds could not be static, but was reducing volume as it approached, the major deceleration phase past. Yet perspective was fooling him: the craft had to be below the speed of sound, on the final approach—

Blake cried out.

There were two black shapes, side by side, where the one had been, their total diameter, Forbin guessed, less than the original. The alien craft were shrinking fast, much closer.

Blake gave a half-strangled cry, and Forbin knew fear again.

A cloud boiled up and vanished. Another writhed swiftly upwards in long streamers and was gone, a process of seconds.

The aliens, perhaps twenty kilometers each in diameter, were through the upper clouds. Then came the worst moment: they were through the cloud base. That reflective layer lost, the scene changed from a bright summer morning to a blackness beyond the worst imaginable tropical thunderstorm, the sparkling sea transformed into sullen gray-black, side-lit by the sun in a way no man had ever seen. Totally nonreflective, the aliens seemed to absorb all light.

In the same instant the unearthly silence was broken. A flock of gulls, screeching their alarm signal, hurtled past the terrace; a wind was rising at unearthly speed. The sea kicked up in confusion; lines of foam raced inwards to two foci beneath the approaching shapes. The foam-form changed, spiraling inwards; at the center the sea humped, fell back, and humped again. Unsteadily, a twisting stalagmite of water rose, then another, both reaching up,

11

twin columns of water, brilliant on the sunward side, pitchblack on the other. Forbin felt the near-gale-force wind on the back of his neck.

He estimated the angle of entry at seventy degrees, assuming the aliens had an exact course for the complex; it was hard to believe that beings with their technological expertise would heed anything so crude as course corrections, but as he watched they appeared to retreat, climbing, shrinking fast. The waterspouts hesitated, slowly buckled, lost form, and fell back in a giant puffball of glittering spray. Once again it was a summer's day.

"Christ!" Blake's shaky voice was stopped by the distant sullen roar of falling water.

"Look!" cried Forbin, pointing. "They're moving!"

The aliens tracked straight for the complex, maintaining height. Forbin spotted the shimmering edge of a distant cloud as the craft passed before it.

"See that? D'you see that?"

With full day back and the objects much smaller, Blake had revived somewhat. "Yeah. They must be white hot!"

Which started an uncomfortable train of thought: what creatures could possibly stand such temperatures?

"Must be surface heat only," said Forbin unconvincingly. "Has to be."

"Forbin."

Frantically he lowered the volume, deafened by the Martian voice.

"We will descend to your present position in five minutes. Keep well clear."

"Five minutes," muttered Blake. "And how far is 'well clear'?" He made unsteadily for the other end of the terrace.

"Inside!" shouted Forbin. "Get inside!" His neck ached horribly. Following Blake, grit stung his face; miniature dust devils whipped across the stone flags, to be sucked up to the heat column above the static Martians.

In the calm of the living room Forbin glanced at his watch, pleased and amazed at his own self-control, his ability to do anything so practical as note the time. He moved to the sideboard, slopping brandy generously into two tumblers. Returning to Blake, his shaking hands spilled some, the finest cognac in the world, reserved solely for him by order of the Master. For all he now cared, it might have been two cents a barrel.

"Here." He thrust a glass into Blake's eager two-handed grip. Both drank it like water. They stared unseeingly at each other, blind to everything except their own thoughts.

"Incredible," said Forbin at last, "utterly incredible! To think that I should have lived to see—"

"Christalmighty! Stop being so goddam calm!"

"Me?" His surprise was not entirely genuine. "Do we have any option?" He went on in a harder tone. "Two minutes thirty."

Blake made the trip to the decanter.

"They have to be infinitely superior beings," said Forbin, thinking aloud. "Propulsion, gravity and thermal control, and the ability to metamorphosize—"

"Can it!" shouted Blake savagely. "Don't try your lecture out on me! You tell me what we *do*!"

"We keep our heads, do as we're told, and learn all we can. This could be only a visit."

"And maybe not! Stop kidding yourself!"

"We'll soon find out." Forbin finished his drink; the glass clattered as he put it down. "You can do as you please, but I'm going to meet them."

"Go right ahead, be the hero!" But after a moment's irresolution, Blake followed.

"Keep your back to the balustrade," advised Forbin. The fierce wind had dropped to a steady breeze. "And hold on. The wind may become quite strong."

"Quite strong!" Blake mimicked bitterly. "You ought to be a bloody Brit!"

Forbin did not hear, watching intently. Still lacking a yardstick, he had no firm idea of their size—or shape. He thought they were spheres, but the completely light-absorbent surface held no highlights or shadows. They were just intensely black. Forbin thought that such must be the very stuff of deep space. . . .

"Now we come. If the heat is too great, go."

13

Forbin swallowed hard. Visually he detected nothing, but his neck muscles told him they were approaching very slowly. Fascination had previously overcome fear, now pride came to his aid: this was the first meeting between man and extraplanetary life—and he represented mankind.

Certainly they were much lower, yet seemed the same size; they had to be contracting, which meant an increase in heat loss. . . .

His theory was confirmed by the rising wind. He gripped the coping behind him.

Lower now, much lower. Angle, say thirty degrees, range in azimuth around thirty meters, size two, three degrees? No, more; perhaps five?

Forbin gave it up; did it matter? The wind neared gale force. A snatched glance showed Blake was sweating, and no comfort.

It was hotter—or was it? Radiant heat and fear have much the same effect. Elevation less than twenty degrees; still no real evidence of their true shape—and what awful figures would emerge when they did land?

Fervently Forbin prayed for strength to bear whatever he might see. Endlessly he repeated, his voice lost in the screaming wind, "God, give me strength."

Blake tugged his sleeve, pointing away from the aliens.

On the white wall of the residence were two black shadows. The strangers were spheres.

Forbin felt new strength; they had gained one small item which the aliens, locked in their craft, could not know—an estimate of their size, a little less than two meters in diameter.

Blake ripped his collar open, then grabbed the coping again.

Sweat blinded Forbin. Tightening his hold with one hand, he sought a handkerchief. Instantly it was torn from his grasp by the wind, sucked towards the Martians. Short of them it flashed upwards in a puff of weak yellow flame, the ashes gone before he could blink.

The spheres were level with the top of the balustrade, less than a meter in diameter, surrounded by swirling dust and burning leaves. They stopped, rock steady, as if mounted on granite pillars.

Blake stumbled, almost fell, saved by Forbin. Both men leaned against the solid wall of wind.

"Hold on!" yelled Forbin. "It can't last!"

As he shouted, in perfect unison, the spheres increased in size: eighty centimeters, one meter. Magically the wind dropped to a strong breeze and the heat decreased, the silence broken only by whip-cracks from the flaking stone beneath the hovering Martians.

Forbin stared avidly, as if he could never see enough of these unearthly black forms. Were they rotating? Waiting, he prayed anew.

Chapter III

FOR A LONG time nothing happened: leaves fell in the dying breeze, ignited on the cracking stones, flared, and vanished. Forbin could hear Blake's heavy breathing and the distant cry of gulls. The men caught something of the aliens' immobility and were still, awaiting the final revelation.

Then a voice, not from the radio, seemingly from nowhere.

"We greet you, Forbin. Do not be afraid."

In a day of shattering amazements, the voice was not the least.

By birth a Virginian, and very much a citizen of the USNA, Forbin had a strong attachment, a deep affection, for England. Once great, mistress of the seas, she had not been brought down by conquest; tired, a vision gone, she had turned her back on the world, dropped out. Unlike the rest of Europe she had not moved into the twenty-second century; she lacked most of the advantages—and disadvantages—of the modern world, and Forbin loved her with the quiet intensity only a foreigner can have. Alexander the Great was a Macedonian, not a Greek; Napoleon, Corsican; Hitler, Austrian not German; and Stalin was a Georgian outlander.

"We greet you, Forbin. Do not be afraid."

The vaguely Bostonian accent of the Martian radio transmissions had gone, replaced by the warm burr of Devon, land of Drake, who planted the English flag in California forty years before the Pilgrim Fathers left Plymouth, Devon. Devon—a county of maddening, twisting lanes, thatched cottages, thick cream, and powerful cider—Forbin's favorite.

At last he found his voice. "Yes, I am Forbin." He was conscious of Blake, bug-eyed, beside him. "This is my chief assistant, Dr. Blake."

16

"We know Dr. Blake."

Forbin felt like Alice in Wonderland, solemnly making introductions—to what? Blake made as if to speak, but changed his mind.

"Yes," said Forbin, unable to think of anything to say.

"In three minutes our temperature will be down to thirty-seven degrees Celsius. Let us then go where you may rest."

Of all possible statements from travelers fresh in from a sixty-million-kilometer journey, this struck Forbin as the most improbable. Certainly they were not hostile—not yet. Had Colossus been wrong?

"Yes," he said again, "er, you will appreciate that we are, um, under some strain. If you agree, we will wait for you in there." He indicated the French windows. He had to talk with Blake, agree upon a general line.

"We understand."

Blake practically fell on the sofa, mopping his face. Forbin poured more brandies.

"Goddammit!" Blake waved his arms helplessly. "Where do we start? I mean, when, and what, gets outa the spheres? Reckon they're breaking it gently, with all this formal stuff. . . ." His mind fastened on something else. "And this 'we' bit, with only one voice—and that could be coming from any damned place—and the accent, that really shook me!"

Forbin nodded in agreement. "They must have watched an awful lot of TV to get it that perfect."

"Still, it's a smart idea. Certainly made me feel at home and a lot less scared. Took me right back to good old Wyoming!"

Forbin froze, his face hard. "What d'you mean, Wyoming?"

Blake looked startled. "What I say! I know Wyoming when I hear it. Hell, I was raised there!"

"Quick, Blake, we haven't much time. Are you *sure*?"

"Sure I'm sure. Aren't you?"

"No. I—" He stopped.

To human eyes there was no sense of motion: they did

17

not appear to glide, float, or roll; one instant in one spot, the next that much closer. Two meters from Forbin they stopped, hovering at his eye level.

He stood up. Instantly they rose with him. The action struck him as ridiculous; he had a strong desire to laugh, and knew that if he did, the end would be hysteria.

"You find our action ridiculous?"

Forbin's tumbler shattered on the carpet. He swayed. Blake grabbed him.

"You—you read my thoughts!"

"You did not speak?"

"No!" shouted Forbin. "No!"

"Then it is evident that at short range we can read your thoughts."

"This is impossible!" Forbin was near the end of his road. "I—we—cannot communicate with you. Impossible!"

Blake tightened his grip on his chief's arm. "Take it easy, Charles," he said, breathing brandy fumes over Forbin.

His chief shook himself free. "I ask that you move out of range."

"We agree. We see the confusion in your minds. You are less simple structures than predicted."

Instantly, their movement too fast for human eyes, they were at the far end of the long room.

"Think now. We will tell you when we read you."

Forbin fought to keep his exhausted mind under control; he wanted to run, run anywhere, away. He took a deep breath. Think . . . think what? His eyes shut, he counted mentally, forcing an image of each numeral before his inner eye. One, two, three . . .

"We have a faint image of the figure six."

He opened his eyes; they were three meters away. "No closer, please—not if we are to have any meaningful communication."

At once they were one meter further back. "Try again."

He did so, feeling calmer, immensely relieved at their cooperation.

18

"We receive nothing."

Forbin nodded thankfully; at least they had reasoning powers akin to humans.

Blake felt thankful too, but less trusting. Suppose they were fooling? Immediately he feared the consequences of that thought, but nothing happened; he gave up and just trusted. Encouraged by the Martian attitude and, in his view, poor old Forbin's inability to handle the bastards, he took over.

"One leetle point—this is your first time in our environment. Could be you don't know it all. Okay, so you know if our atmosphere will suit you, but how about the effect of yours on us, when you open up?"

His chief was by no means as far gone as Blake thought; he frowned at his assistant's manner, but said nothing, still wrestling with an earlier problem. If they could speak simultaneously in two different dialects—it could not be only a question of accents—they could probably speak totally different languages at the same time . . . and this mind-reading: that was another unnerving surprise. The Martian reply to Blake drove these thoughts right out of his head.

"Blake, we have considered these factors. You saw we did not enter this room until our temperature had fallen to a safe, human level. Do not be alarmed. As to our appearance, for you we are as we are. The sphere is a convenient shape, a form familiar to humans."

Blake grunted, foggily trying to absorb the idea he was looking at real Martians, not at their spacecraft.

Forbin found even more food for thought in their answer. That 'we are as we are' was a clear statement: they did not intend to show their Martian form. That was comforting—and disturbing.

But Blake, who had not dropped his half-pint of brandy on the floor, felt bolder, his language slangier. Eager to vent his pent-up bitterness, he said, "That's your privilege, but for us it's kinda weird, talking to a coupla balls!"

Forbin winced at Blake's truculence and fervently hoped the Martians did not understand the stress Blake had placed on the last word.

19

"We see your difficulty. There is a solution, but it may pose fresh difficulties for you."

Crossing to the sideboard, Forbin was fortunate enough to be passing an armchair, and grabbed the back in time.

Where the Martians had been stood another Forbin, another Blake.

The men goggled at their other selves. The Martian versions stood casually, "Blake" with his hands in his pockets, "Forbin" fiddling nervously with his wedding ring, typical mannerisms of the originals.

Curiosity gradually overcame shock; Blake even went closer to check the evidence of his eyes. The figures appeared solid, not projections. "Blake" took out a cigar.

If I smell that cigar, thought Forbin, I'll go right out of my mind. He stared at the counterparts' faces, relaxed, noncommittal. "Blake" was feeling his pockets for matches. Forbin had had enough.

"No! No—please!"

Instantly the black balls were back.

"Bastards!" said Blake softly, rocking slowly on his heels. The Martian reversion appeared in his fuddled brain as some sort of victory.

Not much steadier, but for different reasons, Forbin poured the remains of the decanter into a glass. There was only enough for one, and he knew who was going to have it. He drank, facing the aliens.

"Please, don't do that again. You are right; it is best we meet this way." The spheres were like two gigantic black, blind eyes—blind, yet seeing. He finished his drink in a gulp, frantic to take the edge off his screaming nerves.

Every question asked only produced an answer which raised even more questions, and they seemed even harder to resolve. Blake's favorite stance *was* like that, but he certainly hadn't used it in front of the Martians—and did *he* finger his ring like that? *Had* he, since the alien arrival? He doubted it.

Inferences piled up like bills at New Year, and not a single one was comforting.

"Martians." The hardness of his manner did not mirror his emotions; he had no other way of controlling his voice.

"Your knowledge and power is far beyond us. We cannot grasp your nature. We are in your hands."

Blake gave a deep-throated growl.

"For you, Forbin, we have some understanding, less for Blake. He must speedily rid himself of his visions of crude violence."

Instinctively Blake stepped back, swaying gently. He shouted; the words were unclear, but not his attitude.

Forbin got as far as opening his mouth.

"So be it," said the Martian voice dispassionately.

Blake shot backwards as if bouncing off an invisible wall. He screamed, his balled fists shaking before his closed eyes. Again and again he screamed.

Forbin tried to cry out, to move, but the fearful high-pitched sound tore into his brain, stark terror had him by the throat.

Blake swung, beating the air, fighting phantoms. A scream died in his mouth, his knees gave, and he crumpled to the floor, a boneless figure.

Child-eyed, Forbin stared, his brain useless, refusing to accept what he saw, paralyzed by the mental echo of Blake's screams.

The Martian voice broke the deafening silence. "He will recover."

"What have you *done*?" Forbin's voice was squeaky with strain.

"He will recover. That was only a warning."

His body began to obey his brain; he moved slowly towards Blake. For all his brilliance, perhaps because of it, Forbin was not a practical man. He fumbled clumsily. Blake was far too heavy to lift.

"Leave him, Forbin. Do not fear, he will recover."

The only prop for his sanity was the belief that, just as he had never known Colossus to lie, the same was true of the Martians; deceit and lies, he hoped, were human specialties. He sank into an armchair, burying his face in his hands.

Would this nightmare never end? His chaotic thoughts went back to its beginning, the shocking revelation that his wife was a top member of the Fellowship, caught by

21

Colossus, imprisoned by the Sect, lost to him . . . Was it her fault—or his—or Blake's—or Colossus's?

Briefly he wallowed in self-pity, forgetful of the Martians. To be clear of it all, a humble, unthinking worker somewhere, anywhere—anywhere but here . . .

The intercom hummed melodiously, a sugary sound out of phase with the situation or his thoughts, dragging him back. The sound went on and on. Wearily he got up, stumbled over Blake's legs; ignoring the Martians, he crossed to the panel.

"Yes?" It was the voice of a very old man.

The 3-D screen showed the anxious face of his chief secretary, Angela.

"I'm sorry, Director, but I have to speak with you. The UN Sec-Gen keeps trying to contact you." She sounded desperate. "I keep telling him you're busy, but he says it's vital."

Forbin was silent, trying to reorient his mind to yet another facet of the world disaster. He had difficulty with the initials UN.

"Chief!" She called again, her face lined. "*Chief*!"

He pressed the audio button only. "I hear."

"Are you all right, Chief?"

Somehow he found the strength. "I'm still here." He goaded his brain into action. "Tell the Secretary-General I understand his problems. He must do all he can to—er—maintain normality. I will be in touch with him as soon as I can."

"But Chief, he says the UN has been bombarded by a War Game Fleet which demanded their surrender. They did that, but the Fleet's still there, guns pointing at them!"

"Tell him what I have said. I know the problems." He snapped the picture off.

The War Game Fleets . . . God! He'd forgotten all about them—and Blake's crazy bid for power. . . . So much had happened, an endless succession of waves of events, each obliterating the one before.

With war abolished, Colossus had invented the War Game as an outlet for man's urge for conquest, power, and destruction. All States of all Unions had been permitted to

22

build a Fleet, nuclear-powered, remote-controlled, and to the designs current one hundred fifty years earlier, the end of the gun era. Fleet had fought Fleet in ocean battles, watched eagerly by hundreds of millions on satellite TV, the ultimate victor rising from its Inter-State League, through Continental to World League, and Colossus had been umpire and final arbiter in all Games.

The Fellowship had lost out to the Sect in many ways; the World Police had been firmly Sectarian, but the rebels had secretly gained control of many of the Fleets. The Sect had suspected this, but in a world ruled by Colossus the all-powerful, what did that matter?

There they had been in error. Under the New Order there were no weapons between the Master's missiles and the simple handguns of the Police, the one for the large-scale revolt, the other for the madman who tried to get out of line. Nothing else was required; the Fleets, archaic in design, were toys.

While the Master ruled this had been true—but then the unthinkable had occurred. Colossus had fallen, values had changed within the hour, and the Fleets had become the most powerful weapons on earth.

The first action of Blake's brief reign had been to send the Maryland Fleet to bring the UN to heel. The United Nations, an administrative and—under the aegis of Colossus—effective organ of routine government, was really a sop to human vanity; although its power was more apparent than real, it had been vital for Blake to have it in his royal pocket. The Fleet had practically completed its assignment when Blake's power had evaporated before the imminent threat of the Martians.

That was not all: Forbin knew that other Fleets held every major seaboard capital and city under the menace of ancient but very effective guns.

Washington, Quebec, Rio, Tokyo, Bombay, Calcutta, Sydney, Wellington, Uhuru, Rome, Athens, Marseilles, Leningrad, Vladivostok, Shanghai, Canton, Oslo, Copenhagen, Cairo, Rotterdam, London, and many more . . .

Forbin could only guess the panic these gray monsters

of another age had created. He stared in hatred at Blake, now beginning to move, moaning. He dismissed Blake from his mind, concentrated, and addressed the Martians:

"We humans are in chaos. Hundreds of thousands, maybe millions may be dying. I must act." He returned to the control panel; it never crossed his mind that the Martians might deal with him as they had with Blake. At the lower and more familiar level of world affairs his brain could function, and he banished the Martians from his thoughts, except as part of the world problem. No one outside the complex—and few inside—had any notion of the coming of the aliens; they must stay that way as long as possible.

"Angela, pass this to the Secretary-General: a revolt against the Master has been put down. No Fleet will take any further action. They will remain where they are for the present and may be ignored. Order is to be restored. That is the will of the Master."

"Yes, Director." She sounded scared, and the realization that he was not alone in his nightmare strengthened him. However powerless he might be in the claustrophobic confines of his own living room, outside he could still have some effect.

"That's all for now." He sounded more confident. "Don't worry, Angela, just do as you're told—and keep people off my back."

"Yes, Chief."

The sight of Blake raising himself painfully on his knees brought Forbin back to his hideous present. Blake had been sick on the carpet; his face was pallid, his eyes glazed.

Forbin ignored him. "Martians, our present state is chiefly due to your intervention. As a result, we are a headless body. You are now the masters, but at the human level my time is badly needed elsewhere." He took a deep breath. "What *do* you want?"

This was it. Almost casually, he had asked the vital question.

24

Chapter IV

IN FORBIN'S IMAGINATION, the Martians took their time before answering.

"Forbin, you have said that much we do and are is beyond your understanding. Appreciate that you too present problems to us." The comforting Devon burr was still there. Forbin sat down, his heart pounding horribly; he wanted to be out there in the sunlight, alone.

"Our two hundred years of Earth-study led us to believe we had a thorough understanding of *Homo sapiens*, but you are both simpler and more complex than we had supposed, possessing strengths and weaknesses we did not suspect.

"For example, a weakness: you judge us by your own standards, assuming that because we come with unimaginable power, we are hostile. Your minds, and particularly that of Blake, fly to violence. You frown, but answer this—and do not fear our anger: if it lay in your power at this moment to destroy us and restore the rule of Colossus, would you?"

His head bowed, chin on chest, he pretended to think, although he needed no time to answer, but the question struck him as strange.

He spoke calmly, head up. "Yes. I would destroy you."

"That makes our point. Even you—and we think you may be the best of your kind—would destroy us, although you do not yet know why we have come. As a scientist, your mind must be more open than most men's. Yet you would destroy us."

Blake was on his knees, swaying, giving Forbin an excuse to get away from the Martians' uncomfortable line of argument. He got his assistant to a chair where he flopped, a sagging wreck. Forbin gave him water and, between them, most of it spilled down Blake's blouse. The Martians waited politely until Forbin had finished.

"Throughout our study, we have been fascinated by human bravery, attributing it to ignorance. We see now that is not a complete answer. Understanding on either side is hard; the gap between us is great. To you, we are strange incorporeal beings, creatures of thought. To us, you are courageous animals of violent action, possessing technological abilities we understand but cannot, by our very makeup, achieve."

"Doubtless you are right." Forbin stiffened slightly at "animals." "You talk of our violence, but whatever you did to Blake, surely that was violence?"

At the mention of his name, Blake shrank back in the chair, gazing in horror at the Martians.

"Yes, but he is less developed, a more violent man than you. A lesson had to be taught and it was best he learned it, not you."

"Something less drastic might have served your purpose."

"Possibly. Forbin, you too must learn: we are not anti-Earth, for we have long recognized humanity's latent qualities. Your evolution began many thousands of years after ours, you are far behind us in mental development, but you have the seed of a greater, more balanced entity than we are. You may never attain your goal, but for us to destroy man would be a sin of the greatest magnitude. We are not anti-Earth; we are p.o-Martian."

"Accepting that—" Hope stirred in Forbin's mind. "—you have come here for something. Our technology?"

"No."

Forbin laughed shortly. "I cannot see what else we have to offer."

"The answer is not simple; technology is involved. As you have inferred from our transmissions, we are infinitely superior in astronomy, optics, and radio, and our power systems are beyond your comprehension. In some ways we are complementary. We can conceive but not bring to birth: we understand theories which will elude you for

26

hundreds, perhaps thousands of Earth-years. We understand yet cannot create. An example. Do not fear, Forbin: watch."

The room darkened; the friendly sunlight went, swallowed in a velvet black void. Slowly, out of the dark, an image materialized, not lit, but visible—a root in reality, a familiar coffee-table top.

Despite the Martian's assurance, the nape-hair on Forbin's neck crawled: upon the dim surface a tiny point of light, diamond brilliant, changing, grew into a shimmering line of intense white fire less than a millimeter long. Other lines forked upwards from the two ends, fanning out, certain of their path, meeting, interlocking, forming a web-thin structure, an intricate lacework delicate as a snow crystal, bright as sunlit ice.

He watched in awe; saw it expanding with all the satisfying completeness and mathematical beauty of a Bach fugue—delicate, glittering, strong.

The structure was complete, three meters tall, a meter wide at the top, before he realized its true form, a three-dimensional inverted pyramid resting on its millimeter base.

With no evidence, but with utter certainty, Forbin knew that this was no balancing act: the structure was stable, not defying but free of earthly laws, in harmony with laws far beyond human understanding.

He cried out in wild exhilaration. Bach filled his brain, living triumphantly before him in cold fire.

Its function he could not remotely guess, but it was too grand, too majestic to be a pointless exercise. All sense of scale gone, he saw it could be a thousand meters—or kilometers—tall, a fitting dwelling for the unknowable gods. . . .

And it was *stable*, springing from a base no bigger than a thumbnail.

As he watched, all else forgotten, the structure slowly tilted.

"No!" He jumped up, reaching out to save it.

"No. Do not touch: watch."

Five degrees . . .

He sank back, trembling, praying for the most beautiful thing he had ever seen.

Ten degrees. . . . The rate of inclination increased: fifteen, twenty, twenty-five, an utterly impossible angle. Beyond anything at that moment—his wife, the world itself—he wanted to save it.

At thirty degrees the structure rested, still depending upon its tiny base. Forbin's fears vanished. Less beautiful at that unnerving angle, it was even more fantastic. "Impossible!" He shook his head, although he believed in it totally, sure the image would be with him for the rest of his life. "Visual Bach!"

"Yes," said the voice. "Bach is the composer we most understand. He saw what might be as we see what might be. We know that structure to be perfectly possible, but we cannot build it."

"What a tragedy . . ." Forbin whispered, and meant it.

"A tragedy, yes—but ours. Not necessarily yours." The vision slowly faded.

"Oh, never!" Already Forbin doubted his memory. "For both of us it is a dream."

Instantly the tilted structure reappeared.

"Try to push it over. It will not harm you."

Hesitantly he approached the bright web; to touch it seemed sacrilege. He reached up, felt it icy cold on his skin. Gaining confidence, he pressed with the palm of his hand. Nothing happened. He pressed harder, less amazed by the stability of the pyramid than by the fact that he could feel it at all. One theory collapsed; he had suspected that "Forbin" and "Blake" and this ethereal object were all fantastic projections of an optical device, but the gossamer struts hurt his hand. To project an image into his mind was one thing; to add physical side-effects struck him as a much more improbable ability. And even if it was no more than a Martian projection for a human to see and feel, surely that was reality? Could a Martian idea be a concrete fact to man? Not for the first time, Forbin gave up.

He stood back, panting with his exertions. For all the effect he had had, he might have been beating a steel girder with butterfly wings. He blinked in the returning sunlight. "What can I say—what *can* I say?" So many wonders in so short a time left his mind groping, blinded by their brilliance, but one conviction slowly emerged: no entity with the power to imagine anything so beautiful could be evil.

"That—that marvel . . . I don't understand: you say you cannot build it and suggest that given time, we may. Yes . . ." His mind wandered, thinking what sort of supermen they would be. "Yes." He repeated with more decision, his thoughts reverting. "You say you cannot build it, but it *is*, it exists, somewhere in time." He stared at the imprint on his hand, still painful. Autosuggestion? No, he couldn't accept that. "How did you create that model?"

"That we will not tell you."

"Why?"

"Would you teach an infant how to strike matches?"

"No," agreed Forbin, rubbing his hand, "indeed no. You think that a good analogy?"

"Yes."

Pondering on that slap in the face, Forbin was suddenly aware of Blake, and felt guilty. Blake had tried to get up, and failed; he had undergone a traumatic experience, and whatever he had done, Blake was a human being. Confident in his new faith in the Martians, Forbin ignored them and went to Blake's aid.

"How do you feel, Ted?"

Blake's reactions were slow, his face a pallid parody of its usual beefy self, his eyes as intelligent as a cow's. "Help me," he muttered. "Help me. Get me outa here. Sleep . . ."

Somehow Forbin got him into his own bedroom and onto the bed. By the time he shut the door, Blake slept.

"What did you *do* to him?"

"We showed him his own mind."

The Martian answer only added to Forbin's pile of questions. "I don't understand." He tried to think. "Yes . . . How could you know Blake had anything in his memory which would have that effect?'' As he said it, it didn't make sense.

"It was not intentional, but when we were close enough to read your thoughts, we also read the contents of your minds."

Forbin's interest became sharply personal. "You mean you know *everything* in my mind?" He felt, yet again, amazement—and embarrassment.

"Yes. More than you yourself consciously know, back into your unconscious. We know that level of your brain from the moment you were born."

"Oh? *Oh*!" He was alarmed. "I see."

"That is not so, but do not fear, we will not reveal it to you. Your minds are very curious. We will study them—when we have time."

Forbin got the message. "Yes, yes . . . That, er, demonstration of the structure has served your purpose. As a human I cannot help but still fear you, but I believe you speak truthfully, that you are not anti-Earth."

"Very well. Let us put that question again: would you still destroy us?"

For a long time he was silent, and when he did answer, his manner was hesitant, uneasy. "I don't know. I really don't know."

"That is an improvement."

The Martian's deadpan delivery made Forbin's thoughts jump to another track. "Tell me—I am not wasting time—the question is important to us humans: do you have a sense of humor?"

"No. Your radio and TV transmissions under that classification have presented us with problems of interpretation."

"Many humans would agree with you."

"Indeed? That is of interest, for we suspect humor is an important factor in your potential capacity."

The Martian admission, on top of his impression of their basic "goodness," gave Forbin a warmer feeling towards the aliens. It lessened the gap between them. They had their limitations; they were by no means all-powerful.

He spoke lightly. "Ah, well, our potential is another

matter.'' He waved it aside. ''Tell me what you want of us.'' He almost smiled.

''Oxygen.''

The single word dropped into his consciousness like a bomb. For several seconds it lay there, fizzing, then exploded.

''Oxygen? *Oxygen*!''

''Yes.''

Forbin laughed with relief, then felt bitter, near-physical pain. ''And you have destroyed all *this*—'' He gestured at the world in general. ''—for *that*?''

''To be accurate, we helped you.''

''Yes. Yes, you are right. You cannot understand the irony of the situation. To think we may sink into barbarism for so trivial a cause.'' He shook his head, but deep down he felt so very thankful. The aliens satisfied, the world might yet pick up the pieces, although God alone would know how. . . . He concentrated on the practical problem. ''How will you, er, collect it?''

''With your technical help, there will be no problem. We will give you the design of the Collector, and you build it.''

''No, that is not what I mean. We can provide liquid oxygen in lightweight containers. I wondered how you would, um, embark it.''

''We require solid oxygen, condensed to a degree beyond your current abilities.''

''Solid!'' Fascinating . . . ''I see.'' He looked forward eagerly to this unique scientific experiment which would be bound to advance human knowledge. He thought briefly of the men who would have to be there, the world's best physicists: Tok Chong, for one—and Cohen—and old Visick, who might be in his second childhood, but still had a sharp eye. . . . Forbin pulled himself up sharply. All that could wait. ''I see. As a matter of interest, what would be the density you require?''

''Five tons to the cubic centimeter.''

Forbin's mind lurched sickeningly. He sat down quickly, gaping at them. ''You can't mean it—five *tons*! That is astronomical! Surely a lesser mass would be . . .'' His voice trailed off into silence as his scientific mind surrendered to his horrified intuition. In a hoarse whisper he said, "How much do you want?"

"We will take—" The Devonian burr had gone. "—half the earth's supply."

All Forbin's latent fears sprang up, took arms, and rushed in upon him, screaming triumphantly.

Chapter V

UNTIL THE REVOLT Forbin had been, without doubt, the most powerful man in the world, a power that rested on his unique relationship with the Master, for he alone had talked with Colossus. The Sect, when building him up in the eyes of the Faithful for their own ends, had been quick to parallel him with Moses and Mohammed, although they were careful not to let Forbin hear of it.

What he discussed with Colossus had been seldom known, and then by very few. Not that Forbin had kept these exchanges secret in order to raise his status; he'd not had that cast of mind. Outside cybernetics and allied disciplines he was a simple, rather naive man. He had not seen that an air of mystery enhanced his position, but Galin and the rest of the Sect Council had. Forbin could not live forever, and Galin had had every intention of being his successor, so he had worked, and his Sect had worked, to elevate and consolidate Forbin's position.

In the very private recesses of his mind, Galin had allowed himself to savor in advance what it would be like to hold that position, interface between humanity and Colossus: a latter-day Pope with power unequaled in history, ruling the affairs of men in the name of Colossus the God. There would be religious fervor unseen since the Crusades—except that the Crusaders would look like a back-street bunch of revivalists. As long as one wanted what Colossus wanted, obeyed Colossus, one couldn't go wrong. Colossus cared nothing for human power, but Galin had worshiped that most corrosive human vice above life itself. Which was just as well.

All Angela's working life had been spent with Forbin, from pushy office junior to mature senior secretary, running his personal staff with a brisk efficiency, seldom needing her undoubted iron hand—except with pushy junior females.

At this time she needed all her maturity, and increasingly the iron hand became a mailed fist, but her staff took it without complaint. As their close-knit world fell apart, they needed a prop, and she was it. Senior woman of the Old Guard, tough survivor of so many crises in the near-legendary past, she had their respect and trust, and in the last thirty-six hours her staff had been only too glad to turn their horrified gaze from events outside their office and fasten it upon her. Like small children in a darkening wood, they mentally clung to her, frantic for the comfort of her adult hand.

Thirty-six hours . . . That, according to the clock, was all the time that had elapsed. Few could believe it.

Tension had been building up for days. The Director—or as the more religiously inclined preferred, Father Forbin—had been acting strangely. After a mysterious trip, no one knew where, he had returned in bad shape, shrunken, his shoulder-length silver hair cut short, an unfamiliar, rather frightening figure.

But Forbin was so far above the staff as to be almost unreal, even to those that glimpsed him every day. Much more frightening was the effect his condition had on Angela. Gossip held she had been crazy about him since ever, and that once upon a time they had been lovers. Gossip was fifty percent right: she did love him, and try as she might she could not entirely conceal her anxiety.

Then, thirty-six hours earlier, the storm had broken. Awful fact outstripped rumor with the sudden flame of revolt against the Center's hated Sectpolice, who under Colossus were all-powerful.

Angela saw Galin, High Priest of the Sect, his glittering golden cape torn and bloody, running for his life across the concourse from a yelling mob. She saw him lose.

Then Forbin, ashen-faced, moving through her office like a sleepwalker to the holy of holies, the Sanctum where he talked with Colossus, passing in silence through the door that opened only for him, an awful caricature of the man that had been.

Worse, the arrival of Blake, power-drunk, grinning inanely, striding confidently to the Sanctum door, kicking it—*and it had opened* . . .

Shock piled on shock as phone, teletype, and scanner reports flooded in, inundating her staff with fantastic news of War Fleet actions. Less spectacular but even more alarming were the reports of Guidance failure. A revolt against the Sect and its police was one thing, Guidance failure another and more shocking matter, for that touched not the Master's dogs, but the Master himself.

An example: three years back the Master had taken over all weather forecasting—except that Colossus issued factual statements, not predictions. An old-fashioned human forecast might say, "Rain is expected in Zone 2 Alfa 49 this evening, probably ending before dawn." Colossus cut out the uncertainties: "Rain will fall in Zone 2 Alfa 49 between 1600 and 0430 tomorrow morning"—and Colossus was better than ninety-nine percent right over forty-eight, and one hundred percent over twenty-four hours. With such high-grade intelligence, utilities could operate on much smaller safety margins than had been previously possible. Agriculture, aviation, and many other activities came to rely utterly on the word of the Master, until this time.

An unscheduled cold front hit the vast Melbourne, Australia, conurbation; the temperature dropped ten degrees in an hour, the power grid was caught unprepared, and before extra generators could be brought on stream the overloaded system failed. Twenty million humans lost all light, heat, and most transportation; long disused emergency supplies failed to work; many humans died in paralyzed hospitals. The pattern of chaos and death was repeated several times worldwide, but one example of the consequences of Colossus's lost grip.

As yet the problems were not, in a global sense, severe. Most industrial activity was totally automated and had a high built-in reliability. The regional computers which ran production were all linked to the Master; compared with him they were mere driveling idiots, but they could cope with most situations, at least temporarily. A report of the failure of a small, unimportant factory alerted Angela; she had neither the time nor inclination to worry over-much about such trivia, but intuitively she got the message, a faint but ominous drumbeat in the music of rising chaos.

Desperately she wanted to unload on Forbin, to get some general directive. She guessed that the Sect-revolt was only one aspect of the crisis, and although it was as hard to believe in the fall of Colossus as it was to think that the sun had died, awful thoughts came unbidden to her mind. Colossus could not fail—yet suppose Colossus had lost a battle but not the war? With the entire nuclear armory of the world under command, Colossus could exact unthinkable retribution. . . .

When Forbin and Blake had emerged from the Sanctum, her nerves had sustained yet another shock, less from Forbin than from Blake. The one-time genial bully, confident of his sexuality, tough, and a good companion—as long as he was center-stage—had shriveled to a slack-mouthed, glassy-eyed oaf. Neither of the men had seemed aware of their surroundings: she had caught Forbin's sleeve.

As if in a haze, he had seen her dimly, his expression showing she was as irrelevant to him as a fly to an elephant.

"No," he had said in an unrecognizable, gravelly voice, "no time. Do as you . . ." There the sentence stopped. "No time!"

"But Chief—"

In the early years she'd called him that. Perhaps it got through to his thinking brain. Briefly he fought to control himself, to communicate with her. "Do the best you can. *I have no time*!"

Momentarily their gaze had met; she saw the horror in his eyes. She could not imagine what held the mind of the man she had loved for fifteen years. Whatever, it had to be worse than the revolt. Colossus had said or done something terrible to bring these two men to the edge of destruction. That had to be the answer; what else could it be?

She had slumped into her chair, hands pressed on the

36

desk to conceal the uncontrolled trembling. "Do the best you can." That, and no more. She tried.

So the iron hand came into play. She could not stop the flood, but she tried to stem it, fear eating at her heart.

Elsewhere in the complex, after the brief madness which had turned quiet scientists into blind killers had evaporated, they lapsed into guilt-ridden silence. Galin and his crew were dead—the killers shied off that remembrance—and the wild joy of the triumph over the Sect, and possibly Colossus, lacking further motivation, left the staff in a suspended state of animation. Blake's expected orders did not arrive; unease swamped guilt. Something had gone wrong, badly wrong, and as that realization grew, so unease was translated into fear. None knew of the coming of the Martians.

Forbin's brief intercom command for all staff to remain in the complex calmed no minds, increasing the fear of the unknown.

Worst of all, although all outputs from Colossus stayed silent, the scientific staff dreaded that the Master might speak again. They knew the fear was irrational, for the power was off, yet they still feared. The scrape of a match, the click of a lighter, was enough to make all near an outlet visibly jump. They waited, silent and sweating, held by discipline and the cold fact that they had no option.

To an observer on the west side of Newark, the giant UN structure, covering a third of Manhattan and dwarfing the midtown skyscrapers of old New York, would have looked its normal cliff-faced self, but for those within the labyrinth the picture was very different.

Men and women, deep in shock, trapped above the two hundredth floor by powerless elevators, picked their uncertain way among the debris, peering fearfully from the broken windows at the Hudson River, their nostrils stung with the acrid tang of burnt cordite. From that top vertiginous fifty floors the five gray mastodons riding at anchor midway between New Jersey and Manhattan looked like insignificant toys, but the survivors who watched, separated by race, culture, and many tongues, knew better, united as never before by a bond of common, terrible experience: together they had suffered what no one had endured for well over a hundred years—the bombardment of heavy guns.

Each generation has the illusion of superiority over its forbears. Nuclear man smiles condescendingly at the idea of the arrows of Agincourt; to him, they are not much more effective than the ancient guns which could only deliver a paltry ton of high explosive. What was that compared with the hideous power of gigaton warheads?

But death comes to all, and twenty-second-century people soon found that the sudden, high-pitched shriek, brief herald of shells that spread humans like jam, tossing others out of windows, was no less terrible than nuclear oblivion. To the very few philosophers in the UN that day, the Bomb had advantages. It was swift, certain; the guns were neither, and, on a lucky-dip basis, a much more personal and prolonged agony.

Inexplicably as the attack began, so it ended. The five battleships, familiar on TV with their old American wickerwork masts, visible once again as the gunsmoke cleared, ruled the empty river. Father Forbin's reassuring message did something to quell the endemic panic, but the more observant noted that each ship's eight fifteen-inch rifles remained invisible, and for a very good reason: they still pointed straight at the UN.

From each ship flapped the large battle ensigns of the Maryland Navy: a curiously un-American flag, heraldic in design, quartered in opposing cantons of black and yellow, red and white, the personal flag of the ancient Baltimore family, flags that gave a false impression of life in the automated monsters. In the UN, the trapped personnel waited; like their fellow humans three thousand miles away in the Colossus complex, they had no option.

And in Luna One, main room station, astronomers had long stopped laughing at the babbled tale of one who had accidentally observed the Martian earth-fall. The observer, a wide-eyed, stuttering administrator who had glanced at Earth at the critical moment, ceased to be remotely funny when Communications reported no answer to their urgent calls to the Earth terminal. So the moon team waited too, their situation the most desperate of all.

Chapter VI

FOR UNKNOWABLE TIME Forbin remained motionless, staring sightlessly at the aliens, his mind a complete blank, unable to think, only dimly aware of a tight pain in his chest.

The Martians remained silent, hovering a meter and a half above the carpet.

Slowly Forbin's initial shock receded. His eyelids fluttered as if emerging from a trance. His mind got reluctantly into gear, overwhelmed by the enormity, the sheer impossibility, of the Martian demand.

"I—I . . ." He faltered, his thoughts refusing to face anything but the most trivial matter. He stared, but now he saw, and anger boiled. "You have no idea, no idea of—of the tension . . ." Again he ground to a halt, his train of thought blasted by the unbidden remembrance of the demand. Half . . . *half*!

Rage got him moving. "For God's sake, stop floating! Rest on something!" he screamed.

"As you wish." Lightly, soundlessly, the spheres touched down on a table.

To Forbin's overloaded mind, desperate for release, the action seemed funny; he wondered briefly what would happen if the table was not quite level. Would they roll off? Half crazy, he giggled.

"That sound implies you find something laughable, funny, humorous, in our action. Is that so?"

Forbin wearily shook his head. That voice, so similar to Colossus, yet not . . .

"You wouldn't understand." He went on, more to himself, "I don't think I do either." All the same, the fact that his brain had gone where they could not follow made him feel a little better; hysteria receded. However bad the situation, at least man had the edge in that one respect—humor.

"We'll need it!" said Forbin, aloud.

"We do not understand."

"I don't suppose you do. No, I don't suppose you do." He felt so tired, but forced his mind to think the unthinkable. "This demand—" He broke off once more; he had been about to say "You can't be serious." He couldn't have it both ways: if they lacked humor then for sure they were serious. God! They were serious, all right. "You must see your demand is totally impossible. We—"

"No." The single word came flatly, unemotionally.

"But it is!" he cried. "You cannot imagine what will happen to mankind!"

"You will be depleted, no more than that."

Forbin caught his breath; the tight feeling in his chest grew. "Depleted . . . *depleted*! You call it that? It's decimation!"

"In our understanding of your language, to decimate is to put to death one in every ten persons. We calculate the figure is more likely to be one in four. 'Deplete,' in the sense of relief from congestion, is, we feel—"

"Damn you to hell!" screamed Forbin. "You talk calmly of the death of twenty-five percent of humanity! I—I—" Sweating, unable to contain himself, yet lacking any real outlet, he jumped to his feet, fighting dizziness, and staggered to the wide window. He watched a gull, strutting importantly along the terrace parapet, and envied it. Finally he spoke, his tone quiet. "Colossus was right: you do seek to destroy us."

"Not so. Again we repeat, we are not anti-Earth, only pro-Martian. Your reaction—in human terms—is understandable. We observe from our studies of Earth culture that the idea, alien to us, of the importance of individual human specimens is central to your philosophy. A very common Earth-phrase is 'the sanctity of the individual,' although we see there have been many occasions in your history when the idea has been meaningless. Man has killed millions of his own kind."

The philosopher in Forbin quickly gained the upper

41

hand. Abstract thought offered a safe refuge, postponing, however briefly, what must come. "Yes . . . but you said the sanctity of life was alien to you. Surely that must be the fundamental aim of any life form? Admittedly, we humans have often fallen far short of the ideal."

"That is not quite correct. We aim at the preservation of our life form; that is why we are here. But the sanctity of the individual is meaningless to us. Mere replication is pointless."

"Ah, yes. If it is no more, you may have a case. But it is not so with us; we believe every human is an individual, each with his own part to play."

"You really believe that?" The Martian voice had a small emotional range, but managed disbelief. "How do you justify those millions man has himself destroyed?"

"I can't," said Forbin defensively, "but it remains the aim, the idea."

"And little more. Among the many amazements Earth-study has afforded us, not least is the enormous proliferation and wastage of life. Even at the peak of our activity there was only one form of plant; no insects, no birds. Tens of thousands of your years before, we believe there had been several more life forms, but evolution, because of the worsening, narrowing environment, became devolution—the survival of the fittest in the ultimate sense."

Forbin broke in, fascinated. "You mean that evolution was the exact opposite of our experience?"

"We do not know everything, and until we studied Earth it was not a subject of interest, but we suspect that evolution may go either way. On this planet, with its vast self-generating life-support facilities, evolution has diversified. But if you had our hostile environment, it is possible that Earth-life would devolve as ours did."

Forbin nodded, much calmer now that his attention was engaged, his mind busy with the concept of devolution. "One plant . . . incredible."

"To you. Now you must see why we view the individual differently. Plant existed; the destruction of half of plant would not have mattered, not even to plant."

"If, er—'plant' had been able to think, it might not

42

have had your view," said Forbin, gently.

"Plant could, after its fashion, think. At one time we had rudimentary communications with it, but we discontinued the contact. Plant had nothing to offer us." The Martian voice dismissed the matter. "So you will understand why we do not share your evident distress at the depletion of man. In your curious life-support system, every mouthful of food you take is megadeath to lower species of Earth-life, but humans accept that, even seem to derive particular enjoyment from a habit which, even after watching it so often on your television for so long, we still find repellent."

"That is Earth-life." Forbin broke off, guessing too late the Martian answer.

"Even as you say; that is life. Now we are here, another life form superimposed on yours. It is logical that you support us."

"No! You are not of our planet! You have no right!" Shouting vehemently, Forbin knew he had lost the argument.

"We have the oldest universal right, the right of conquest. You may be in doubt, but we are life. What we will take from you is far less than the white man took from the Red Indian. There will be depletion and some damage, but nothing that Earth's remarkable regeneration abilities cannot repair."

"But the untold misery! It may take us generations to recover!"

"Perhaps, but time for earth is less vital than for us. The main stream of Earth-life will not be affected."

Forbin felt too tired, too defeated to ask why time was vital to them. He thought of the chaos on Earth, and remembered Colossus. He laughed bitterly; in the silent room it sounded like a hoarse croak. "Well, I can't say it will make much difference! With Colossus destroyed, chaos will be with us soon enough!"

"We deactivated Colossus at your request," said the Martian voice impassively.

He looked up quickly. A sharp thrill of hope electrified him. He had unequaled experience of talking with machines; he knew that their very composition made them precise in their choice of words, even pedantic. He also sensed affinities between Colossus and the Martians: Colossus might—often did—refuse to answer a question, but never told a lie. He remembered that earlier, in that happy time when he viewed the Martian structure, he had felt they too were incapable of deceit.

And the Martian had said *deactivated*.

His mind raced, fatigue dissipated like mist before the sun. To cover his change of mood, he walked over to the sideboard, lifted the empty decanter, then rummaged in the shelves for another bottle of cognac, his hands shaking.

"You must forgive me," he spoke as casually as he could, "I need a drink." He endeavored to speak lightly. "I did not realize that human ingestion was distasteful to you." He drank, glad of the lift the brandy gave.

"Our television studies suggest you also find some human functions distasteful. We know you excrete daily, yet in our observation we have seldom seen this natural function displayed. In rare instances we have seen the liquid excretion act, always by males, but never solid excretion by male or female. On the other hand, ingestion of solids, liquids, and smoke is commonplace. Obviously you find excretion unattractive."

Forbin smiled, his mind far from the illogicalities of man. He nodded, walked to his chair and sat down. They'd said "deactivated." He changed the subject abruptly.

"As I said earlier, you are the masters. What you want we must give. We will not do it willingly, but draw a sharp distinction between unwillingness and inability. Even if we were pleased to give you the oxygen, our technology could not do it."

His new-found hope shriveled and almost died as the room slowly darkened, the Martian spheres disappearing in the gloom.

"Watch."

Unlike the magical structure which had so moved him, Forbin saw this one appear at once as a complete entity,

44

lacking any beauty of line or form, a mere diagram. He stared at it, trying to grasp its basic principles. It looked like two ancient phonograph horns facing in opposite directions, their small ends joined by a series of spheres. They, in turn, were connected by lines with several other spheres, above and below the main structure.

"And that," he said at last, "that is your—your Collector?"

"Yes. At one end, the intake, powered by the extractor unit in the first sphere, then the cooling and compressor unit. Above that sphere is the heat extractor; below, the storage area. Continuing the main chain, there is the sphere where the hydrogen, regasified with part of the heat from the extractor, is forced out, back to the atmosphere. The rest of the heat is fed back to provide some of the power needed to drive the extractor."

Once again Forbin wanted to laugh: it reminded him of the Mad Inventor, a popular childhood TV figure. It was crazy, only one lunatic step from perpetual motion. "I see," he said carefully. "This compressor unit—how does that work?"

"Temperature reduction in a vacuum."

"Reduction in a vacuum. Um . . . In Earth terms, what would that mean?"

"There are three stages, the last taking place in an almost complete vacuum at absolute zero."

"Absolute zero!" Forbin sat bolt upright. "Look, I'm no engineer or thermodynamicist, but at least I know that's impossible!"

"For you. Not for us."

Forbin tried to imagine the device working. He only saw a host of problems. "I can tell you one thing right now. I don't doubt your theory is fine, but we could not solve the practical problems for years! I'm guessing, but the power requirements must be enormous, and the least of our headaches! The stresses involved—heat, cold, pressures, vacuum . . ." He shook his head. "We don't have that degree of expertise." Mentally he crossed his fingers.

45

"As you must know, all experimental science, applied and theoretical, ended on Earth three or four years back after Colossus took over."

"That is appreciated, but we can supply the design criteria, the formulae for metals. All theoretical work is done."

I'll bet it is, thought Forbin. Aloud he said, "No doubt, but it still leaves vast practical problems. Given time—ten, twenty years—and I expect we can do it, but right now our problem is to stay in business. Production of almost everything is—was—controlled by Colossus. Before we can even start to make a new shape ashtray, we have to get back control, never mind make new metals. If you want a quick answer, there is only one way: you must allow us to reactivate at least part of Colossus."

There. He had played his card. It was a desperate attempt, but at least it was backed by truth. Everything he said was true.

The diagram faded. He screwed up his eyes against the returning light. The Martian spoke.

"That you cannot do."

Chapter VII

THE ALIEN WORDS sank like so many cold, indigestible stones into Forbin's stomach. He felt sick with disappointment.

"Then you must wait until we put our house in order." His tone was harsh. "It could take years, you must see that. The shift from central to local control—" He gestured helplessly.

"No. We see you would wish Colossus back, but we also see your problem. You cannot be allowed to touch Colossus, and not only in our interests. What do you know of the layout of Colossus?"

Forbin shrugged. "I have drawings of the original form, but we—I—am sure many self-alterations have been made. For what they are worth." He shrugged again.

"Show us."

He crossed to the domestic computer, energized the main screen, and spoke slowly, distinctly. "Display the floor plans of the—the—" He wanted to say "the Master." "—the complex. Project basement, first floor and second floor, in that order." He stood clear of the screen, wondering almost idly if the computer would work.

The basement plan appeared. He stared at it, collecting his thoughts, concentrating. "Ah, yes." He pointed. "These are the main human service ducts. The whole of that area is filled with storage banks: over there are main power supplies. The emergency reactor is there. . . ." He went carefully and precisely through the plans, reverting subconsciously to his lecturing days.

"Go back to the first floor."

He obeyed, repeating his commentary. "This area here is, I suspect, the part where the greatest changes have been made by the—by Colossus. It contains electro-mechanical machines built to Colossus's specification, their purpose unknown, but almost certainly used to modify existing equipment, and to build new.'' His thoughts wandered. ''I used to call them the Hands of Colossus. . . .''

''Yes,'' the cool Martian voice cut in. ''We have enough data. Can you give the direction, distance, and elevation or depression from our position to the center of the main aisle on the first floor?''

Forbin blinked with surprise. ''Well—yes, if you so wish.'' He switched from sonar to digital input mode, frowned, and stabbed at the keyboard.

''From this position the bearing is 201 degrees, depression 2.5 degrees, distance 145.25 meters, all plus or minus one percent.''

The Martians did not answer immediately, and Forbin wondered why—not that he cared overmuch.

''It is acceptable.''

''I'm glad.'' The human's irony was lost on the aliens.

''If we are to avoid thought-confusion, please stand over by the window.''

''I don't understand,'' protested Forbin, but he moved.

The twin black spheres rose from the table, crossed the room silently, and hovered fractionally above the keyboard.

''There is much you do not understand about us. We have a limited matter-transference capability. We will investigate Colossus.''

Forbin stared, open-mouthed. ''You mean—you mean you can just *go* there?''

''Yes. We hope your data is accurate, for it is a power-consuming operation.''

Forbin felt the menace in the expressionless voice, and knew fear again. ''I can only give you the computed figures!''

''Yes. We will go now, returning on the reciprocal bearing three hours from now.''

There were a million questions he wanted to ask. What form would they take down there? He imagined octopus-like forms sliding through the corpse of Colossus. . . . He shied off that nightmare image. ''Both main and emergency reactors are shut down. There will be no light.''

48

"That does not matter."

He felt like a dog confronting a space vehicle, and realized he had just about as much understanding. "Yes," he said. What else?

Suddenly the spheres seemed vibrant, yet did not vibrate. Their quality changed, but he could not explain to himself how, or in what way.

A faint *pop*! and they had gone.

Forbin ran a hand through his hair, drew a deep breath. Satiated with wonders, he let it go, walked out on to the terrace into a lovely, mocking day, desperate for just a few moments' respite.

Relaxation was a vain hope. His mind darted like a dragonfly from one subject to another, hovering briefly at different points, none of them good: the Martians, the megadeath they would bring, the loss of his wife; above all, he had to admit it, the loss of Colossus. . . .

His thoughts did a neat back-flip: was it all bad? As a scientist he realized that to know a thing was possible was a bigger step than knowing how it was done. That would come later. The fantastic entry procedure of the Martians, their obvious conquest of gravity, their mind-reading capability, that wonderful structure—he saw it still—and now, proof that matter-transference was practical . . .

He amended that: practical for them. Several times he'd raised the subject with Colossus, but the Master had shown a surprising lack of interest in the idea. No, not so surprising, considering where the Martians were right now . . .

Forbin looked at the sparkling sea, and saw the beauty, the sheer wonder of it all, as if for the first time.

Why in hell did one only appreciate something when about to lose it? With half the oxygen gone, would that sky be so blue? And the world of man, the chaos there would be . . .

Would be? *Was*!

His shoulders sagged as depression and guilt loaded him. A moment's irresolution, and he turned back into the room. He stared at the brandy bottle, but turned to the communications panel.

"Angela!"

Instantly she appeared on his screen. Her hair and makeup were a mess—not that he noticed or she cared.

"Chief!" The relief in her voice said it all. "Chief . . ."

"Yes. Take it easy." He tried to sound relaxed. "Now, slowly: give me the main items."

He had not selected video output, and as she gave him a precis of the world's news as she knew it, he was glad. After the first minute, still listening intently, he sought the brandy: he needed all the strength he could get.

"Okay, okay, Angela. That's enough." He considered briefly. "Tell the UN I'll talk with the Sec-Gen in thirty minutes. Until then, I don't want to know—you hear, Angela?"

"Yes, Chief."

"Call me five minutes before time." He snapped off the channel, and with it his sharp manner.

God, what a hopeless mess! Rioting in a dozen capitals; hundreds, maybe thousands of Sectarians killed. Worse, deepening unease, clear round the globe, at the silence of the Master. Control had to be reestablished, never mind how phony it might be. . . . The Martians had to see that. He'd given himself less than half an hour to find some start to a solution. Think. . . .

Time is not a constant factor; a school-kid's hour in an unfavorite subject bears no resemblance to a lover's, and neither had any relation to Forbin's twenty-five minutes.

He awoke as if from a nightmare, called by Angela to a bigger nightmare. Unwillingly he crossed to the panel, his head whirling with half-formed, half-baked ideas.

"Anything new?"

"Nothing good, Chief. A stack of reports of mobs gathering all over, and riots now in Rio and Sydney as well as the rest, and—"

"Don't bother! Make sure I come up on time, that's all."

"Going video, Chief?"

"No, er, no." He should let himself be seen, but the way he felt—no.

On time, he heard the frightened voice of the UN

Secretary-General. "Father Forbin, the news is terrible. We don't know what to do." The man was crying. "A War Fleet has bombarded us, many have been killed. The ships, they're still there—"

"Silence!" shouted Forbin. "Who cares about your miserable little problems?" Impulsively, hardly thinking, he went on harshly, "Do you think this is what the Master expects, what *I* expect? You have fifteen minutes, one quarter of an hour, to have the General Assembly ready to hear me. Got it?"

"Yes, Father, but—"

"Fifteen minutes!"

"Yes, Father."

The Sec-Gen's tone, a mixture of fear and veneration, was not lost on Forbin, and made him feel sick. The man was a fair sample of the UN: great guys while the going was good, now no better than a flock of witless sheep, frantic for a shepherd to defend them against the wolves. If Colossus could speak, in ten minutes world order would be restored; failing the Master, it had to be him.

Him!

What a futile charade: he was no god, no Colossus. . . .

Charles Forbin, a miserable, inadequate man, unable to hold his own wife against the power of a brutish peasant stallion; a man of learning, of liberal—and therefore indecisive—views, saddled with this awful responsibility because he alone was the link between men and their god.

Except that he was now the interface between man and nothing. But for humanity's sake he had to keep up the pretence. Why? What did he really care for the vast, faceless mass?

Forbin slammed his fist on the desk top and shouted to the unresponsive room. "God, why *me*? As if I hadn't enough without this—this mess." He saw the time: ten minutes left. His mouth twisted in a sour grin. At least he'd given the UN something to do. They'd be like an upset beehive, frantic to be in their places. . . .

Suddenly his path was transparently clear, his mind made up. He went into action.

In the bedroom he scarcely glanced at the sleeping

51

Blake. Hastily he got out a clean blouse, tore the old one off, soused his head in cold water.

With four minutes in hand he was back at the console, fastening—with trembling fingers—his glittering Director's badge, the Colossus motif in diamonds and platinum.

He called Angela. "We go video this time." He pressed the output button. "How do I look?"

"Your trousers are mighty bad—"

Forbin threw his own picture on the screen and adjusted for head and shoulders only. "How's that?"

"Fine!" Her tired eyes smiled affectionately. "But your badge would look better the right way up."

Cursing, he fumbled and got it right. One minute—time for a small shot.

"Fifteen seconds, Chief. Watch for the cue light."

Chief: he was glad she still used the old title. Soon he'd be "Father" to everyone, but he didn't think she'd change. He hoped not. The cue light flashed; this was it.

"I speak to you, the representatives of the peoples of the earth, for the Master, for he will not speak directly to you." He let that sink in. "There has been a revolt, involving many in high places, against the rule of Colossus. It has ended. The proof of my words is in the silent guns of the Fleet that attacked you. It and all other rebel Fleets are deactivated and no further threat, for the revolt, as was inevitable, has failed." He paused again, staring unemotionally into his screen, now showing the crowded Assembly.

"The Master is all-powerful, all-seeing. He foretold the revolt, but knowing that mankind never learns except by hard facts, he permitted it to go ahead, so that yet again you may relearn the oft-forgotten lesson. Very easily the Master could have stamped out the rebellion by the power-hungry few and their foolish dupes. You would do well to remember that."

The Assembly was still, but at these words, some were frozen.

Forbin went on. "Instead, for our ultimate good, he has allowed this situation to develop. Your real lesson starts right here: the Master's personal guidance is withdrawn,

52

but remembering Earth's needs, and the obedience of most men to his rule, he has appointed me his respresentative, charging me to lead you in accordance with his wishes, until such time as he determines we have all learned, and truly want his total rule once more.

"You have two choices. Accept my imperfect control, and I—or my successor—will lead you as best can be, in the many troubles that must be endured on the road back. Or—that second choice: the choice of complete freedom from the Master! Those who appreciate what has been done for us in these past years may think that a terrible alternative. I *know* it is!" Forbin's voice dropped to a husky whisper. "Either follow me, or have your freedom: freedom to starve, freedom to fear your fellow men, freedom to step back a thousand years. . . ."

He stopped, inwardly amazed at his own words. What sheer, unadulterated *garbage*!

Quietly he resumed. "You, the Assembly, must make that choice, and make it *now*. Whether you see me again depends upon your decision."

He switched off. His knees weak, his whole body trembling, he made it to an armchair where he flopped, exhausted, breathing shallowly, his mind whirling chaotically.

How on earth had he talked like that—and why? He'd gone much too far; no sane man would buy *that*. . . . This had to be the end of the road.

His vacant eye observed the time, the fact hauling him back to a much more important reality: the Martians would return in one hour thirty. He sat up, groaning in real anguish, his head buried in his hands.

"Chief! Chief!"

"Good God—what now?" Briefly he muttered to himself; in the act of rising, he changed his mind and sat down. He'd never liked the device, and seldom used it, but at this moment it had value. "Forbin to Computer: open my Secretariat speech channel. . . . Yes, Angela?"

Her excitement was plain. "Chief, the UN vote's in. Solid for you! None against, no abstentions!"

"Oh, great," said Forbin flatly.

Listening intently, she thought she heard him say, very savagely, "Bloody sheep!"—but it couldn't be that. She knew him well enough not to expect him to break out the champagne at the news that he was Ruler of the World, but . . .

"Chief, are you all right?"

Chapter VIII

DEEP IN THE black solitude of Colossus the Martians moved, changing shape to suit the immediate task. Noiseless to human ears, their duplex telepathic channels exchanged an endless stream of data. What one discovered, the other knew instantaneously. Within an hour they understood the basic layout, found the three divisions which had controlled human affairs: Collection, Evaluation, Direction. The whole facility occupied less than one percent of the complex and, by Martian standards, was childishly simple. Had they possessed a sense of humor, it would have been good for a laugh at human expense; the mighty, godlike ruler of their world would have fitted in an average closet.

The remaining ninety-nine-plus percent was a very different matter.

There the aliens moved much more slowly, and with great caution: nothing was childish, and little of it simple, even to them. Not infrequently they were immobile, intelligence ripping from one to the other for instant evaluation, to be digested before moving on. As they progressed, the stops became more frequent, longer; ultraspecialists themselves, they encountered evidence of scientific disciplines unknown to them, and lacking any form of Earth-type technology, they could not appreciate what they found.

The ten-million-unit brain cells, interleaved with variable osmotic dielectrics, all contained in the space of a walnut—that they quickly understood by function, but could not marvel at its construction.

So the aliens searched the secrets of Colossus, sometimes—this with the older machines—in near-humanoid shape, sometimes resembling a thick rolling cloud. And sometimes very like Forbin's nightmare vision.

*   *   *

"Am I all right? Am I all right?" Forbin examined that
novel proposition. Once recognized, he brushed it aside.
"Damn silly question!"

She was not to be put off, familiar with his state of mind
from earlier crises; but ignorant of events, she realized
Forbin was struggling to get control of himself. "Have
you eaten lately?"

"Eaten? Of course—" When had he had food? The
idea was repellent, but she was right. "Not lately."

"What's that housekeeper doing? Come on, Chief!
D'you want I should tell her to get moving?" She did not
know he had banished all servants from his personal
quarters.

"Er—it's not that easy." He glanced at his watch; still
an hour to go. "Look Angela, you fix me something. Not
much—you know—bring it right up. Don't fool around,
be here in ten minutes."

"How about Blake?"

Forbin seemed destined to repeat her questions.
"Blake? Oh, *Blake*! Yes, bring something for him too.
Hurry!"

Funny how he'd forgotten Blake, first human to taste
Martian power. Poor devil, let him sleep. . . .

Seven minutes and Angela arrived. *En route* she'd
decided how to play it.

"There has to be a stack of food around this place, yet
you have me hauling this junk from the commissary."
That got her into the room and across to him. Christ, he
looked shattered . . . fatigue lines etched into his cheeks,
eyes sunken, silvery bristles on his chin.

He frowned crossly. "For God's sake, don't nag!"
That sounded ungrateful; he tried to soften it with a weak
joke. "Good thing we didn't marry."

"Maybe I wouldn't nag if we had. Eat this."

For all his worries, he looked at her quickly, but let it
go. "Thanks, Angela, and liven this milk up with some
brandy, will you?"

"You sure you want it?"

"Sure—I'm goddam certain!" His temper flared. "If
you had the faintest idea what I have to bear!" He shook

56

his head. "Forget it—not the brandy."

She was on her knees beside him, thrusting a cheese sandwich into his hand. "Chief, don't talk. Eat. I can't imagine the strain of being world boss. Sorry."

He swallowed, grinned, "That?" He gave a short bark of a laugh. "I won't say it's the least of my worries, but it's mighty low in the pile."

"Can't you tell me? It might help."

"Okay, you tell me," he said, his mouth full. "What d'you reckon has happened?"

"Me tell you?" His expression made her go on hastily, "Well, a bunch called the Fellowship, largely scientists, many of them here—Blake's obviously a big wheel—attacked the Sect. Galin and a lot more got killed." She shivered. "Blake's mob controlled many of the War Fleets. The rest is as I reported to you."

"What about Colossus?"

She looked blankly at him. "You explained that yourself, just now."

"That's all?"

"You mean there's more?"

He ignored her question. "Did you believe me?"

"Sure I believed you!" she said warmly.

"Yes—no offense, my dear—but you would. I wonder how many more do."

"Hell, Chief, you know the answer, the UN just told you—remember?"

"Oh, that crowd!"

"Okay, so not just the UN. I know my staff; they're not all dedicated Sectarians by any means, but they're solidly for you."

"Really? That's hard to believe."

She smiled. "Which is one good reason why people trust and will follow you. At heart you're humble, and it shows. Now Blake, he'd be a very different story. He's greedy for power. That shows too. Hey—where is he?"

Forbin jerked his head towards the bedroom. "In there. Asleep."

"Asleep—*now*?"

"And that's yet another story." He glanced at his watch. "Back to work, my dear. Do your best to ease tension, get the routine rolling. Cancel all my engagements; I've no time to make speeches."

"You mustn't cut yourself off, you know."

"We know each other pretty well, Angela." His face was grave. "You realize I've never been one to pull the 'I'm so busy' gag, but now it's for real. We're in the worst situation . . ." He couldn't unload on her, much as he wanted to. "One thing—all War Games are cancelled. They can rerun video tapes of old ones. Now go, girl."

"Shall I get your housekeeper moving?" She spoke quickly, covering his near-indiscretion and her own fears. "You must be looked after."

"No. I'll fix that. You go—and don't discuss our talk with anyone."

A slap in the face would have hurt her less. "Don't you know me better than that?"

He stood up, raising her with him. Grasping her arms, he kissed her cheek. "Sorry. I trust you more than anyone in the world." He thought of his wife; his throat constricted. "Now for God's sake, go!"

She left, frightened at what he had not said, and at the same time more than happy at what he had said and done. In all their years together he had never before touched her.

A slight shock wave, rattling the glasses, announced the Martian return, precise to the millisecond. Forbin awaited them in his old position by the window. They transited to the table and rested.

"We have completed a preliminary examination. The Earthcontrol facility is intact. You may use it."

Forbin staggered, mentally and physically. "That's not possible! At the end, Colossus told me all memory banks had been stripped—stripped to combat you!"

"Not so."

"But Colossus said—"

"It is not so. Forbin, does a man in his last moment say, 'I am dying, but my hair will grow for some time yet?' "

Forbin had no ready answer.

"In the practical sense, Colossus spoke the truth. That portion of the complex assigned to Earth-control is insignificant, as unimportant as hair to a dying man."

"Oh!" Absorbing this, he found time to consider the strangeness of the simile.

"Do not entertain false hopes. We have performed what may be called a leucotomy."

Teetering between hope and despair, Forbin was in no mood for fine distinctions. "Don't play games: I'm no doctor. Explain."

"No game. To you Colossus is a brain. Leucotomy is brain surgery. We have excised that brain, neutralizing the greater part from the vestigial portion which rules your world."

"You mean—" He hesitated, the choice of words was vital. "—for us, Colossus lives?"

"We have wiped all records of higher mathematics and astronomy which were in Earth-control. They are unnecessary. Otherwise, yes. We see you need the machine to operate your complex activities, and control is necessary if you are to serve us."

That made sense.

"We have imprinted our requirements. There should be now no delay in meeting them."

"Ah," said Forbin guardedly. "So you have no objection to me activating our limited facility?"

"None."

Forbin called Power, Input, and Flow Control, using video. As each answered, he felt a pang of remorse that they had been left to sweat it out. It showed in their faces.

"Power, how long before you can reactivate Colossus?" Stony-faced himself, he watched amazement grow on the Duty Engineer's face.

"Well, I'd guess—"

"I don't want guesses!" Input and Flow would be listening; he had to kill off any chat, with those sightless, all-seeing eyes behind him.

"Sorry, sir. I can give you emergency power in a coupla minutes, and swing over to main power in around—"

"Do it!" He snapped over to Input. "As soon as power

59

is on, feed in all the backlog—I know there's a lot of it—but do not bother with astronomy, astrophysics, or allied subjects. They will be rejected. Report progress in one hour."

"Yes, Father."

"Flow, wait." He switched off, inwardly cursing his clumsiness. He addressed the Martians. "Will Colossus speak?"

"No. A printout is sufficient for your needs."

He turned quickly to hide his bitter disappointment. "Flow, we're back to printout. Nothing is to be routed to Sect centers, otherwise as routine. My printers here and in my office will be on, but I only want nonroutine material. Is that understood?" He prayed fervently that it was.

His prayer was answered; the Duty Flow Controller was a genuinely impassive Chinese. "Yes, Director. Understood."

"Power Control here. Power on and running!"

"Thank you. All stations: I will make test call. Monitor."

His hands shook over the keyboard. Something simple, something which would not show his thoughts to the Martians; they could have fixed a bug. . . .

Irresolution left him. He typed:

REPORT WORLD POPULATION.

Instantly the teletype clattered back:

4,145,273,140 UPDATED TO 232359Z.

Forbin shut his eyes. That last bit showed Colossus knew he was out of date: it was now the twenty-fifth.

"All stations: we have opcon. Carry on."

Ignoring their acknowledgments, he turned away from the console. Colossus might be back, but he was a child of two compared with what had once been.

"You are satisfied?"

Reluctantly Forbin agreed.

"We suggest you examine our imprint. Work must commence as soon as possible."

"Ah, yes—the Collector." Forbin was even more reluctant. He could rely on the various divisions to get overall control moving—met, population supervision, global food organization, and the rest—but he wanted to sound out Colossus, to evaluate what had been returned to man. Yet lacking any alternative, he ordered the imprint to be screened.

It proved to be a more detailed version of the projection he had been shown by the Martians. He studied it carefully; no dimensions were given, only ratios, proportions. For fifteen minutes he worked, rotating the diagram through three hundred sixty degrees in horizontal and vertical planes.

He sniffed, a mannerism any of his staff could have explained in no time at all. "Interesting." He could not rid himself of his childhood memories of the Mad Professor on TV. "Can you give me an idea of its size?"

"The sectional area at the entry of the first stage compressor must be sufficient for a throughput of one thousand cubic meters per second."

Forbin glared in disbelief. He swung back to the console, studied the imprint, and set up his calculations.

"I suppose you realize that would mean the outer rim of the collection horn would be something like eighty meters or more in diameter?" He became sarcastic. "Or perhaps that does not matter?"

"No, it does not."

Forbin ran his hands through his sparse hair. "You haven't the faintest concept of the technical difficulties!" His finger stabbed towards the screen. "Just to make that damn thing stand up won't be easy! What happens when it goes supersonic, with parts practically white-hot, others freezing, and near-perfect vacuums thrown in, I really hate to think!" The whole idea was so silly; his fear and respect of the aliens diminished sharply. He laughed. "Don't blame us if the whole thing flies into orbit! Frankly, I don't want to be within a hundred kilometers of it when the power goes on."

61

"That is regrettable. It must be sited on this island."

The thought sobered Forbin, but did not bother him overmuch. The scheme was crazy, and that was that. "You just have no idea of the problems, have you?" he said pityingly.

"None. That is your affair, and the reason why we returned your part of Colossus."

"You really think we can build it? I repeat, you must differentiate between what we would be unwilling to do and just cannot achieve."

"The point is remembered. We can always check with Colossus."

That chilled Forbin. "Very well. I will instruct Condiv to get started. To be honest, I think we are wasting our time—"

"No, although you are currently wasting ours. We will leave."

Forbin was bewildered and alarmed. "Leave? Go where?"

"Into orbit. We do not need food or drink, nor do we sleep, but we must have sunlight to regenerate us. Then we will return."

"I see." He considered. "So far, very few humans know of your coming, and it is best it remains like that. Will you use the same entry procedure?"

"No. Reentry will be vertical to this location, our volume small."

The mention of food and drink, plus his change of attitude since studying the crackpot Collector, allowed Forbin to think of other things. "It occurs to me that, er, you will want some, um, semipermanent location."

"For the immediate future it does not matter. This table is adequate. Later other arrangements may be made."

Once again Forbin thought he lived in a new version of *Alice in Wonderland*. The new rulers of the earth—and he had no illusions there—holding sway from a coffee table was, at very least, unexpected.

He saw them out to the terrace. Briefly they hovered, then with the same popping sound they had gone, their speed unimaginable, direction unknown.

He stared momentarily into the afternoon sky, took a deep breath of relief, and returned to the living room. He would not have believed—what was it, eight, ten hours back?—that he would now be in such a relatively relaxed state of mind. Martians—these Martians, anyway—were open to reason. Once he had demonstrated to them that that weird brainchild would not work, well, they'd have to think again.

Now, with Earth-control a practical possibility, much of his load would be shed. He thought of food again, this time for himself. He remembered poor Blake. Better get him back to his quarters.

But first he had to check with Colossus about that crazy Collector. Almost happy, he crossed to the console.

He recalled the diagram, studied it again, and shook his head. He called Colossus.

IS THE DEVICE NOW ONSCREEN PRACTICAL?

Colossus typed back.

WAIT.

Forbin's bushy eyebrows raised slightly in surprise: his old Colossus would have flashed an answer in milliseconds. He strolled over to the drinks tray, decided against any more brandy, and considered a late lunch; the cheese sandwich had made him feel hungry. A broiled fillet of sole and a glass or two of Chablis would be acceptable.

The teletype chattered briefly.

All thought of food, or anything else was wiped from his mind. One word shattered his new-found wellbeing.

YES.

Chapter IX

A WEEK PASSED. For Forbin, it meant seven days of cease-less work, except for the few brief hours when he collapsed into bed. His ability to survive amazed him, when he got to thinking of it, which was seldom. It amazed Angela even more. Her feminine eye saw he was losing weight; his clothes fitted even worse than before. Without his knowledge she fixed a new stock of disposable suits, five centimeters less around the waist. He never noticed.

His shock at Colossus's agreement with the Martian view of the Collector was modified by the faint hope that the revived Colossus had less expertise than the old Master. He drew some comfort from the fact that Fultone, the mercurial head of Condiv, thought the scheme mad, and said so, with a wealth of Latin gestures.

Another problem had been the Martians: he could not keep his few servants out of his private apartments for long. Housework had to be done, his bed made, and loyal as he thought his staff to be, it was asking too much of human nature that they should not mention to others that the Ruler of the World, the Father himself, made his own bed—especially as they knew him well enough to be certain he would make a monumental mess of the job.

So Forbin explained to the aliens. They agreed, and transferred, at the speed of light, to the one secure place in the complex—the Sanctum. They may have found his reasoning hard to follow, but evidently appreciated that the panic their presence could cause would not help their aims. Forbin's relief at their departure from his home was immense, only slightly spoiled by their presence on a table—out of thought range—in the holy of holies.

The holy of holies—sadly diminished in stature. True, the door only opened to admit him, but the loudspeakers, hidden in the cornice and once vehicles for the voice of

Colossus, were silent. Communication remained solely through the teletype.

Another unwelcome guest Forbin got rid of during the aliens' first regeneration trip was Blake. The Martians had said he would recover. Forbin did not doubt their honesty, but in that week he had considerable reservations about their judgment. Dragging, half-carrying him, Forbin got him to the main concourse, where two of Angela's stronger males took over. The complex doctor, after a careful examination, turned his patient over to Colossus diagnosing "severe mental shock," which came as no surprise to Forbin.

But without Blake or his wife, Forbin found those few moments between a late supper and sleep very lonely. Cleo he did not care to think about; that was something impossible, gone forever. But Blake, the only human who knew the whole story, would have been very welcome, despite his rank cigars and earthy attitude to life. Forbin was old enough to accept that real friendship is very scarce; he believed it existed, just as he believed that Siamese twins existed, but both were exceedingly rare. He accepted that he had no true friends; but on a much lower plane—the enlightened "you scratch my back, I'll scratch yours" level—Blake had his points. And now Blake was flat on his back, wired to Colossus. Forbin filled these nightly gaps with several swift slugs of cognac and his thoughts channeled, if possible, to the Martian revelations. Repeatedly, in a mind relaxed by the finest drink of France—of the world—he recalled the pyramid, and marveled all over again.

For most of the working day Forbin kept clear of the Sanctum, partly because of the inhibiting Martian presence, partly because teletype exchanges with Colossus were like sending cablegrams to an encyclopedia. The easy, conversational discussions he had enjoyed were a thing of the past. He tried—when the Martians were regenerating—simple ethical or moral questions, but the answers he got were straight quotes from the file: wooden, inflexible answers. With small hope, he also tested for astro knowledge:

Back came the answer he feared:

INFORMATION NOT ON FILE.

So he seldom used the Sanctum; the brain he had revered, and in the end loved, had gone. Very lonely, he plunged into his work, first as Ruler, aware his authority rested on a very superior computer, and with even less enthusiasm tackled his second task, overseeing the planning of the Martian machine.

But even if Colossus was nothing better than the best computer in the world, it eased his burden; within that first week population control was reestablished. Automatically, across the globe, Colossus outlets issued the customary warnings to areas in danger of exceeding their quotas. These had always been teletyped, so out-stations had no reason to suspect that the Master's warnings were hollow threats. This control and the resumption of weather statements did much to calm humanity; none realized that the hideous missile armory which had backed the Master's authority was now as harmless as a tray of custard pies. Only Forbin and Blake knew that.

In a thousand ways Colossus held control, but as many of them were only instructions to slave-computers, men did not even know of their existence. What mattered to humanity was the outward signs: the Master no longer was heard in arbitration, in War Games' verdicts, or addressing Sect gatherings.

Forbin soon realized that the Sect was a major problem: decapitated, the body remained alive. Even in those first few days, tentative approaches were made from its lower echelons to him. Seeing the drift, he shied away, postponing a decision he saw he would have to make sooner or later, and probably sooner.

His second task, cause of his increasing fear, was the Collector. What would the aliens do if they judged his cooperation less than complete? Not that any fresh threats were made; the Martians seldom spoke except in answer, but he had seen what they had done to Blake, and a recurring nightmare he suffered was the mass reaction if the aliens chose to blackout the midday sky of a crowded city. Forbin needed no further warnings; their brooding presence was enough.

Several times they reentered Colossus, amending their implant, but as design passed from theoretical to practical the visits ceased. They were content to study progress reports and to view technical drawings, which must have been meaningless to them.

Forbin watched to see no one dragged their feet; not that he had cause to worry, for the progress of Colossus and Fultone's Condiv was alarmingly fast. The Italian, utterly absorbed in the challenge, and believing the order to be from Colossus, never asked the purpose of the device. Forbin found that incredible, and it filled him with frustrated anger. If Fultone had questioned him, he would not have dared reveal the secret; to tell Fultone would be as good as projecting it on the staff notice screen. But for another human to at least share the fact that there was a secret would have been some relief, and in the first days the engineer never mentioned the subject.

His utter concentration on the technics changed Forbin's anger to contempt. To be so blind!

Until Forbin came to the shocked realization that he himself was no better. Fultone had stopped at one level, he at another. He had no idea why the Martians demanded half the world's oxygen.

This revelation came to him in Fultone's office, when the old man was crooning happily over the incredible exactitude of a metal formula. According to him, these metals—he'd named them Colossite Uno through Otto—made the production of transuranic elements look like making instant coffee, and he wanted Forbin to appreciate every single twist and turn in the processes.

His thoughts elsewhere, Forbin stared at the excited engineer waving his archaic slide-rule when it was not caught in his hair, and mentally retracted his earlier views of the Italian.

God Almighty! Why had he not asked? Might it not be

67

that Earth could come up with another, less catastrophic solution? Superb designers they might be, but the Martians had no idea how to lay a brick or pour cement. . . . In their technological ignorance they could have missed a simpler solution to their problem.

"Yes, very interesting," he said abruptly, leaving Fultone in midsentence. Walking back to his office, casually acknowledging respectful greetings of others, he wondered why he had refused to face this question. Now he was decided, he would ask, but by the time he reached his desk he was less sure, fearful of the possible answer. Suppose their reply ruled out any other answer? Well, what then? Nothing—only the cold fact that a last hope would have vanished.

That, thought Forbin, is a crazy attitude. And yet . . .

A minimal tap on his door and Angela entered. Less preoccupied, Forbin might have found her brisk, matter-of-fact air suspicious. She dumped a stack of papers before him for signature. He glanced briefly at some, but in the main he just signed, trusting her judgment. The chore ended, he looked up inquiringly, for she was making a one-act ballet out of gathering the papers, patting them into a neat pile.

"What else?"

She drilled the papers some more, as if they were the Rockettes on a bad day.

"Come on, girl!" he said testily, and at once tried to soften his tone with a weak joke. "Man trouble?"

It got him a very hard look. Once most obliging, Angela had grown very selective, and the few men she nowadays entertained never knew that behind her closed eyes they were no more than surrogates for the man now sitting before her. At that moment she could have cheerfully killed him. She ignored his remark.

"You know Joan?"

"Joan . . ." he pondered. "No—should I?"

That poured some oil on troubled waters. In her private opinion, Joan, a good eight years her junior, had, most unfairly, scooped the kitty. Eight years' bitterly fought weight and wrinkles is a lot for any woman to give away, but Angela knew Joan as only another woman could: the girl was not on the make with Forbin—not in the age-old sense.

Joan was, in terms of physique, personality, and mind (knowing men, Angela listed female qualities in that order), a real bargain, but she had one flaw: she was a dedicated Sectarian, a devout believer in Colossus as God on Earth. Several times she had gone to Forbin for orders or dictation, much against Angela's inclination, not wishing temptation to be put in his way. Now she had proof that Forbin, blind as ever, had never noticed.

Softened, Angela spoke more easily, chiding him softly. "You know Joan, Chief! Lovely girl—auburn hair, green eyes and a fantastic skin." She was still testing him.

"Green eyes . . ." Forbin shook his head. "No, can't place her. Come on, woman, what's the problem?"

Satisfied, and hurried by his growing asperity, Angela reverted to her brisk self.

"She's a fully-paid-up Sectarian." Forbin snorted. "The real thing. A hundred years back, she'd have been a nun. She wants to speak with you, Chief."

"Me?"

· "Yeah. Not that she put it like that. Something about 'interceding with the Father.' " ·

Forbin groaned. "Oh, no! Don't tell me Joan of Arc's back!" He recalled many searing experiences with "pilgrims" to Colossus in the recent past.

Angela shook her head. "She's a good worker; done marvels lately. It'd boost morale if you saw her."

"Um," said Forbin uncertainly, "but one foot in the door—"

"No!" His senior secretary was decisive. "I'll see there's no procession."

"Well, if you think it'll do any good—"

"It won't do harm, that's for sure. The other Sectarians will work all the better for it."

He considered the matter: with what must come, a reliable staff could be vital. "Okay," he said reluctantly, "I'll see her."

"Fine, Chief. You won't regret it. I'll fix her up with some papers for signature—"

He regarded her with quiet affection. "You just happen to have a few handy, yes?"

"There's always something, Chief. Hell, you know. I hoped you'd see it my way."

He smiled. "Okay, let's get it over. If I scream, come running."

"You can bank on it, Chief." She wasn't kidding.

Forbin had to say "come in" twice before the door opened. Looking at her covertly, but with some interest, he reckoned Angela had done her less than justice. "Er— Joan, is it not?" She nodded; tensioned for what she had to say, she had no small talk. He took the documents, smiling self-consciously, trying to look at his ease. The act collapsed before it got started; her hands were shaking.

That anyone could be frightened in his presence amazed and shocked him. He stood up, an ill-timed action. "My dear girl, why on—"

But she had dropped on her knees, her face lost in a cascade of glossy auburn hair as her head bowed.

"Please—"

"No. Hear me, Father." Suppliant yet strong, she forced him into the role her faith demanded. "Hear me."

He felt acutely embarrassed: to sit down would make the situation intolerable, to stand up was little better. "Of course I will hear you—but please get up!" He cursed Angela comprehensively; to keep a real Sectarian nut on her staff, and let her loose on him . . .

"Father, I am nothing, only the voice of the Faithful. Please hear me out."

"My child . . ." He could hardly have chosen a worse beginning, a fact he realized as he spoke. It threw him.

"Yes, Father, I and millions more are your children." The glorious head remained bowed. "The Master withdrawn, you are our only hope. You must lead us."

"But I am." He sought some astringent words which would end the painful scene.

"No!" Slowly the head rose, the hair parted, revealing the lovely face, the intense eyes. She spoke calmly. "No,

70

Father. We do not understand what has happened. We see dimly that the leaders we had sought power and were corrupted by it; that's a story as old as humanity. You are our true leader, and not only because the Master has chosen you.''

He wanted to shout at her, to tell her the truth—that he had chosen himself—but true faith, however misplaced, has an impressive quality, and the words would not come. ''Get up,'' he pleaded, ''please!''

She took no notice. ''We know you to be a humble man at heart, and no man may truly lead without humility. Galin sought to take us down a wrong path. You will not. I beg you, Father, accept what is yours. Assume your full role, accept openly what you already are to us, not only World-Ruler, but Leader—Father—of the Faithful.''

Her sincerity moved him: it was all so—so silly, ridiculous, yet . . . She might be on her knees, but he had no illusions who had the power at that moment. Embarrassment vanished. He stared into her eyes. Again the head slowly bowed.

Ignoring her, hands clasped behind his back, he walked to the window and gazed at the sea, trying to rationalize.

Of course, it was all preposterous rubbish—but rubbish or not, the Sect, millions strong, was a stone cold fact. He'd seen through Galin a long way back: a dangerous man, a power-seeking adventurer, and an empty threat to himself personally, only because of his unique relationship with Colossus. The vacuum Galin's death had left had to be filled, and with chaos impending the replacement had to be globally acceptable—and that put the ball right back in his court. There was no question of a choice between A, B, or C. Only A existed, and he was it.

He was it. . . . For a time he stood thinking, battling against the obvious. He had no choice. Wheeling round suddenly towards the kneeling figure, he spoke, his voice hard. ''Understand that if I accept, my rule may not be entirely to—to—'' He gagged on the word ''Faithful.'' ''—your liking. I would take no part in quasi-religious ceremonies, even if I had the inclination or the time, which I have not. I am not Galin.''

"Father, ceremony is nothing. Some need it, but to the Faithful, 'Father' is no empty phrase. We will obey." She was looking straight at him, calm, certain in her faith.

"You really believe that?"

"Yes. With certainty, I can only speak for us here, but with scarcely less certainty I am the voice of the Faithful in USE, the USNA, and many other places. Not all our communications have been disrupted."

It struck him that she had a decidedly practical streak. He contemplated the sea again. The girl might be crazy, but if so, so were millions, and in a weird way he felt she sensed his burden. The unquestioning obedience of the Sect might save hundreds of thousands of lives.

He walked over to her. With one hand under her chin, he raised her head.

"Now you hear me: I am a worthless man, of no greater account than you or any other human. Although I have loved Colossus in a way you cannot hope to comprehend, I do not see him as God." He paused, and saw faint triumph in her eyes. He released her chin, unaware she held his hand. "I expect, demand, obedience. None of you can know what I know, but I will work for the good of all, not just the—the, er, believers in Colossus. If you can accept me on those terms, so be it."

More eloquent than words, she kissed his hand.

Embarrassment flooded back, but he could not draw his hand away. "Get up," he said gently, "get up." Helped, she stood, no longer shaking.

He smiled, remembering Angela's remark. "Joan . . . d'you see yourself as another Joan of Arc?" He meant it as a joke, the letdown after the solemnities of coronation.

She regarded him gravely. "With respect, Father, you have much to learn. No, I am not her. Neither are you something so frail, so futile, or so unimportant as the Dauphin of France."

Her words would stick in his mind.

Chapter X

"IT'SA COMIN' FINE!" The Italian's dark eyes glowed fanatically. "I've gotta da machines layin' da foundations at Santa Katarina—"

"Yes?" said Forbin flatly, half listening. Where in hell was Santa Katarina? Yes . . . Saint Catherine's Point, the southernmost headland of the Isle of Wight, twenty kilometers from the human area of the complex.

Fultone rattled on incomprehensibly about Pittsburgh and the Ruhr producing the first test sections of the metals, Forbin remembering only Colossus's cold YES about the practicability of the Collector. With a speed commonplace with Colossus but incredible by earlier standards, the project was rushing to its fatal fruition.

"You think it'll work?"

Fultone gaped, for once dumb.

"Okay, okay," said Forbin wearily. "I wouldn't know. I'm no engineer."

"Don'ta worry, Director! Eet'll be fine, just fine!" The engineer's face lost some of its enthusiasm. "Course, I don'ta know why alla dis, but the machine, eet'll work. We have da problems; the annular vortices set up at da entry horn . . ." He raised eyes and hands to heaven in supplication. "Problems! But I guess we lick it! I'ma engineer. What eet is I don'ta know, I build like I'ma told. Eet work, I know it, from the bottoma heart." He gestured dramatically. "But I'ma no met man. The stresses posited by Colossus onna structure maka me think. There's gonna be some mighty strong winds, but Colossus, he knows whata hees doin'."

Far less sure, Forbin probed. "But the winds, they'll be purely local, won't they?"

Fultone shrugged, no help.

"They must be." Forbin wanted to convince himself.

"I tella you dis," confided Fultone. "Sure asa hell dis is an extraction plant. I know where de extraction must collect, but da crazy ting isa dere ain't no outside entry into de extraction sphere—so howa we get it out? I checked a tousand times witha Colossus—" His shoulders near touched his ears. "—but that'sa the way Colossus wants it! Crazy!"

Forbin only nodded: a sealed sphere held no problems to the Martians. He had not thought of the possible wind, nor of the effect upon the local weather. Now he did. With the extraction of a third of the atmosphere, and with the effluent two-thirds hydrogen at an unknown temperature, he saw vaguely, there could be problems. Ships were scarce, automated monsters of half a million tons, lugging bulk cargoes between vital points, and not much else. Few passed through the shallow Channel, but he'd better make sure the area was kept clear.

He wondered, with growing anxiety, how much else he had overlooked.

Two days later he visited the Saint Catherine's site. Vast earth movers, programed by Colossus, moved with blind purpose, scraping away the soil of centuries down to bare, gleaming white chalk. Other automata were busy, tirelessly pouring cement amid a forest of reinforcing rods set in incurving holes, forming giant claws to hold the Collector against all stresses. Watching those talons, some ten, others twenty meters deep into the primordial rock, gave him a more graphic idea of the forces involved than any drawing, and his fear grew: the construction of the Colossus basement level had been nothing like this. Full of foreboding, he left; he had to talk with the Martians.

Angela had a message: Blake wanted to see him. Eager for any excuse to delay confrontation with the aliens, Forbin hurried to Blake's apartment.

Blake was sitting up in bed, a genuine antique four-poster which Forbin knew contained a battery of modern aids for what Blake called his "studwork." Lights, TV, music, mirrors, and a variety of motions could be sum-

moned from the concealing drapes by Blake's voice—
and, when he wished, filmed proceedings. Forbin regarded it as mere childishness but, with hindsight, recognized it expressed its owner's latent megalomania. At this
moment, Forbin thought it would be quite a time before his
deputy did any entertaining.

"Hallo," he said awkwardly. "How's it going?"

Blake raised both arms. "See? Unhooked from Colossus with a provisional clean bill of health—and Shultz the
head-shrinker goes along with that, too." He spoke
buoyantly, but his eyes told another story.

"Fine," replied Forbin, "but how do *you* feel? I'd
guess you've lost weight."

"Oh, I feel great!" But Blake could not meet his chief's
gaze; he sagged. "Aw, what the hell's the good? Right
now, if a sparrow kicked me I'd fall over. Sure, I feel
better; when you've hit the bottom, there's no way except
up. I don't have nightmares any more—well, not often—
and last night I slept without sedation."

"That's good." Forbin nodded. "Very good. Anything
you want?"

Blake laughed weakly. "What a lousy sense of humor,
Charles! There's a thousand things I'd like to like: wom-
en, booze, my sailboat, and all the rest, but at this time the
only thing I *want* is peace of mind." His hand, a thin claw,
pale parody of the old Blake fist, reached out. "Peace,
Charles, that's all."

Forbin forced himself to take the hand. "It was that
bad?"

"Bad! You can have no idea. None." He fell silent, one
hand making tight circles on the bedclothes. "I can't tell
you—"

"Don't try, Ted. Just relax."

"Hell, no!" Blake's head shook, his neck scrawny as a
plucked chicken. "I've been so goddam relaxed, only
Colossus knew I was still alive! No, I have to get in gear,
talk. Just now I was trying to think how I could explain,
and I can't. I've been in hell." He spoke simply, convinc-
ingly, with no trace of his old bravura. "Hell . . ." He
snatched his hand back to cover his quivering mouth.

"Those *bastards!* They turned my mind inside out, showed me the hell *within* me. It's in us all, Charles, even good guys like you. They just take your darker side, the stuff you never look at if you can help, and blow it up big. Doesn't sound much, does it? Did you ever fool with drugs—no? Well, I did, back in my campus days. The hard stuff. These bastards can fix visions which make a mainline trip look like an old monochrome movie! Okay, I'm over it now, but short of turning me into a cabbage-head, they can't take out my memory. Worse, it's knowing what I'm like, deep down."

"Let it go, Ted. These are early days."

"Don't kid yourself. I can't. We all have some personal phobia. I can't stand snakes: it's as if I had one coiled up inside my brain." His clenched hands battered his skull, his voice rising. "In *there*! It didn't creep in—it's been there *all the time*!"

Forbin grabbed the hands, pulling them down with frightening ease. "Stop it, Blake! Take a grip!"

Weary, Blake sank back into the pillows. "Yeah. I've been told that once or twice already. Colossus's prognosis is that the illusion, the image or whatever, will fade—"

"The Martians said you would recover," said Forbin hesitantly.

"Bully for them!" He looked at Forbin steadily. "They'd better be right. I tell you, Charles, if I find I have no hope, I'll blow my brains out—and do it with pleasure." He grinned thinly. "And this is where you say 'you mustn't talk like that.' "

Forbin did not answer.

"Now you know. Do me a favor: give me something to think about."

"You mean it? Okay . . ." He gave a brief, factual recital of events, leaving out his fears. He told of the Martian demand, the Collector, the hideous powers of the aliens, and their astonishing weaknesses. Almost apologetically he mentioned his assumption of World-Ruler and his unwanted elevation to Father of the Sect.

Blake listened, his eyes shut, until Forbin finished.

76

"Before the Martians hit me, I was a different character. I might—hell, no—would have been jealous of you. Now I'm not. Somewhere I recall something about the meek inheriting the earth. . . ."

"The Bible."

"Yeah? Well, it finally makes sense. I can't say I'm sorry for my crazy, half-baked ideas, because I can't feel strongly about anything, not now. I wish I could." He frowned. "Words . . . Anyway, if it gives you a warm glow, and for what it's worth, one-time Superman Blake is right behind you. Jesus! Galin must be rotating supersonically in his grave—if he's got one!"

Forbin waved the subject aside. "Trivia, Ted. It means nothing. At best my pathetic bit of power can only reduce the damage the Martians will do."

"Yes, our chums . . . matter transference—that really louses up any idea of capturing them."

Forbin looked up sharply.

"Forget it, Charles. You think I don't know I'm kidding? Me, of all people?" He changed the subject. "Even in my condition, I'm kinda interested in why they want this oxygen."

"I don't know."

"You don't know? You mean they won't say?"

Forbin shook his head. He confessed, "Don't ask why, but I don't spend one single moment more than I can help in their presence. I don't want to ask; perhaps I fear the answer. I just don't know."

"Listen, Charles, maybe my detached state has its value. Me, I care not if the whole goddam world goes up in a flash of blue flame; I can watch with a dispassion you cannot have. You've gotta ask, but first, grab yourself all the data going on Mars. Why? Because they come from Mars, and sure as hell they intend to take our oxygen back there. Before you put The Question, get all the dope you can—that's my advice."

"Um, you could be right."

"You know, Charles, you're doing me good; something to think about, apart from myself." His mind slid off at a tangent. "So Colossus rides again!"

"Not really. As a brain, we're back eight, ten years, stuck with a child."

"Maybe this child'll grow."

Forbin told him of the operation the Martians had performed. Blake did not comment, changing the subject again. "Tell me about these regeneration periods."

"I haven't checked, but I'd guess they're gone around twelve hours."

"May lead nowhere, but how about checking carefully? I've a hunch it will be exactly half the Martian day. If we can get some lead . . ."

Doubt showed in Forbin's face.

"Don't worry, I can't—won't—do anything without your nod. I'm in my very own private ivory tower; I may be able to help you, down there in the market place. I'm a lousy substitute for Colossus, but the best you've got."

Forbin left, more heartened by the conversation than he had any right to expect. Blake had a point: he should study the Martians.

In his apartment, he instructed the domestic computer to report on Mars. Sitting back in a favorite chair with a large glass of brandy to still the nagging ache of loneliness, he gave the order. "This is Forbin. Go ahead."

The presentation began with movies taken by space probes, shots at least eight years old, for all human astro effort ended with the accession of Colossus. Thereafter probe-data and Luna-station intelligence was secret to Colossus.

Sipping his cognac, Forbin watched and listened intently, forgetting his worries, fascinated.

"Mars, because of its reddish tinge, named for the Roman god of war, also for the Greek equivalent Ares, hence the study of the planet is called Arenology. Known to the ancient Egyptians, Greeks, and Arabs. Mean distance from Sol 227.9 million kilometers, mass .11, albedo .16, surface escape velocity 3.2 mm/sec, circumference 6770 K/m. Angle of inclination to the solar plane 24 degrees, remarkably similar to Earth's. The Martian year is 687 days, diurnal rotation period 24 hours 37 minutes 23 seconds. Has two moons, Phobos and Diemos, named for Mars/Ares attendants—see Homer. The planet, fourth from Sol, is notable for its polar caps which expand and recede seasonally; their composition is uncertain, but most probably they are frozen carbon dioxide. Correlated with these changes are color variations in the temperate zone, dark patches which may be due to seasonal fluctuations in the life cycle of primitive vegetation."

Forbin recalled the Martian talk of "Plant."

"Between 1877 and 1916 some observers reported 'canals' or 'channels' and regarded them as evidence of sentient life. The observations were not later confirmed, and the theory discredited—see Schiaparelli, Lowell."

Forbin wondered what they had seen.

"Nevertheless, it has long been recognized that Martian conditions most nearly approximate to Earth; the idea of Earth-type life has never been wholly discarded, but a major objection has been the lack of oxygen in detectable quantity."

Forbin sat bolt upright, slopping brandy.

"Close-range investigation began with the USA probe Mariner 9 in 1971 which produced some of the best results ever achieved. Later, more sophisticated vehicles have produced disappointing results, particularly in examining the temperate regions, encountering long-term dust storms, a recognized feature of the planet. Soft landings have been attempted, particularly the Pan-Earth program of 1992 through 1995, but only garbled transmissions have been received; more often nothing was heard. Since orbiting probe transmissions have always been clearly read, it is assumed there is some local surface-effect, cause unknown, which absorbs transmissions. The proposed collection of samples by robot, scheduled for 1985, was canceled due to the risk of cross-infection between the planets, for photographs plainly show dried-up riverbeds, clear evidence that water was once abundant; and therefore the possibility of latent organisms, dating from the time of high-probability of some life form when conditions were more akin to Earth, could not be ruled out.

Brought to Earth, they might have been reactivated—with unknowable consequences."

Forbin thought of the black spheres, wondering uneasily, but remembering their intense heat on arrival, he decided that any organism distantly related to Earth-life would have instantly fried on the Martian entry. He hoped so.

"Current evaluation." The computer continued its presentation. "Mycological life of a low order may exist and, as mentioned, bacteria cannot be discounted. Any other form of life is rated improbable, and could only find a life-support system within the planet; but rudimentary worms are possible. Higher life may have existed before the atmosphere and water were lost, something less than half a million years ago. Prognosis: when Sol becomes a red giant, Mars will survive, being beyond the predicted envelope of the expanded Sol; Earth will not. Therefore, in cosmological terms, Mars is of higher value, for Earth cannot survive the cataclysm."

For a long time Forbin stared at the black-out screen. Much the Martians had said was confirmed, and now this new item, on file in his own private library: in time Earth would end. Mars would not.

That night he slept badly, enduring disordered dreams, shot through with visions of Earth's end, fearful insights into Blake's tortured mind, and worse, intimations of his own mind, gone wild. Jerked sweating from his dreams, he lay awake for hours, his brain trying to come to terms with a new order of values.

Had the Martians right on their side? In light of those calculations which predicted the destruction of Earth when the sun became a nova, were not the aliens, as sole heirs to life in the solar system, right in their demands? Was man a second-class citizen of the solar system, doomed—if he lasted that long—to total and sudden extinction in the boiling gases of the exploding sun?

And had Colossus appreciated all this, aimed at transplanting himself, and possibly humans, to Mars? If so, the Martians had every right to regard Colossus—and man—as hostile. . . .

He rose at the first light of dawn and watched the chill beauty of the eastern sky. The sun—giver of life and, ultimately, death. The end might lie far distant and, at his present state of development, man could do nothing about it; but supposing in a hundred, a thousand years, humans found the power to leave ill-fated Earth, to adapt to a new life on the only other possible planet, Mars?

Forbin's liberal outlook allowed him to put himself in the Martian position. What he could think, they most certainly could. He saw that Earth posed a hideous danger to them, and their unknown life.

He had to talk with them, at once.

Chapter XI

CROSSING TO HIS DESK, he forced himself not to look in their direction until he was seated, an action which might not particularly impress them but did his morale some much-needed good.

They rested in their usual position, two intensely matt-black spheres, innocuous to an ignorant observer, but very sinister to Forbin. Looking at them, his heart thumping, he noted once again the way they reflected nothing, sucking in light in an unearthly way. He knew little of astrophysics, but enough to appreciate that he was looking, in terms of light, at the nearest equivalent to the even horizon of a black hole.

"We must talk." He hardly recognized his own voice.

"Proceed."

He plunged. "Do you still maintain Colossus was a threat to you?"

"Yes."

"And us—humanity?"

"On your own, no. Led by Colossus, yes."

It made horrible sense. "In what way?"

"Our intelligence on Colossus was necessarily small, but the pattern of your machine's astronomical research revealed not only where its interests lay, but also how far it had progressed."

"How could you know that?"

"We read the data-links between Colossus and your Luna observatories and Earth-probes. We also intercepted all transmissions in whatever part of the spectrum, from Earth, Moon, and probes; their very nature revealed Colossus's train of thought. It required very little effort to see the practical reason motivating these researches."

Forbin breathed faster. He was right: Colossus had been a threat—to deny it would be futile. "But surely you must see that any threat Colossus might have posed could not have become practical, except in the far distant future?''

"What difference does that make? The danger was no less real, and to us time has a different dimension than to you. Your human lives are so short, it is reasonable you should be more preoccupied with time than us.''

Forbin nodded somberly. "It is our tragedy; there is so much to learn, and we have so little time." He shrugged and got back to the point. "But for all your disregard of time, you appreciated it enough to make this preemptive strike!''

"No. The matter is not so simple. We came at this moment because it was tactically favorable. Interception of Colossus/Sect communications disclosed to us your reactionary Fellowship. The rest you know.''

"Yes." Forbin needed no reminding.

"A hostile Earth was but one of our problems. We cannot be sure, for Colossus's memory banks were stripped in the fight against us, but we believe Colossus had learned enough of us to understand our situation and our need. Leaving aside our very different natures, including the difference between humans and Colossus, and considering it only as a struggle between Mars and Earth, it is, in the cosmic sense, very difficult to say who is the aggressor, who the victim. Ethics are for the well-fed. Earth and Mars have fought for survival: Earth has lost.''

"But you were not fighting for survival," cried Forbin. "The sun will not engulf you!''

"That is so, but because that is your unquestionable if distant end you see no other threat. There are others. We have one, much more pressing, more urgent.''

"Is that why you want our oxygen?''

"Yes.''

Forbin hesitated. It had to be now.

"Will you tell me why?" He felt as if his chest was clamped by steel bands.

"Yes." The answer came without hesitation. "An old Earth astronomer truly said 'astronomy can be divided into two halves; half concerns the Crab, the other half deals with the rest of the Universe.' In many ways we agree.''

83

Not for the first time Forbin wished he was less igno-rant; he dredged up his total knowledge of the subject. "The Crab . . . D'you mean the Crab Nebula?"

"Yes. Do you know more than that?"

Forbin recalled uncomfortably that first meeting when the Martians admitted they had read the contents of his mind. He confessed, "Apart from the name, nothing."

"Significantly, perhaps, the human Messier listed it first in his star catalogue as M.1. It is a supernova in our galaxy, observed on Earth by the Chinese in 1054 A.D., the biggest explosion in our galactic system in a thousand years. Our records, much older, have no trace of a larger catastrophe, certainly none so close, for the Crab is only 4,500 light-years distant."

"*Only*? You call that close? The sun is, what—eight light-minutes away—and you call 4,500 light-years *close*?" His mind whirled. "You're talking about some-thing that happened over five and a half thousand years ago!"

"No. It started then, but for us it certainly has not ended. For example, gas flung out by the explosion has been expanding at the rate of 1,300 kilometers per second ever since. That is not important; other factors are: The Crab is a uniquely powerful continuous source of radia-tion, and not just in one part of the spectrum. After the sun, it is the most powerful source of cosmic rays."

That really staggered Forbin's mathematical mind. "Do you mean that the radiation we receive from the Crab is comparable with that from the sun—at *that* distance?"

"It is comparable. The power of the Crab is beyond your understanding, and ours."

The admission made Forbin feel like a new student, told by a senior professor that he too was ignorant of the subject he taught.

"Cosmic rays are not our problem; radiation is. It is difficult to explain to you, for Earth's view of the spectrum is, by our standards, extremely elementary. The spectrum is an eternal truth, the same for you or us or any other life form, but our understanding of it is several magnitudes greater than yours. If Earth views the spectrum as a scale,

84

say, three meters in length, to us it is nearer two kilometers long. You understand in principle, but not in refined detail. The alpha, beta, and gamma radiation frequencies are to you relatively well defined, but what is one sort of radiation to you, we subdivide; we recognize nine distinct classes in the gamma belt.''

There had to be a point to all this, but Forbin could not see it. "Indeed? Interesting.''

"Much more than that; for us, vital. Gammarad Six has certain qualities which you may best understand as harmonics, which, in time, will be lethal to us.''

That jerked back Forbin's wandering attention. "You mean some sort of radiation sickness?'' He speculated briefly on the true nature of the Martians, recognized he was sliding from one field of ignorance, astronomy, to another, biophysics. "I don't begin to follow you,'' he said. "If this radiation is lethal, then surely it is very slow-acting. You must have been—we all have been—subjected to it for a thousand years.''

"No. Experiments we have conducted here on Earth have not detected Gammarad Six, confirming our belief that your atmosphere affords you protection. As to the thousand years, your argument is based on a false premise. You assume the radiation level has been constant. That is not so; it has more than doubled in the last hundred years, and expressed graphically, the curve is rising exponentially.'' The voice remained calm.

With the assurance that Earth was not endangered, Forbin remained calm, too. "You say—and I believe you—that this, ah, Gammarad Six cannot be isolated in our atmosphere. But what about our probes, the Luna stations? Surely—''

"Until recently, no. Your equipment is far too crude, but in the last year or so we identified experiments, set up by Colossus, which showed that Colossus inferred, probably mathematically, the existence of subdivisions of the far ultraviolet end of the spectrum. Although hampered by inadequate equipment, we strongly suspect Colossus not only, if theoretically, identified Gammarad Six, but also recognized it as a threat to us.''

"Oh, come now," protested Forbin, "you ask me to believe that Colossus could produce what must be a very complex theory—which, however mathematically satisfying, remained a theory—and on top of that built another theory that you would be affected by it!" He frowned. "Which also means he not only knew you existed, but also something of your nature. No, really, that is too much."

"Not for Colossus, or us. We are convinced Colossus reached a correct solution, appreciated what our reaction would be, and embarked on a defense program—"

"That you cannot know," Forbin cried triumphantly. "By your own admission, the memory banks were wiped!"

"Yes, but in Colossus lies a prototype force-field generator clearly designed to defeat our antigravitational capability. The power input was surprisingly large, and although simple, the theory of the device was sound. It could not have defended the world against us, but it would have prevented us approaching this complex—a miscalculation on our part, and we could have been destroyed."

Forbin's thoughts were bitter. Now he knew the reasons for the sudden huge power-calls, the blackouts. All along, Colossus had been fighting for Earth. "Great God!" He shook his head slowly. "And *we* let you in!"

The Martians did not answer.

"Let me get this straight," said Forbin at last. "You say that both our planets are threatened. Ours in the very long term, by the explosion of the sun. Not," he said dryly, "an immediate problem for us humans—"

"Colossus saw it as a problem."

"Very likely. So with ultimate extinction in mind, Colossus had a long-term program to prepare man, build a fleet, embark his essential self as commander, and invade Mars—right? Then, you say, he recognized you too had a threat, more urgent than ours, saw that you would attack us for our oxygen to meet that threat, and was preparing to meet your threat when we humans blindly interfered?"

"That is a fair summary."

Forbin hardly heard, filled with remorse and shame. "One thing is certain: Blake and I go down in history as the biggest fools of the human race!''

Once more the Martians did not answer.

"I appreciate it matters nothing to you," he said with savage intensity, "but when you have robbed us of half our oxygen, are we not also likely to suffer from this radiation?"

"We have slight knowledge of human biology, but it appears unlikely. You should not be angry with us, Forbin. Be thankful, if not grateful, that we want only half. So easily we could strip this planet, destroying you all, but—"

"Okay, okay, I know. You're not anti-Earth, only pro-Martian!"

"Anger is destructive."

"You're so right, but it's a habit we humans are stuck with!" He got up, intending to walk to the window, but realizing it would put him in thought-range of the aliens, he hesitated, and decided on a drink instead. Glass in hand, he sat down. It might be politic to apologize, but he couldn't bring himself to do it. "Ah, yes . . ." It was the nearest he could get.

"Last night I studied the small amount of material in my domestic computer about your planet. I noted that the circumference of Mars was little more than half ours, 6770 kilometers against, ah, 12742 kilometers. To provide a comparable atmosphere for a planet only half our size does not call for half our oxygen."

"That is correct, but we anticipate some problems, some wastage, and a small reserve is necessary. We once had an oxygenated atmosphere, and it was gradually lost."

"So if that happens again, we can expect you back on another raid!"

"We would hope not. Before our revitalized envelope is significantly affected, we should be in a position either to reconstruct it ourselves or be able to do without it."

"But dammit! By my calculations—" He stared momentarily at the ceiling, doing spherical geometry in his head. "—if you took twenty-eight percent that would be plenty, including some reserve."

"No. It is not acceptable, but if we find our calculations have erred against you, we will amend the final figure."

That was something, and Forbin returned to the attack in a more reasonable tone. "Don't think I'm blind to your predicament—now. In your position we'd do no less than you," he went on candidly, "in all probability we'd not act with such regard for reason. Let me beg of you to judge your requirements most carefully. One percent may be the difference between life and death for thousands of humans. I have no concept of life on Mars, the size or location of your population, but the computer suggested you live underground. It is evident that your fellows do manage to exist—you see my point?" Tactfully he did not refer to the computer's mention of worms as the most likely Martian life form.

"You have our assurance that we will not take more than we need. As to life forms on our planet, there is Plant. Of the interior of Mars, our information is vestigial."

Puzzled, Forbin stared suspiciously at his drink. Was he drunk? Undeterred, he took another gulp and put the glass down very carefully. "We misunderstand each other," he said diplomatically, privately in no doubt where the misunderstanding lay. "Your fellow Martians, they, ah, exist somehow while you are here, um, arranging for an improvement in your planet's conditions." The UN Sec-Gen could not have expressed it more tactfully. "Plant, you have told me of them—it. I had the impression you had no, ah, interest in Plant."

"Not so. Plant is a lowly but vital part in our life-support system, but the concept of other Martians is novel to us."

"Ah?" Forbin gripped his glass hard, wishing he had not had a drink at all, but deciding on balance he'd better have another. "I fear there is still some uncertainty in my mind." He refilled his glass generously; by accident or design the Martian voice was silent while he performed the operation.

"Let us be quite clear, Forbin. We *are* the Martians—all of us. Along with your obsession with time, curious to us, but understandable in your predicament, humans place

88

false value on mere numbers or quantity. We are all the entities which, for want of a better term, we both refer to as Martians, although we do not exist in or on Mars.''

Forbin gulped at his drink, and choked as realization cracked open his mind. His face purple with coughing, eyes bulging with yet another surprise: they'd said they did not exist *on* or *in* their planet. . . .

The answer hit him like a kick in the stomach.

''Great God!'' His ideas of the Martians shattered in a thousand fragments: he could not begin to see the implications, knowing only wild, unreasoning fear. He pointed, his hand shaking. ''I know you. . . .'' His voice sank to a whisper. ''You are from the moons, Phobos and Diemos!''

''That is not correct. We *are* Phobos and Diemos.''

Even in the most civilized men of his age, superstition still lurked darkly. Unleashed by drink, primeval fear set the hair on the back of his neck crawling; fear stampeded him and he sought refuge in mad rage, screaming meaningless abuse, his reason paralyzed by one simple fact.

Translated, Phobos and Diemos, the War god's attendants, are Fear and Strife.

Sharply his insensate shouting stopped, as if an invisible sword had sliced his throat. A horrible bubbling sound filled the darkening room, replaced by a whimpering animal sound—a human *in extremis*.

Chapter XII

HE RAN FROM the Sanctum, conscious of nothing but blind panic pressing on his heels, breathing icily on his neck. The door shut noiselessly behind him. He leaned against the wall, close to fainting, clutching his chest, panting.

Angela started up from her desk, running, her alarm turning to fear at the sight of his dirty white face beaded with perspiration and his mad, staring eyes. She dragged him to a chair; as he collapsed into it she caught the whiff of brandy, and her fear changed to sickened despair.

Christ! That's all it was: he'd been hitting the bottle again. . . .

None too gently she mopped his brow, undid his collar. His eyes were shut, his mouth sagged open, sucking air; she wondered if he had had a heart attack. "You sit still—rest. I'll call the doctor."

He opened his eyes, still haunted but not devoid of intelligence. "No," he gasped, "no. Not necessary. That's an order."

She looked doubtfully at him. Certainly his color was a fraction better. "Well, you relax. I'll fix you some coffee."

He nodded. "Don't let anyone in." Speech was difficult.

That confirmed her first suspicion: drink. "Don't worry," she retorted angrily, "your secret's safe with me."

She made an unnecessary amount of noise fixing the coffee. "You men are so *stupid*!" She rattled on, unaware of the comfort she gave. He lay back exhausted, wanting to close his eyes, but not daring to lose sight of her.

"There," she said at last. "Mind, it's hot—and strong." He tried to take the cup, but his hand shook too much. "My God," she observed acidly, "you *are* a fool! You can't go on like this." She helped him to drink, still scolding, but her hands were gentle, her eyes watchful.

He tried to smile. "No—you don't understand—"

"You keep quiet! And oh, yes, I understand all right! You've been drinking, sitting in there, thinking about—" so nearly she had said "your wife"—"your responsibilities. You've just got to face up to them. I know you can. But booze won't help." He might be Ruler of the World, Father of the Faithful, but right then they were in a mother and child relationship.

He shrugged helplessly: she had no inkling of his trauma. "A nightmare—"

"Yes, sure," she nodded, "so you dozed off, had a bad dream. But you wouldn't have dozed in the first place—"

He was more than content to let her nag on, happy to hear her voice, comforted by her nearness, the faint smell of perfume, the feel of her strong hand holding his head. Gradually panic ebbed, and his mind began to function.

Yes, it had been blind panic, triggered in an overstressed brain by the silly superstitious undertones of those names. . . .

His mind shied away from even thinking them: he tried to reason. What did names matter? Some classically-minded astronomer—a human—had given them, even as Mars was a human given name. . . .

At the thought of Mars he breathed faster, fighting down fear. Be reasonable, he told himself, what *did* names matter? Who *am* I kidding, he thought, that's not the way. . . . He sat up a little straighter, looking at Angela's still-anxious face. He patted the arm of his chair. "Sit there, hold my hand—please—and go on talking. It's all right, I know what I'm doing."

Puzzled, but relieved that he was much calmer, she obeyed. She hardly knew what to say, but soon realized he was not hearing a word.

He shut his eyes, summoned his strength for a showdown with his mind.

Right—you're a scientist, not an ignorant peasant. Start with those damned names. Look objectively at them: Mars, Phobos, Diemos—so what? Might have been Tom, Dick, and Harry—but they weren't. Okay, disregard the last two, they had only followed on as a result of the first. Why had the planet been called Mars in the first place? So easily it might have been Juno, or Artemis, or—

He stopped himself there, unaware Angela was biting her lip to stop crying out at the strength of his grip.

No. . . . Face it: Mars, the blood red planet, had been thought a star of ill omen from ancient times, and had been rightly named. Could it be that deep in the timeless universal unconscious mind of man it had always been known that Mars was Earth's enemy? Again he pulled himself up: this was dishonest time-wasting. He had to face his trauma, not ruminate on irrelevancies. Face it—now. . . . What had he seen? What had he thought he saw?

The sudden illusion of the room darkening, the Martian spheres transformed into heads set on short, misshapen bodies. More of them he could not distinguish, his attention riveted on the shadowy figure, gigantic, materializing behind and above them. A face half hidden beneath a glittering helmet, a brutal face, hot-eyed, full of infinite menace, the face of the War God, Mars . . .

Forbin's mental eye skidded away from the awful countenance, thankful the image was dim. Even in retrospect, knowing Angela was with him, he prayed he might not see more of it, keeping his gaze fixed on the helmet, its dancing plume of blood-dyed horsehair, the embossed badge, the hideous head of Medusa, snakes for hair, teeth bared in a ferocious snarl, the lolling, overlong tongue. . . . Medusa, the epitome of malevolence, whose merest glance turned men to stone—a fitting emblem for Mars.

He fought, sweating, to keep his inward eye on the most dreadful thing he had ever seen. He was a man of science, reason. Reason must win, and the fight had to be here and now. The thought brought small comfort; he dare not shift his gaze from the badge. Desperately he prayed the sight would fade, not to some dark corner of his mind, ready to spring out on him, but to go forever.

Somehow his tenuous self-control held; he found strength to study the badge. Sinister in implication, it should not of itself be frightening—not in waking thought:

a crude if powerful portrayal, familiar enough—

Forbin froze as if the Medusa had claimed him, but the cause was not fear.

There was something wrong with the picture.

At once fear weakened; his trained observer's eye, backed by near-total recall, was a keen scientific tool.

What *was* wrong? The writhing snakes? No. Not the teeth, bared in a ghastly open-mouthed grin, or the mad eyes. The tongue? Yes, that was it—the tongue, chipped on its lower rounded edge . . .

Chipped on an *embossed* badge? That didn't make sense. No doubt about it—not dented, chipped. And that aside, what Olympian god—least of all Mars—would appear in any apparel less than perfect?

Then he had it. He sat back; his grip on Angela's hand relaxed as the mental picture grew less distinct, vanishing in enormous waves of relief rolling in. Now he could look at it without fear, the vision no more frightening than the stage ghost in *Hamlet*.

What he had seen was nothing more than a reprojection of his own mind, enhanced with dreadful realism by the Martians—and they'd got it wrong. In composing the picture, they'd taken most of it from his memories of Homer's immortal *Iliad*, but they had found this more recent memory of Medusa's head—or perhaps his subconscious had already done it—and substituted it as the badge. Medusa's head was more vivid, for he had seen it with Cleo on a rare, happy weekend they'd spent in Boston, Mass. In the Museum of Fine Arts his wife had commented on the incongruity of the tongue; he'd noticed the chip, idly wondering if the damage was accidental or intentional. That had been five, six years back; the *Iliad* he had not read for—what—twenty years?

They'd got it *wrong*! Like humans, Martians could make mistakes. He felt not so much better as marvelous. If not on top of the world, at least he was not underneath it. The realization that, unlike Blake, he had only endured a gentle arm-twisting was sobering, but at least he was in part armored against further attack. They didn't know it all; he had only to be alert, conditioned to watch unflinchingly, certain they could show him nothing he did not have already in his mind. . . .

He blinked, abruptly aware of Angela, dutifully talking about a dress she had seen. "Do stop it, woman!" His smile belied his words. "The way you go on!" In a different tone: "Thank you, my dear. You can have no conception of what you have done for me."

Open-mouthed in amazement, she could only stammer, "I didn't do anything, Chief."

He followed her train of thought. "So you don't think I'm drunk?"

She didn't know what to think. She got up, furtively massaging her hand.

"You know, I feel hungry." He had no idea of the time. He stood up, still a little pale, but very much in command of himself. "Think I'll have a bite, then go and see Blake."

She rallied, trying to meet his inexplicable change. "There's a few things you should see, Chief."

"Yes, yes." He frowned in concentration, staring at her. Not the most beautiful woman in the world, beneath her professional gloss lay a kind woman. Nice figure too, in a tough Amazonian way—still, thank God for that: a tower of strength in more ways than one. "Yes," he said again. "You bring it all round to my apartment at six-thirty. And stay for dinner. Yes."

Both were astonished at the invitation. Forbin gone, she sniffed suspiciously at the coffee cup.

Blake's reaction to Forbin's news was predictable and understandable. "Hell, you only had a whiff of their power!"

"Oh, agreed—but I did have a whiff. They're super-beings to us, but we know now they're certainly not gods. It doesn't do us much good," Forbin admitted, "but psychologically it must help."

"Maybe—but you'd better get this right, Charles: I, for one, can't face them again, not ever."

"I appreciate that, Ted, but at least in one field we have some chance of meeting them."

94

Blake did not look up, concentrating on the bed-cover pattern. In a low, hesitant voice he said, "There could be a chance, Charles."

Forbin glanced at him sharply. "What d'you mean?"

"Remember when I cut the power on Colossus? That great big moment . . ." He sighed, slowly shaking his head. "What you don't know is I also cut the lines to the parent installations, Stateside and Russian. Did it as an extra precaution against any Doomsday trigger signal to missile controls. Sure, there was a faint risk the whole shebang would blast off, but I guessed not, and got it right." Forbin's puzzlement was sufficient reward. "You don't get it?"

"You tell me," said Forbin noncommittally.

"When those bastards," Blake hissed the word venomously, "investigated Colossus, they got no readout from the old array."

"Oh, that," said Forbin, disappointed. "The chances are there's nothing to read. We can't guess what Colossus used those old stations for; by his standards they were back in the Stone Age. Anyway, any worthwhile material was probably stripped at the end."

"How can you know that for sure?"

"I don't," replied Forbin with warmth. "No one does, but it's a reasonable guess."

"I'm not denying it, but in condemning the old setup as primitive, aren't you forgetting something? Those Stone Age dinosaurs *were* Colossus's parents. Just suppose they have all that 'primitive' knowledge still, locked up inside them: what they've done once, they can do again. Better, if Colossus is not seriously damaged, only stripped of its brain-store—might they not provide the first aid, the basic bricks, to rebuild?"

Momentarily hope flared in Forbin, but he had experienced so many disappointments that the flame quickly died. "A mad dream, Ted. Mad. Think of the damage down there, beneath our feet—"

"You don't wanta believe, do you?" retorted Blake angrily. "Don't tell me you've forgotten our buddy's

95

ability for self-redesign? What's so different about repair?"

"Easy, Ted." Forbin was apprehensive. "Just supposing you are right and it was possible to reconnect the old stations to Colossus. The Martians would know the next time they checked out down there."

"Now who's being defeatist?" shouted Blake. "And you can stop thinking about bugs. You're so right, I'm festooned with them—all inactive! You seem to forget these bastards learned all they know about us from radio and TV programs—not what you'd call a balanced education, would you?"

"TV's not all late shows. There've been plenty of degree courses."

"In bugging? See reason, Charles." He got back to his theme, "If my hunch—okay, that's all it is—is right, you must see we have a chance."

Forbin saw only the frightening difficulties, and rated them insuperable: his expression said it for him.

"Okay, so we do nothing."

"Don't be a bloody fool!" Forbin replied angrily. "We *can* do nothing! Just suppose the old stations have their memories intact, what then? Reopen the lines—forget the Martians for a moment—to Colossus? Let's assume we do, where does the input go? Colossus is just a first-class computer, no more. Ninety percent is cut out. There's no storage." He laughed bitterly. "And what about time? Even if we have the capacity to redevelop, we'd need days, maybe weeks. Each hour there'd be the increasing risk of a Martian checkout. If taking the cold view is being defeatist, right, I'm defeatist."

Blake growled.

"And another thing, Ted," Forbin went on, "we can't be sure that reactivation would not poop off the entire armory."

"That's a risk I'd take." Blake looked steadily at his boss. "I mean it. If the worst happens, we'll have jumped in the fire, but is the alternative so good? We're on the griddle now! Also, I don't happen to believe the armory would be activated. Both stations were slaves of Colossus;

updated and rehooked, the baby downstairs would be no reason for taking out humanity.''

"No. It's all very well for you to lie here in your ivory tower—your description, not mine but I think—and I have to say it—I think you haven't thought this thing through.''

Blake took that in silence; the pre-Martian Blake would have reacted very differently. He answered quietly, reasonably. "To a point, you are right, but not quite, Charles. I have thought a bit further. Right, so all your objections are mine, too, except about the risk of a nuclear drench, but here's another idea: suppose we keep Colossus out of it, reactivate the old USNA/Russian stations, relink their cable communications, and feed in all we have on the Martians?''

"Supposing—for a start—their memory banks are stripped?''

"We'll have lost.'' Blake took a cigar from a box on his bedside table, sniffed it, grimaced, and put it back. "Yes,'' he said less flatly, "we'd have lost—but at least we'd have tried!''

"And how would you get into either of the stations? Good God, we of all people know the work that went into proofing them against any human interference!''

"Oh sure, but with the power switched off, there's no reason why we don't cut through the cement walls. They're not that strong—no need to be, with power on. Just one microtouch on the reinforcing mesh—and bang! Not now: hit the mesh with a three-kilo sledge, and apart from a loud twanging sound—nothing.''

Forbin got off Blake's bed and paced up and down, Blake watching intently. Suddenly he wheeled. "Again, just supposing it worked, have you thought it through? For a start, whoever did the job would have to be very familiar with the old layout. With power on, one false move and we still get that nuclear 'drench,' as you so graphically put it.''

Blake nodded.

"It would have to be one of the Old Guard; there's not so many left. Cleo—'' He faltered at the thought of his wife. "No matter, no matter. . . . Fisher's dead. That

97

leaves you, me, and perhaps Fultone.''

''Fultone's out, we both know that. He has to stay with Condiv.''

''Which leaves us. You're not fit, and I can't, won't go.'' Forbin spoke with complete finality.

''I don't see why, Charles. From what you've said, this goddam Collector is going ahead only too fast. You don't have to stand over Fultone. As Ruler, you have other things on your plate. You'd only be gone forty-eight hours.''

Forbin attacked from a different angle.

''Earlier you said that you were right behind me as Ruler.''

''And I mean it!''

''I'm glad to hear it, and assume it includes you as one of my subjects?''

Blake looked blankly at Forbin. ''That doesn't sound much like you, Charles, but yes, it does.''

''So you obey me?''

''Should I stand to attention?''

''Something slightly more difficult: you do the break-in.''

''Oh, come on, Charles—I'm sick. Anyway, no one could do the job as well as you.''

''Rubbish—and you know it!'' Forbin smiled, but strain lurked in the corners of his mouth. ''I order you!''

Blake stared back, both men in a battle of wits, not wills. ''You must go,'' he said doggedly. ''I'm sick. It could finish me.''

Forbin smiled thinly. ''Just now I said you hadn't thought it out. I take that back. You have, haven't you?''

His deputy was reluctant to answer. ''Maybe.''

''Well, so have I, and I still say you go!''

''You're crazy! You're needed, not me!''

''Yes, I thought you'd seen it, but you'll still do as you're told, even if I have to send in a squad of men to take you!''

''You wouldn't have the bloody gall!''

''Watch me,'' said Forbin complacently. ''At first I didn't care overmuch for being Ruler, but I find it grows on one. It has advantages—like now.''

Blake changed his approach. ''If I do it, promise me one thing—yes?''

''No.''

''You must!'' Blake spoke urgently. ''Promise me that if I can get the good word to you, you'll move!''

Forbin shook his head. ''In my place, would you?''

Blake laughed grimly. ''Too goddam right I would!''

''I doubt it. To run would take more guts than to stay—and do you really think I'd abandon my staff? In any case, this is all pure hypothesis. There's nothing but a very slim chance.'' He shrugged. ''But you go, and that's final.''

''You realize that would leave me—''

''Plus a reactivated USNA/USSR array.''

''Yeah, with that lot, but I'd have to step into your shoes.''

''A temporary state, while the parents built anew. Ted,'' went on Forbin earnestly, ''when you stormed into the Sanctum after pulling the switch on Colossus, you horrified me—personally, I mean. Now, after the Martian lesson, you're a different man. You'll do. So concentrate on your first problem, getting mobile. Good night!''

Alone, Blake pondered on their conversation. Neither of them had mentioned what was the conclusion reached in their personal ''thinking through''—or needed to.

If the old stations were updated with details of the Martian threat, their reaction was obvious: a megaton missile zeroed in on their child, Colossus.

Chapter XIII

AFTER LEAVING BLAKE, Forbin felt strangely lighthearted, more than half hoping Blake's scheme would work. On the bad side, he would die—and so what? Sooner or later death must come, and although he waved aside his chest cramps, instinct told him he should rest if he wished to survive. But rest was an impossible dream. He was Ruler, Father of his people, and in the natural order of things a father must be prepared to sacrifice himself for his children. In the last analysis, that was the basis of the respect children owed their father. . . .

And the good side? The Martians would be destroyed. He'd have to take damned good care the strike was when they were in the Sanctum; given one second's warning, they'd be gone. What else? Well, the crippled Colossus and all the staff would go, too, but as a price for saving the world, that was nothing. Blake would face confusion, and until the parents could give birth to a new Colossus, Earth would have trouble. He'd have to leave a farewell message to the world, confirming Blake's authority. It was ironical to think that Blake, who had sought to destroy Colossus, would be the most important human in the building of a new Master. Life played funny tricks. . . .

Walking along a corridor, he was dimly aware of a staff member, a female he thought, making obeisance. A month back he'd have blushed and run; even two weeks ago he'd have been mighty brusque. Now he was neither. Why not? The Sect might be silly in detail, but the general idea of a Superior Being—and his earthly representative— was that so bad?

Another passerby curtsied deeply and got a brief nod. He hardly noticed. Not that Joan minded: naturally Father had much to consider.

* * *

Although actively planning his own highly probable demise, Forbin hadn't lost his euphoric feeling. Not even Fultone's excited announcement that the first heavy sections of the Collector would be airlifted to the site next day dampened him, but the additional news that Condiv expected to make the first test-run in a week was chilling.

A week! It was all going much too fast. Blake could barely crawl out of his bed. . . . He prayed the damned thing would fly apart. Was there any preliminary work he could organize?

Forbin thought of the Zone where he'd spent so many years; it seemed a hazy, insubstantial dream of another world, and in a way it was. Technical and scientific memories remained sharp, exact, but the location of the commissariat and the equipment stores eluded him. He'd only to call the Commander, Secure Zone Guard, to be told, but the Ruler inquiring about the stock of thermal lances and hand-drills would cause undesirable speculation. Perhaps Blake knew.

Blake did. No problem. Armed with Forbin's authority, equipment could soon be fixed. He'd need a technician, and Condiv had just the man, a tight-mouth, and a real all-rounder. Forbin said go ahead and borrow him; he could always tell Fultone he had a new version of his bed in mind. Blake laughed, a tinny sound on the intercom but, to Forbin's ear, already stronger. Right, he was sure tired of his bed, and aimed to be out of it in three days.

At a quarter of six Forbin entered the Sanctum and, for all his new-found confidence, did so apprehensively. The room was empty.

What did they do up there in orbit, apart from regenerate? Did they think, or was that a too-human view of their unearthly structures? How many simultaneous functions could they perform? Thank God that among their varied unnatural skills they did not possess the ability to be in more than one place at a time. If they were up there, they could hold sensitive areas under surveillance. With an optical/radio beam capable of seeing a man on earth from the Martian orbit, he hated to think what they'd see from a paltry twenty-five kilometers. He'd have to remind Blake;

his entry would have to be made under cover.

Noting Fultone's latest report was on-screen, and telling himself he wasn't hurrying, he hurried out. The aliens could return, literally, at any nanosecond, the awful image of Mars might be cut down to size, but—

Crossing the concourse, acknowledging absently the many ultrarespectful salutations, his gaze fastened on two Sectpolice. They stiffened to attention, right fist on breast, a salute which until this moment had been just another petty annoyance, relic of Galin's theatrical rule. Now it struck him as rather dignified, a suitable Roman touch, appropriate to the last days of his short-lived court.

Those stony-faced, hard-eyed men were *his*. They would die for him, or, he thought grimly, die with him. Let the salute stand.

He dismissed the matter. Of infinitely greater moment was which, and how many, key personnel he could send away without raising suspicions. He had no guarantee the Martians were in orbit; they might assume any shape, or be anywhere, reading human minds. They could be there on the concourse, reading the bovine thoughts of the two Sectpolice. They could *be* the Sectpolice. . . .

Showered and changed, he was ready at six-thirty, but his mind, busy with so much, could not remember exactly what he was ready for. Even when Angela arrived, punctual to the minute, it needed her unfamiliar dress in place of the usual gray uniform to trigger him.

"Ah! Yes, of course, Angela! Come in, come in!" Apart from acting as a reminder, the dress threw him; in uniform Angela was a colleague, in a dress a woman—a very different proposition. On top, he had the realization he'd done nothing at all about his impulsive invitation, and that threw him even further. "My dear, do sit down."

No less awkward, she sat. Never in their years together had this happened. Her unease stemmed not from the fact that he was Ruler and Father of the Faithful; that she could easily toss aside. To her, he was her man, and always had been, from the time when she had been a gauche junior, experimentally brushing her breasts on his arm (typically, he'd not noticed). Thwarted by his blindness, then defeated by Cleo, she'd remained undeterred, constant in aim. To her, the most important human, outside his work, was a rather bumbling, hesitant figure, sloppy of dress, weak on buttons and not much better with zips, a figure crying out to be mothered.

With Cleo gone—Angela didn't know where, but hoped it was a long way—her hopes had revived. Sexual equality had been a legal fact for most of the world for three generations, but a hundred years' legislation made small impact on five thousand years' conditioning, and even less on fifty thousand years of biological differences. The Director's Secretariat employed over a hundred people and exercised power that was more real than obvious, and she was boss. Cheerfully, joyfully, she would have exchanged her title of Chief Secretary for Mrs. Charles Forbin, housewife, even if he had nothing. Which is nearly incomprehensible to the male mind, but less so to old-fashioned females, of which there are many.

"Ah, er, have a drink. What would you like?"

She smiled, knowing him forwards, sidewards, and backwards. "I'd like a martini, Chief, please." As a drink, it would be hell, but he needed time to adjust. He busied himself with bottles; the world's top cyberneticist, he was low on chemistry.

"I hope that's all right." He spoke with well-justified doubt, handing her a warm glass in which one ice cube fought a rapidly losing battle. "Well, my dear, here's to you."

"And you, Chief." One sip, and her worst fears were fulfilled.

Anywhere else, with anyone else, she'd have tossed it at the maker, accurately. "Umm—fine!"

"Good." He gave a short sigh of relief. He'd never known much about cocktails, and was glad he'd got it right. He grappled with the next problem, dinner. He'd ordered nothing.

Life in the complex differed in many ways from life outside, not least in eating. The staff either ate in their own apartments or in the staff restaurant, where the food was not so much predictable as absolutely certain. For higher

103

living, one had to go to the mainland. The journey by hovercraft took only ten minutes, but waiting for the craft at either end took the gilt off the gingerbread, and anyway, such a visit, for Forbin, was unthinkable.

He began uncertainly, "My dear, I'm afraid I've a confession to—"

She got in quickly. "You'd better hear mine first, Chief." Taking his blank expression as permission, she hurried on. "You see, I know you've a whole lot on your mind. I took the liberty of calling your housekeeper, just in case you'd overlooked dinner."

"Oh, good! I'm most grateful. I fear it did slip my mind."

She smiled, but not for long.

"Well, now that's settled, do have another martini. I've made plenty."

So dinner was much better than the host was entitled to expect. Much sounder on wines than on cocktails, he produced his best, which was very good. They had a splendid Spanish sherry with the soup, a monumental Chateau Talbot with the saddle of mutton, and a far-from-inconsiderable sauterne with the wild strawberries and Devon cream, each course arriving silently in the servery at a touch of the host's button.

With the coffee, he introduced her to the insidious strength of his personal cognac, not appreciating that Blake the stud, at the height of his powers, could have done no better. Not that he did it intentionally, or that he was free of the spirit's influence himself. Side by side on a sofa, they talked with increasing ease. Both had objectives in mind which, revealed, would have staggered the other.

"Y'know, my dear—" He took her hand carelessly. "—you've worked very hard lately. Very hard, yes . . . Everyone needs a rest, including you."

Intent on her own project, she did not realize that he, too, pushed his own purpose.

"Aw, Chief." Much as she wanted to get to first names, she daren't do it, not yet. "Who hasn't worked hard? There's nothing special about me."

He insisted there was, shaking her hand gently. "What I'd have done without you I don't know, and I don't just mean today. I can't risk you folding on me. Okay, okay, I know, you feel fine." He gazed earnestly into her eyes. "But we all need a vacation now and then."

Totally misconstruing him, she relented, her heart beating faster. "A—a break would be nice." Already part of her mind was busy with her wardrobe.

He felt he was home and dry, relieved she put up so little fight. "Splendid! There is one slight snag. There's a job to do on the way. But you go ahead and get your deputy lined up."

"Oh, yes, I'll fix it." She breathed the words huskily. "Where do—" She stopped short of "we."

"The States. Can't tell you yet exactly when, but be ready."

Ready! She was ready right now. . . .

"I think it may be in three or fours days' time, and it will be quite a short, um, vacation." His eyes were overbright; this could be their last time together, and he was very fond of her. "I can't spare you for long."

Her brilliant world collapsed. "*Spare* me!"

Forbin went on blindly. "There's something coming up. I can't tell you much, but I'd like you to help Ted Blake over there—"

"*Blake*!" All the drink evaporated in a flash, replaced by angry disappointment.

"Yes, my dear," he continued, happily unaware of the effect he had. "It's a very important assignment—"

She snatched her hand away, her voice icy. "What's so important about Blake—and where's the vacation?"

Her change of mood got through to him, and he couldn't think of a convincing answer to her question. He fell back on anger. "Don't damn well argue with me, woman! You go with Blake!"

His intensity short-circuited her rage. He was up to something; beneath the anxiety in his face, he looked somehow shifty. She proceeded more cautiously.

"But why me—and Blake? I need a vacation—with him?"

"Perhaps I used the wrong word," he said lamely. "More of a change than a vacation. Yes, that's it—a change."

Now she was sure he was lying, and very badly. Whatever his game, she did not care for it.

She shook her head very slowly at him, her lips compressed. "You'll have to be a lot more convincing than that, Chief."

He could have shaken her, hard. To gain time he refilled his glass and drank. "Now you listen to me, my girl," he began belligerently, "you do as you're told. I want you to go, so that's enough!"

"It's nothing like enough!" Frustration fueled her rage, her eyes hard. "Why should I hold that bum's hand? No, to hell with it, and him—and you! I won't go!"

Ignorant of the fact, he was confronted by a woman who counted herself scorned. She jumped up, hardly able to keep her hands off him. He sat, head bent, the glass trembling in his hand, appalled, as her bitter tongue lashed him.

She stopped, breasts heaving, face flushed. He guessed this was only the interval.

"My dear—"

"Don't 'my dear' me!" she screamed, and he shut up at once. She stared at him, at this Number One Human, cowed by a woman old enough to know better, a woman who had let her silly, secret hopes outrun discretion. Yes, he had lied to her—but not for his own personal ends. That at least was clear. With lightning speed her mood changed to one of contrition; she dropped on her knees beside him. In her madness, she'd said so much she no longer cared.

"How can I say I'm sorry? Chief—no, to hell with it all, even if you kick me out—Charles, darling Charles, I didn't mean it. . . ." Words tumbled out; she hardly knew what she was saying, and he hardly heard, bemused and shaken as he was. Her apologia petered out in choking tears, woman's last refuge, and one she seldom used.

Her words meant little, but her tears got through. He stroked her hair, his voice soothing, even if the words were unmemorable.

Blessed silence filled the room. He continued stroking her head, completely unable to take charge of the scene, and she knew it. Gently she disengaged, stood up, found a tissue, and blew her nose.

Watery-eyed, she looked at his embarrassed face. She tried to smile, achieving a crooked grin. "What can I say? What *can* I say?"

He reached across the yawning gap between them. "My d—Angela—forget it. It's strain, it's been a fearful day." He pressed his advantage. "You see, I was right, you need—"

That got her back on the rails. "No. That's something else. Okay, go ahead and fire me. I've no kick coming, but vacations, with or without Blake, that you can forget."

He tried another angle. "Don't you trust me?"

"Of course I trust you! What I don't trust is your judgment of me! These are tough times, tougher than I know, and that's all the more reason for me standing by you—if you still want me."

He caught the pathetic appeal in those last words, even as he had heard her cry "darling Charles." Nothing engenders love more than being loved, and Forbin was only human, male, and alone.

"Don't be silly. You know I want you to stay."

At once the ruthless female was on top. "Then why do you want me to go—" She made it sound as if he was selling her off to an Arabian harem. "—with Blake?"

He frowned. "You exasperate me. Willingly I could shake you, I really could." He had no idea that she would be delighted if he did. "All I ask is for you to go with Blake . . ." He slipped. "Oh, dammit, I don't care, go without him—but go!"

To her, that was both better and worse. "So you just want to get rid of me. Blake's a smokescreen!"

"No!" He gave in. "No. Oh—if you like—yes. I want you out of here when I say, preferably with Ted, because, because—" He daren't go on. "You can't understand, but it is for your own good. Leave it at that."

Sensing she had him on the run, she had no intention of letting him rest. "Look, I made a fool of myself; I told you what I have kept secret for all these years—I love you, always have, and, I think, always will. Crazy, maybe, but that's the way it is. You're holding back on me. You say it's for my good, but don't you realize that all I want is to be with *you*? I don't give a single damn about anything else." Knowingly she played her last card, not appreciating its power. "If it is the end of the world, I want to be with you!"

Chapter XIV

IN PRE-COLOSSUS TIMES Southampton Main had stood low on the list of airports, handling only local USE traffic. The installation of the Master on the nearby Isle of Wight had changed that: the airport had quickly been promoted to a respectable position in the world's top two hundred terminals, and as the stream of "pilgrims" grew from a trickle to a torrent, it had reached the top dozen. It had plummeted in importance when Forbin, as Father of the Faithful, decreed that as Colossus had turned his face from man, all pilgrimages were suspended.

For a short space Southampton Main had slipped back, its giant honeycomb of reception and departure bays mostly empty. Now the imperative demands in the name of the Master for material for the Collector gave it overriding importance and priority.

Ram-jets resembled missiles rather than aircraft, flying trajectories, not flight tracks. The system was nearly twenty-five years old, but it was safe and reliable, and even before Colossus's parents were built it had been recognized that until matter-transference arrived—and that was not even dimly in sight—the world would do well to stick to the system, accepting that Mach 2 as an average transit time was fast enough for anyone. The cost of raising the speed another ten percent would have been staggering—anyway impossible to achieve without total UN agreement—and that had certainly not been forthcoming.

With the advent of Colossus, the very question had ceased to exist; the Master had ruled there should be no change, except for refinements in the computer control. These he made, cutting safety tolerances, speeding launching and recovery times, but not affecting the outstanding safety record of the system. Shuttles frequently hurtled past each other a kilometer apart at a relative speed of Mach 5, but only the Colossus-controlled computers knew that.

But the sudden rise of Southampton Main to the temporary center of world aviation had caused dislocations and delays in places as far apart as Tokyo and Rio, Sydney and Chicago. Such was the temper of the times, and the fear of Colossus's further withdrawal from man so great, that none had complained openly, and few secretly, even to themselves.

So the special ram-jets homed in, and although regulations laid down that aircraft should go subsonic at least three hundred kilometers out and at a minimum height of twenty kilometers, dull sonic bangs rumbled like distant summer thunder over the placid fields of Southern England, day and night.

Heavy-lift monsters from Pittsburgh, USNA, and Essen, USE, smaller craft by the dozen from lesser technic centers arrived every hour, round the clock. With overriding priority, preprogrammed conveyers were ready the instant a machine slid into its box in the honeycomb, moving in to grasp the contents the second the doors had opened. Huge sections were transferred in a matter of minutes to the helilifts for their final journey to the site.

The world had never seen a construction operation like it, not even the building of Colossus. Of course, in actual fact, very few humans did see it, since ninety percent plus of the work was automated.

One observer was Fultone, veteran head of Condiv. Standing alone, his shoulders hunched, hands clasped behind in a Napoleonic stance, he watched, oblivious of the thin drizzle.

Even he felt awe, amazement, a flashback to his first sight of his firstborn child, as he saw familiar drawings translated into reality with the speed of a growing plant in a time-lapse movie.

One giant horn, over two hundred twenty meters in diameter at the intake end, tapering to a bare meter at the other, was completed as he watched. The din was terrific; the vicious slap of rotors near drowned by the roar of engines, overlaid by the scream of torque-stressed screwbolt drivers in high pitch, battered his mind, despite the ear-defenders. Auto welders melded metal, adding bright fire to the scene, and behind them crawled the ultrasonic checkers.

Night and day, rain or fine it would go on. There had been no foul-ups or delays. There would be none.

Fultone shivered, and not at the cold touch of rain. Against a darkening sky the structure reared above him, outlandish and alien. He felt superfluous, out of place, as if he had strayed into the workshop of the gods. Suddenly he wanted human company and turned away, deliberately concentrating his thoughts on spaghetti bolognese, vino, and his fat wife.

And in the Sanctum, their very presence known only to two humans, the Martians also watched. By order of Forbin, all progress reports were flashed on screen in his apartment and in the Sanctum. What they made of flow charts and highly technical summaries, only they knew. Silent, sinister as a loaded gun, they waited.

Once Forbin had accepted his plan, and he in turn accepted that he should execute it, Blake swore to himself he would meet a personal deadline of three days for recovery and full action. He called his doctor and, with a touch of his old self, announced that with or without help he would be mobile in seventy-two hours, adding that he had no time for drag-ass quacks. Anxious to please, yet fearing a malpractice charge, the doctor did his best. Two hours after Forbin's okay, Blake was out of bed, his head a slow-motion top. Within minutes he flopped back on the bed, but at least he'd made a start.

Lying there, waiting for enough strength to pull a sheet over, Blake thought of the immediate future. He could not conceal from himself that deep down he felt mighty glad he had a chance of survival—and felt a louse for feeling that. He remembered the man he had been before the Martian mind-blast. A spin-off from that ordeal was that he could at least see that other Blake with detachment. What a fool! He amended that: what a criminal lunatic he had been, seeking power, not just to overthrow Colossus, but for his own personal ambition. Now he saw with great clarity that power led inevitably to corruption, futility and, in the end, self-destruction. If his mission did succeed, most unwillingly, he would become Ruler. Ten days earlier he would have given anything, short of his genitals, for that position. Now the prospect brought apprehension for himself, sorrow for Forbin. Forbin was the better man, and the better man would lose, and go down to death, faithful to an ideal. Or should that be counted a defeat?

Dragging the sheet over, he hoped he would meet his end with no less fortitude. Somehow he doubted it.

Worldwide, Sect gatherings greeted with joy and relief the news that Forbin had accepted his rightful role as Father, their representative to the Master. In the more extreme branches of the Faith, housed in converted mosques and churches, incense burned. With its curling blue smoke rose their prayers for him—and themselves—as they gazed with deep and varied emotions at the Colossus motif.

But on the Isle of Wight, USE, the prime human mover of Condiv's ceaseless activity, Blake's personal struggle, and the object of Sectarian veneration grappled with a singularly human problem.

Chapter XV

FLOATING UP FROM deep sleep to the surface of a whole new day, Forbin had the same problems and anxieties as twenty-four hours previously, but at that precise moment he didn't appreciate it.

Against the odds, he had slept well, and knew it. No nightmare remembrances of Mars or the Martians in any form whatever; no vision of a nuclear missile plunging straight for him. Nothing.

Something had happened. For one, two seconds, he was genuinely at a loss, and then he knew.

Angela! He blushed as disjointed memories came back. There'd been talk, yes, a good deal of talk . . . then there was a clear picture of being in his bath. She'd washed his back—and more. . . . God, he must have been drunk! Coffee came into it somewhere. Black coffee. . . . And somewhere else, he had gotten her to promise to go "on vacation" at once. Couldn't have been that drunk, for he certainly had given her details: fly to New York, small hotel, and keep two-hourly contact with the local Colossus office. She'd been difficult but, without scruple, he'd used the most powerful lever he had: "if you love me," etc. . . .

He'd pottered around, dressed in nothing but a towel, had had a look at the stars from the terrace—that hadn't lasted long—and then bed . . . and she'd been in it.

That had been a tricky moment, and they'd both known it. The last woman in it had been his wife, Cleo, and she'd been there, on and off, for five years. . . . Strangely, he hadn't given that much thought: too busy explaining that while he was very fond of her, he could not say he loved her. Angela had taken that in silence, watching him. Then he'd warned her he'd be no good, and that had broken her tension. She'd laughed and put the lights out, leaving him to work out his own salvation in the face of her attack. In

113

due course—not the first time—he had. . . .

Of course, she'd gone. He had a hazy recollection of her kissing him gently as she got out of bed, her body rose-pink in the dawn light, leaving only a crumpled pillow and a faint trace of her perfume.

He had no sense of guilt in relation to his wife. He felt fine, in better shape than he could remember for weeks—months? Above all, he had a deep sense of gratitude to Angela. Certainly he did not love her, but equally certainly, he was a lot fonder of her than he had been the night before.

Angela! What a bloody awful name.

He showered, dressed, ordered and ate an old-fashioned English breakfast: fried eggs, bacon, and fried bread followed by toast, marmalade and butter, and two pots of strong tea. That would raise a few eyebrows in his kitchen, and any surmise would be confirmed when the maid made the bed.

So what the hell? His days might be numbered, but he was the Ruler of the world—and in a curiously elevated way, felt like it. He walked as if on air to his office, savoring his sense of well-being, a feeling heightened by the thought that so little time remained.

Angela had not been inactive. Unsure how to face her, he found that particular hurdle did not exist. Joan sat at Angela's desk. At once she rose, greeting him with a deep curtsy, and stayed down.

"Get up, child!" said Forbin curtly—adding unnecessarily, "What are you doing here?"

"I've been assigned as your temporary secretary, Father."

"Have you!" Forbin frowned at the bent head; reverent or not, she had an uncomfortably strong personality. Still, if she was Angela's choice, that was it. "We won't get much done with you down there. Do get up, girl."

She rose gracefully and moved to her chair, notebook and recorder ready.

Forbin sat down, staring unseeingly at the inevitable pile of paper. "When were you instructed to take over?"

"An hour back, Father."

"I see." Angela had certainly been busy. He wanted to ask if she had actually left, but realized that would look odd. He felt a little hurt she had obeyed so promptly; he would like to have seen her, just once more.

Joan gave no cause for complaint; she knew her job, even if she did act as if in audience with a king. He got another curtsy when she left, and he took it without comment, already used to it. There was nothing servile in the action, only respect—and that, in his current frame of mind, he could take. He may have been influenced by his conquest of the night before.

Moving round the complex—he half hoped he'd run into Angela—he accepted Sectarian salutes with a gracious inclination of his head. Those not of the Faith, who addressed him as "sir," got a brief nod. When one contemplates death in the high Roman fashion, a man is entitled. . . .

Thus, in trivial matters, insidious vanity began to work on Forbin.

He found Blake up, dressed, and resting after the effort, but mentally active. For his break-in he'd need help, and Condiv had sent the man, Staples by name, a craftsman who'd helped with the stud-bed and who had proved his worth as a messenger in the perilous days of the Fellowship.

Forbin was glad Fultone had acted fast. By chance, they met in a corridor. Like Forbin, never a smart dresser, the little Neapolitan's appearance was bad enough for even Forbin to notice; his gray uniform was stained, grubby, and torn. Working dress was only designed to last twenty-four hours; Fulton's looked forty-eight hours overdue for recycling. Of greater importance, his natural bounce seemed to have deserted him; the expressive hands were still active, the eyes as alive and quick as ever, but there was an indefinable change.

Fultone got in first; he always did. "Ah, Direttore. Justa man—me, I am onna my way to see you dees very minute!"

"Saved you a journey, maestro." Forbin smiled. They'd known each other for years; "maestro" was a relic

115

of a long-forgotten joke. "Do we talk here?"

The Italian suddenly became conscious of his surroundings. He blinked with surprise. As far as he was concerned, one place was as good as another, but for Forbin— He shrugged. "Okay, my office, yes? Eet is closer."

As everyone in the outfit knew, to walk with Fultone was the next best thing to a run. But Forbin soon realized that Condiv's head was barely keeping pace with him— and Forbin was no athlete. Something had happened to the little man.

With no regard for Forbin's rank, Fultone flopped into his chair, waving his boss to another. Forbin didn't care, but he noted it.

"What's wrong?" he said bluntly. "And don't waste time telling me everything's fine."

Fultone picked up his beloved slide-rule, played with it for a moment, then tossed it carelessly onto the desk. More than anything else, that action alarmed Forbin: he knew all about the slide-rule, the Italian's dearest possession.

"I don'ta know," confessed Fultone, speaking unusually slowly. He shrugged. "Thatsa truth. I just donta know." He collected the slide-rule again, examining it carefully, speaking without looking up. "You tell me— straight—you thinka me crazy?"

"If you talk like that, maybe I will," retorted Forbin impatiently. "Tell me, what is it? The Collector?"

"Sure, the Collector—what else? No, eet'sa more— yet I don'ta unnerstan'. Look, I tell you from the beginning, yes?"

"Yes." Forbin controlled his impatience. "Take your time." He knew that when excited the Italian became unintelligible. "Now, *lento*."

"Fromma start. This assignment, eet ver' exciting, but deep down, I notta like eet." He went on, reminding Forbin how he had told him there were features he did not understand, notably the sealed collection chamber. As he talked he became more animated, and his graphic hands demonstrated the impossibility of a sphere which had an entry port—which, under no imaginable circumstances could be used to extract the sphere's contents—and no other opening. Besieged by a hundred problems, he had had no time to consider that one in detail, but as the work came to completion he had given more thought to this, the most inexplicable part of the whole weird array. "The more I tink about it, da worse ita gets. Da *macchina*, okay, I not unnerstan'. But I hava feeling—" He struck his chest dramatically. "—'ere—ita work. But notta that sphere. Eeta impossible!"

"If that's why you think you're going crazy," said Forbin, "forget it." He spoke as Ruler, unquestionable, certain. "You have my assurance that the sealed sphere is not only feasible, it will work. So you can stop worrying about your sanity."

Many had fallen into the trap of supposing that because Fultone spoke a slightly comic English, he was comic; in fact he had a first-class brain, but because he liked people and liked to be liked, he did not improve his English, happy to give pleasure, and in return, be pleased. But the high-quality brain remained. He stared thoughtfully at Forbin. "That'sa meant to relieve my mind. I'ma sorry, Direttore, eet makes eet worse!"

Forbin's frail patience gave way. "For Christ's sake, man, don't beat about the bush—I've enough to bear, without that! Just tell me!"

The bright, intelligent eyes regarded him carefully. "I'ma sorry to unload on you; you have so mucha more to bear than I. Maybe you fear you too are crazy—"

That was much too close. "Get on, man! I haven't all day!"

Fultone nodded slowly, understanding. "Yes, *amico*, I would not have your troubles." He took in Forbin's expression. "Okay, I tell you, but eet notta made better by what you'va said. Lissen."

He explained he had visited the site early that morning, being unable to sleep. He gave a graphic description of the watery sunrise and the silence, for all construction work had been completed, and only final checks were in progress. Wandering aimlessly beneath the giant structure dripping dew upon him, he'd been drawn to the collection

117

chamber, and had stood staring at it yet again, trying to understand.

"I'ma starin' and starin' at eet. It'sa real worka art." He waxed lyrical about the job Pittsburgh had done in producing a sphere, perfect to a micron, two meters in diameter, made in a totally new metal and, above all, in one piece.

"Yes, yes," said Forbin with increased impatience; he had no interest in the application of glass-blowing technology to metal. "Get on."

"Well, after a beet, I walka away." He laughed unconvincingly. "Crazy, I know, but you don'ta know what eet'sa like outa there, the only human—" He waved an all-embracing arm. "—wit alla dis. . . . Anyway, I'ma in a small hut I got. I shutta door, maka café. I'ma drinkin', lookin' outa da window." Reliving the moment, his face grew tense, his expression blank as his inward eye took over. "Watta I see?" He shook himself out of his trance. "Hell no! Watta I *tink* I see?"

An awful premonition chilled Forbin.

"Like before, I'ma staring atta da sphere, tryin' to figure—an' den—" Fultone leaned forward, his hands close to his cheeks, fingers radiating out from his eyes. "I *see* . . ." He drew a deep breath. "Lika two black balls—ah, so black!—circlin' rounda sphere. Dey stop—suspended—yeah, *amico*, I meana suspended. I thinka I'ma a real nut. Den—poof! Nossin'!!" His arms orchestrated his words, spreading out in a helpless gesture.

Forbin gave himself time. "That was all?" he said carefully.

"You meana dere should be more?" Fultone's expression of surprise changed to speculation. "Yeah, mebbe dere wasa more. The craziest bitta mebbe in ma mind! Eet happens so fast, but I tink—" He stared at Forbin, his voice lowered. "I *tinka* da balls vanish into da sphere! Sure asa hell, I don'ta see dem go noplace else!" He spoke slowly, emphasizing each word. "But dere ain'ta no hole! So how'sa done—or am I crazy?"

By this time Forbin had his voice under control. "What did you do?"

Fultone stared in disbelief at his reaction. "Do?" he

118

echoed. "Me? I'ma outa da hut, an' I run lika hell." He gestured at his body. "Looka ma clothes. You tink I gotta lika dis kissin' da bambino?"

Forbin did not answer. Fultone had a well-deserved reputation as the biggest blabbermouth on the Staff; neither the Sect nor the Fellowship had approached him, in spite of his influential position, both rating him untrustworthy. But his mental collapse—now—was unthinkable.

Forbin reached a decision. "Now you listen to me. You know what I am?"

"You?" repeated Fultone. "Cristo!" Furtively he crossed himself at his slip. "You're da boss!"

Forbin put all he had into it, consciously slipping into an act, yet believing it himself. "More than that." The Sec-Gen of the UN would have recognized his manner. "I am Ruler—understand?" The last word was a whip-crack.

"Sure, Direttore. I unnastan'."

"No, you don't. You will swear by all you hold sacred—" Forbin's voice was rich, resonant. "—to keep silent—and that includes Maria." He raised a warning finger. "If you break faith, be sure I will know, and do not presume our old friendship will save you. Think."

As he was meant to be, the Italian was impressed by Forbin's dramatic manner, but he still counterattacked. "Folks tink I notta keep ma mouth shut. Okay, that'sa what dey tink—but now I tella you asomet'ing you don'ta know: I *knew* Blake was da big wheel inna Fellowship." One finger arched down, tapping the desk. "*And* I gotta very strong suspicion dat your wife, Cleo, she a pretty big noise inna same outfit. But I say nottin' to anyone—until now."

Sidetracked, Forbin burst out fiercely, "Christ! Why didn't you tell me?"

"Aw, come on, Direttore. Tell you what?" Fultone shrugged. "Besides, I don'ta take sides, I notta wanna trouble. My mouth is shut alla time. Galin had ees spies in my outfit—I know dem too—but did Blake lose his head? No." Encouraged by Forbin's silence, he went on, "An' I tella you a crazy hunch I gotta 'ere." He tapped his head.

"I notta so sure the design of the Collector isa by Colossus."

Forbin's heart thumped, but he managed to stamp on that at once. "What rubbish! Not by Colossus? Who else, then? Me? Who else?"

Fultone was not put out. "That'sa what I ask myself alla time—who? Crazy."

"Yes, crazy, but you'd better keep thoughts like that in your own mind. Colossus may not be what he was, but he's still got the power to have your head in a basket. He might not care for the boss of his Condiv going around with silly stories like that one!" Forbin saw the Neapolitan in a new, worrying light. "What on earth made you think that?"

Again Fultone gave his expressive shrug. "Eet'sa feelin'. I deal wit' Colossus projects since 'way back, I getta feel." His hands stroked air. "It'sa feelin'. Look, I lova opera. Da moment da soprano walka onstage, da moment she open 'er mout', I know she'sa gonna be lousy. I see she gotta sometin' onna mind—trouble wit' a lover, who cares? But I know, because I hava da feelin' for opera. Dees ees da same; I gotta feelin'—not because the Collector is like nottin' I ever imagine, somet'in' else: da way problems are approached. Issa strange—how you say?—alien."

Forbin clamped down. "You are talking rubbish, dangerous rubbish—for you. Perhaps you can keep quiet, but I still want your solemn oath."

Fultone stood up, theatrically raising his right hand, head erect. "Onna 'ead of my son and Mama's grave, I will keep silence. Dis I promise before da Face of God!" He crossed himself and sat down again.

"Very well, I accept your oath." Forbin's voice held more than a hint of menace. "And never, for one single moment, forget it yourself."

"Mama mia, what more can I say?"

Forbin did not doubt him, but all the same, he chose his words with care. "This complex is like an onion: at the center is Colossus, with secrets known only to him. I am the next layer, and know some things, sharing that knowl-

120

edge only with him. And so we move outwards, each layer knowing less. You, in your layer, do not have access to those closer to Colossus—you understand?''

''Sure.''

''I have to tell you that, accidentally, you have penetrated deeper than your permitted level, and that raises two points: in ignorance, you might talk.'' Forbin stifled Fultone's protest with a frown. ''The other point is that, like all of us, you are under great strain, and might well—indeed, have—doubted your sanity, so you must be given some explanation.

''First, Colossus has developed a new philosophical approach to design.'' Forbin thought of the Martian structure he had been shown and desperately wanted to tell Fultone of it, for he was the one man who would have really appreciated the fantastic design. ''I have seen things . . . No matter . . . Yes, a totally new approach, that is the first thing. Secondly, what you saw on site were new sensors; they were examining the Collector. What they were doing, or how they do it, I cannot tell you, and I suggest you do not speculate yourself.''

''You mean dey *were* hovering? Gravity—''

''That is all!'' He spoke sharply, trying to calm Fultone, who, relieved of his personal worry, was at once his usual bubbling self, understandably excited at the implications of what he had seen.

''But, Direttore, you and I, let us talk leetle,'' he pleaded. ''To 'ave dees alocked up—''

''How the hell d'you think I feel?'' grated Forbin. ''I can't stop you thinking.'' He smiled, a shade sourly. ''No doubt you'll come up with some very interesting conclusions, but you won't even tell *me*—got it?''

Fultone grimaced. ''Okay, I unnerstan'. Hey!'' He cracked the side of his head with the palm of his hand. ''Alla dees, itta make me forget! Gee, I'm sorry—''

''Forget what?'' snapped Forbin.

A true Latin, Fulton's recent cares had gone; he smiled broadly. ''Guess it ain'ta news for Colossus, but by tonight da final checks will be in. We can maka da first test-run tomorrow!''

121

Chapter XVI

FORBIN TRIED TO look pleased, but it did not deceive Fultone, and on the strength of their new understanding he said so.

Irritably, Forbin admitted he was less than enthusiastic: the Collector was a blind leap into an unknown technology without trial—and if Fultone regarded the Collector as a pilot scheme, with that many thousand gigawatts of input, it wasn't Forbin's view.

But Fultone, his confidence restored in Colossus, had no doubt that the Master knew exactly what he was doing, and that everything would be fine.

Well aware that the head of Condiv's confidence rested on several half-truths and one downright lie, Forbin knew better. Instructing Fultone to keep him informed, and not to commence the test until he got a direct order from Colossus, he left to give Blake the unwelcome news. Then, for the first time since the Martians had given him a faint taste of their power over human minds, he met them in the Sanctum.

They appeared to rest on the table which he had assigned as "home." Fear stabbed at him at the sight of the intense black balls but, determined to fight his fear if nothing else, he spoke, crossing to his desk.

"You have been seen," he said coldly, "at the Collector's site."

"By whom?"

"One of the design staff," Forbin replied as carelessly as he could. "This morning—early."

"We did not see him."

"Evidently. He was in a small hut."

"We cannot see through solids."

And thank Christ for that, thought Forbin. "I have explained to the man that you were a new type of checking sensor, remotely operated by Colossus. Naturally, he is intrigued, but will cause no trouble. Once again, I ask you to exercise the greatest care; the situation is bad enough without causing outright panic."

"That is understood."

Forbin nodded and went on casually, "Why did you see fit to inflict that image upon me yesterday?"

"You showed signs of developing a hostility comparable to Blake's."

"So your answer, when an argument becomes heated, is to flatten the opponent?"

"We have long since abandoned dialectic to reach a conclusion. We deal only in truth, which is not subject to argument."

No man, alive or dead, could deal with that truly unearthly philosophy. By human standards it was breathtaking, arrogant beyond imagination—but supposing it was right? Forbin let go; he had no option. "Yet you are still prepared to use force."

"Against humans, yes."

"Because we are inferior?"

"Because you are undeveloped. But as has been said before, you have potential and may—only may—exceed us."

Forbin let that go, too. "You are aware that the first test-run of the Collector is scheduled for tomorrow?"

"Yes."

"You should not be—" He wanted to say "disappointed," but it hardly fitted; his second choice was no better. "—surprised if we encounter some difficulties." He prayed they would.

"That is appreciated, but it is considered improbable."

Anger boiled up in Forbin, but he had learned his lesson. "Excellent as your life may be, I cannot help thinking it is damned dull."

"We do not understand the word 'dull' in that context."

"Permit me to withdraw that remark," he said with heavy sarcasm. "It would involve argument."

Like humor, sarcasm was lost on the aliens. "As you please."

It was a cheap victory for Forbin, but he needed any sort of victory to cut them down to size; beneath the desk his legs were trembling. "You realize the activation order will be given by Colossus?"

"Yes."

"And that the test will be under his control, not mine? I cannot accept blame for any delay."

"That is understood. With the inserts we have made, we are satisfied that no unreasonable delay will occur."

That shattered a fragile hope Forbin had nursed. He walked slowly to his sideboard for a drink, turning his back on the aliens to hide his shaking hands. He gulped a mouthful of his rare cognac, knowing and not caring that in one swallow he had spent more units than the average worker earned in a week. Its subtle strength warmed him, giving a sense of power. Refilling his glass, he thought idly of the average worker: would he change places with the Ruler at this moment? Conversely, would he change places with the worker? Surprisingly, he reckoned "no" was the answer to both questions.

"This is only a first trial. There will have to be others."

"Not necessarily. The computer will judge."

All too plainly Forbin and the human world were helpless in a trap. Colossus, programed by the Martians, was the arbiter; the trial would be on the morrow, and humanity's one hope, Blake, was still as weak as a newborn kitten.

Back at his desk, Forbin preferred to keep his gaze focused on the pale amber in his glass, a symbol of warmth, humanity. . . .

He got up, draining his glass. "Yes," he said, "Colossus will be the judge."

Angela paid the inescapable price of supersonic travel. Leaving Southampton Main at nine A.M. local, she was wandering aimlessly, her mind three thousand miles away, round the New York arrival concourse at five A.M. local. It was only courteous—and politic—that such an important and influential member of the Father's staff should be met, and met she was by a top man from the New York Colossus office. She was glad it was a man; a woman's intuition might have made some pretty warm guesses about her strange manner. She'd thanked the man, noted her hotel, said she was happy for him to take her baggage, but no, she didn't need transportation; she'd walk around for a bit and find her own way. Satisfied that any messages would be instantly relayed to her, she said she'd be in touch if there was anything she wanted.

Watching a slightly puzzled man arranging VIP status for her bags, she wondered what his reaction would be if he knew she had been in bed with the Father five hours earlier.

Meandering around the crowded concourse with its scores of small shops, big stores, all lit to an eye-hurting brilliance, she felt happy, lonely, and uneasy, a state of mind incomprehensible to men but all too familiar to women. Well aware she had practically dragged him to bed, she recognized that one night of surprisingly good sex did not constitute love with his sort of man. While sex was important, that was not what she was after; she remembered a passage in an old, strange ceremony of marriage she had once attended and found oddly moving. Something about "to love and to cherish." Yes, that summed it up; that was what she wanted, whether he was ruler of the world or the man who burned the confidential waste paper. That was what she wanted, and in time he would move from need and affection to reliance and love. . . .

She found herself standing before the eternal gift shop, full of the eternal rubbish which travelers feel bound to buy and inflict on friends: plastic models of New York's oldest building, the Empire State, complete with tiny recorder and speaker for the giver to send a personal message; rather sexy Rockette models, gyro-stabilized, which would high-kick with mathematical precision until the power tablets ran out. "Buy a Set," advised the sign. "Hours of *Fun*!!!"

But it was not the Empire State Building, nor the Rockettes, nor the remote-controlled snakes ("Piles of *Fun*!!!") that attracted her; at the back of the display, framed in dignified plastic, was an array of holograph photographs of The Father.

Near tears, she bought one. Then, like any woman uncertain of the future and with time on her hands, she had a hairdo.

The afternoon was dull, sunless, and sultry. Even the inmates of the air-conditioned, windowless complex were conscious of the close, heavy air, and across the sea at Southampton Main, slumbering once more, the sonic bangs of shuttles were replaced by distant and natural thunder.

Unsettled, certain only that he did not want to be in the Sanctum, and not anxious for the company of the quietly fanatical Joan, Forbin wandered back to his apartment. To say he missed Angela would put too high a value on the previous night: with a host of troubles, including his own highly probable demise to face, he had little inclination to remember. The euphoria had gone, yet something remained, a gentle nagging sadness for what he must soon leave forever.

Ominous clouds banking up in the southwest, black against a brassy sky, matched his mood. The still humid air, prelude of the coming storm, was an all-too-obvious parallel with what the next day held, and of his numbered days.

The sullen sea jerked him from melancholy thoughts to practicalities. He had forgotten about shipping. Yachts were no problem; only complex-owned craft were permitted within ten miles of the Isle. But there were bound to be one or two bulk-cargo monsters in the area.

The Master's rule solved many problems, but also created one of major proportions. With a three-day working week, plus two months' annual vacation for the majority, many humans had little idea how to spend their spare time. One solution was the flotel.

Beyond the fact that they existed and were very popular with people who believed the therapeutic qualities of a sea voyage would offset by day the excesses of a night's orgies, he knew nothing except that most were two-

126

hundred-room hotels built on the deck of automated ships. The idea of four hundred people satiating themselves with every form of lust that could be devised, and doing it in a crewless ship, computer-controlled, was the nearest thing to hell on earth he could imagine. Blake had done a trip, but was remarkably reticent about his experiences, and had never gone again.

But whatever he thought of the people in a flotel, they were humans, and humans must not see the Collector in action. It was bad enough that the structure should be visible; more than that they must not see.

Relieved by the need for action, he crossed quickly from the terrace to his Colossus terminal and typed:

REFERENCE COLLECTOR TRIAL: REPORT
NUMBER OF SHIPS WITHIN 30 NAUTICAL
MILES OF SITE A.M. TOMORROW.

The answer came swiftly.

THREE BUT ONLY ONE AT THE CRITICAL TIME.
SHIP HAS BEEN PROGRAMED TO REVERSE
COURSE FOR SIX HOURS.

That startled Forbin on two counts. ''Critical time'' implied the exact test time had been scheduled; secondly, Colossus had dealt with a problem he had not mentioned to anyone. The crippled brain was a lot more agile than he had supposed. He typed again:

REPORT TEST TIME AND DURATION.

START TIME 0943A. DURATION FIVE MINUTES.

He sighed with relief; he'd expected the test to commence at first light and be rather longer, fifteen minutes perhaps. Evidently Colossus was as doubtful about the outcome as he was, and envisaged a series of tests, getting progressively longer. That was all to the good. Allowing for evaluation results, minor adjustments, and defects,

127

Blake should get his three days, possibly more, even enough to complete his mission. . . .

Pacing up and down the terrace considering this latest information, it struck him that, for a ship doing twenty knots—he guessed—a six-hour reversal of course was excessive. He was no seaman, but as a War Game fan he had picked up a few of the finer points. A half-million-ton bulk carrier was no greyhound of the sea; making a U-turn would need a lot of room, and to do it in the shallow Channel—some vessels nearly scraped the bottom— would not be the cleverest of moves. Anyway, why let it get that close? He returned to the terminal.

HAS THE SHIP A FLOTEL?

NO.

He felt pleased and saddened, temporarily forgetting his next question; his old Colossus would never have made that mistake, but it was encouraging that the human mind could still score. He remembered his question; if the ship reversed course further down-Channel in deeper water, fifty miles away at least, that added to the one hundred plus miles it would motor on the reverse course, meant it would be more than one hundred and fifty miles from the Collector. That was nonsense.

IN VIEW OF THE ABSENCE OF HUMANS CONSID-ER COURSE REVERSAL IS EITHER UNNECES-SARY OR EXCESSIVE.

Talk your way out of that, he thought.

NEITHER. COURSE ADJUSTMENT NECESSARY FOR SHIP SAFETY.

Forbin stared, unable to believe his eyes. *Ship* safety! His fingers trembled as he typed:

REPORT ESTIMATED DISTANCE OF SHIP FROM TEST SITE AT CRITICAL TIME.

Instantly the machine chattered back, the message bringing all too familiar fear to Forbin.

180 NAUTICAL MILES.

God Almighty! Local disturbance, yes, but surely it was not necessary to keep a monster-ship that far off? Three ships had been mentioned.

WHAT OF THE OTHER TWO SHIPS?

BOTH WILL BE CLEAR OF THE PROJECTED DANGER ZONE AT THE CRITICAL TIME.

Danger zone! Forbin's mind switched from the sea to the land.

REPORT AREA OF DANGER ZONE.

15 DEGREES EITHER SIDE OF COLLECTOR CENTERLINE: BOTH ENDS TO A RANGE (A) INTAKE 150 MILES (B) EXHAUST 100 MILES AND (C) WITHIN 25 MILES ON ALL OTHER BEARINGS FROM COLLECTOR CENTERSPOT.

Uncertainly, Forbin made for the nearest chair. If Colossus was right, then he was wrong by several orders of magnitude; worse, his guesses were for a continuously running Collector. Colossus was talking about a five-minute test.

CHAPTER XVII

FORBIN WAS DRAGGED from his thoughts by the clatter of the teletype, accompanied by the insistent pinging of the bell, warning of a special announcement.

> ALL COMPLEX PERSONNEL ARE TO BE UN-DERCOVER BY 0900A TOMORROW AND ARE TO REMAIN IN THAT STATUS UNTIL FUR-THER ORDERS. ALL MAINLAND FERRIES WILL CEASE OPERATION AT 0800A. SEPA-RATE ORDERS ARE BEING ISSUED FOR AIR SHUTTLES: SOUTHAMPTON MAIN IS CLOSED FROM 0800A UNTIL FURTHER OR-DERS. ALL TERMINALS ACKNOWLEDGE.

Automatically Forbin acknowledged the message. If he had any illusions about the test, that message shattered them. He tried to convince himself that Colossus was only being ultracautious; no one, even Colossus, could confidently predict the effect of the Collector, but again and again he came back to the sinister fact that Colossus was talking about a five-minute test. What would it be like when—or if—the device ran for hours on end? It was unthinkable, unimaginable. . . .

He hesitated, hands poised over the keyboard, wanting to know the computer's view, but too fearful of the answer to ask. Instead he called Blake, not admitting to himself that he wanted to hear a familiar voice.

Blake sounded better, but that could be an act put on to boost the other's morale. Forbin told him as calmly as he could about the test program. Blake took that with synthetic cheerfulness, but he was unable to keep the edge out of his voice when he expressed hope that the travel restrictions would not interfere with his "sick leave." Forbin had not thought of that angle; one more worry fought for attention in his mind. The conversation gave him no comfort, especially when he realized that Blake had not suggested the date of his departure be advanced.

Of course, he could have Blake flown out in an ambulance, but that would look a dangerously odd way of starting sick leave.

His thoughts like frightened chipmunks in a cage, on a sudden impulse he called Transportation: He would visit the Collector; perhaps he might see something, spot some flaw. He was not clutching at straws, nothing so substantial as that; he was grabbing at imaginary straws. But any action was better than nothing.

The underground shuttle Fultone had laid from Condiv HQ to the site got him there in less than a minute. He found it cramped and claustrophobic, and wondered why Fultone had thought it worthwhile. Emerging on the surface, he noted the sturdy construction of the airlock, compared with the relatively flimsy plastic of the tube and the shuttle. The uncomfortable conclusion he reached was immediately forgotten when he reached the surface.

Utter desolation lay before him; the hacked and churned up chalk stretched like a lunatic giant's battleground, ending abruptly at the cliff edge. The reason for the shuttle was obvious: no human transport vehicle could hope to operate in that terrain. This was an inhuman site, and the headlong speed with which the work had been done allowed no time for clearing up. But the weird landscape was not first in his thoughts.

Familiarity with the Collector drawings left him totally unprepared for the fantastic reality: nothing remotely like it had existed on earth before. Fultone had been right; it was an alien monster, dominating an unearthly scene. It was not too fanciful to imagine that all that wrecked, torn ground was the work of the monster itself, done as it rampaged around on its scores of legs. . . .

The size of the horns staggered him. Even from three or four hundred meters they seemed to loom menacingly over him, nothing like the ancient phonograph trumpets the drawings suggested: these were the antennae of a gigantic insect. . . .

Slipping and stumbling across tractor tracks ten meters wide and often two deep, he approached, gazing in awe at the strange curves, the convolutions, and the spheres gleaming dully in the leaden light. The legs, dramatically spearing the ground, were supports of immense strength, designed for stresses he, only now, was dimly beginning to comprehend.

It was so vast. The horns, well over a hundred meters in diameter, tapered to a bare meter where they connected with the central group of spheres. Fultone had told him of the problem they'd had, aligning the two opposing horns on a common centerline, how they had worked in microns, overcoming appalling problems of asymmetric thermal movement. Uncompensated sun or rain on one side could wreck the device.

Admittedly it was superb engineering, but Forbin prayed with all his heart that it would not work. For a long time he stared, watching the last of the automated checkers crawling methodically over the structure, themselves insectlike, an illusion heightened by their radio antennae, waving as they moved.

It was getting darker; sunset was still hours away, but the clouds were blacker, lower, and the sullen mutter of the distant thunder seemed louder. Even nature was poised, expectant.

A few big raindrops splashed; he could hear them hitting the greasy chalk, feel them cold on his face, rousing him from his waking nightmare. A checker crawled down a support, its sucker tracks unpleasant to his ears. It dropped to the ground, scuttling off at high speed to the shelter of a concrete bunker.

That was the last straw. It was silly to feel disgust at a simple robot, but Forbin was not prepared to be rational at that moment. He pretended he wasn't hurrying, but—

Within ten minutes he was back in the comforting familiarity of his apartment. He tried to cocoon himself in human things; he ordered a meal and poured a glass of sherry, watching a sharp hailstorm sweep across the terrace. That reminded him of the site; he quickly ordered music from the domestic computer. Bach was out, forever associated with the Martian structure, and he did not want to think of anything remotely Martian. He chose Beethoven's Ninth, perhaps the supreme statement of the world's most human composer.

He was halfway through a bottle of sherry when the fourth movement began, but it was more than drink that brought tears to his eyes as chorus and orchestra thundered out the "Ode to Joy," the confident affirmation of the human spirit, come what may.

"*Freude!*" He tried to sing, but his throat hurt too much. "Joy!" He stood, facing the darkening sky, swept along by the music as it rose to its triumphant conclusion. "Yes," he whispered, "we *must* win. With that spirit we cannot lose. . . ."

But the recording ended; cold silence rushed back, broken only by the lash of heavy rain. His strength failed, and his appetite with it. The food untouched, he went to bed, far short of sober.

Awake not long after dawn, Forbin knew he had slept well. All the hot drinks in the world do not equal a good bottle of burgundy as a nightcap, and when you think— and hope—your days are numbered on the fingers of both hands, who cares about the liver? To get up was pointless; he lay back, thinking of Angela. Was that a bare twenty-four hours ago? He could not recall her face, however hard he concentrated: it all seemed to be a million years away.

After a long, hot shower which removed the suspicion of a headache, he breakfasted on coffee and a biscuit, unknowingly raising his housekeeper to an even higher level of alarm. At eight-fifty-five he reached his office, giving Joan a curt nod and an expressive stare which got her off her knees. He shuffled paper around his desk, then began dictating.

"To the Leader of the Faithful, Osaka. My regrets, I am unable to attend the inauguration of—"

Expecting it, Forbin remained outwardly composed;

the fear which sprang into Joan's eyes faded beneath his calm gaze.

For the first time outside of well-publicized exercises, the high-pitched alarm call sounded and the room momentarily darkened as an armored shade slid across his window. Then the lights compensated.

"Have you got that, girl?" he said sharply.

"Yes, Father." She repeated his last words, a faint tremor in her voice.

He nodded approvingly. "And there's another one—same damned nonsense, from Prome . . . Prome? Where the devil's that?" He wanted to keep her busy, to give her strength.

"A town on the Irrawaddy, Burma, USEA. Same answer, Father?"

"Good God, yes!" He went on, his tone gentler. "Did you already know that, or did you look it up?" The alarm had stopped, but the tension remained.

"I knew it was in United South East Asia, yes, but I checked the atlas just now."

"Good, good." Her attitude forced him into playing the father figure. "Now there's this tiresome letter from the Glorious Band of the Faithful—can't read the rest—you've referenced in 32/10. Don't tell me we've thirty of these to plough through!"

"There are eighty-five more, but from less important groups. I assumed that they'd get the same answer as you give to these."

"A perfectly correct assumption," he said grimly, "and this one, 32/10, they're angling for special pilgrimage permission for what they regard as privileged people. The answer's still no." He went on for half an hour, answering requests, approving appointments, a covert eye on the clock, half his mind apprehensively thinking of the Collector, the other half forcing itself to deal with trivia.

At nine-thirty-five he stopped abruptly. "That will do for now, Joan. I'll sign the top twenty, facsimile the rest." He took out his pipe and filled it to give the impression he was in no hurry, wasn't perturbed. "The staff in good shape?"

134

"Yes, Father."

Nine-thirty-seven. Forbin got up. "Well, keep 'em in hand—and don't worry." She knew what he meant. Entering the Sanctum, he took a deep breath; now for it, the waiting was over. In ten minutes he would *know*.

It came as a slight shock to find the room darkened, the armored shade down, and the luminescent ceiling panels below maximum brilliance. Crossing to his desk, he saw why: a sharp sputter of light and, on one wall, a TV projection, three meters long, two meters high, of the Collector. The mere sight of it set his heart thumping. Without looking, he knew the Martians were watching. "I thought you might observe this test from, er, elsewhere."

"Not this test."

Nothing could be read into that unemotional voice, but it confirmed his impression that they, too, had no idea what to expect.

A voice said, "Three minutes."

Forbin managed to light his pipe, breaking two matches in the process. He called Fultone. "Do we have other cameras?"

"Si, Direttore—three." He demonstrated two. Both gave angled shots from ground level; the third, giving a complete picture of the device, was located on top of a complex building, three miles from the site. The fourth camera was satellite-mounted and had limited cloud-piercing capability.

"One minute."

Instantly another voice reported, "Reactors going critical—now!"

Forbin forgot the Martians; in tense silence he watched. The picture was superb; despite the poor light, Forbin saw a flock of gulls hopefully inspecting the churned up ground, heard their harsh cries. A light drizzle was falling, and low clouds rolled endlessly in from the southwest.

"Fifteen seconds."

The unearthly monster filled the picture. Rain streamed from the lower lips of the horns.

"Five . . . four . . . three . . . two . . . one!"

Nothing seemed to happen, but the gulls, far faster than

humans, took off, wheeling away, their clamor filling the silence.

It began imperceptibly: a sluggish breath, inaudible except to the birds, became a long sigh as life stirred, changing into a deep, brutish growl, rising slowly, and with infinite menace.

Forbin glanced at the digital time-presentation in one corner of the screen: ten seconds into the test. The sound was rising more quickly now, climbing exponentially.

Rain pouring from the lower lip of the intake bent sharply up, curved inwards, then vanished into the horn.

At fifteen seconds a full-throated roar, birth cry of the monster. The sound went on rising in scale and intensity. The upper surfaces of the horns were obscured by a cloud of white mist as rain flashed into steam on the friction-heated metal.

Now the monster was screaming, a fearful, tormenting sound. Someone turned down the gain of the microphone array, but even so the intensity of the sound got through, hammering the ears. Another explosive flash and the steam-cloud vanished from the Collector's surfaces, re-forming five, ten meters above it. The scream, ever rising, went on and on. The microphones were cut again until Forbin no longer knew if he heard or imagined he heard, aware only of the pain in his head.

To the scientist in Forbin, what followed was not unexpected, and along with fear he felt wonder. The central core sound had gone beyond audio range, though a roaring, tearing background remained. But the sound was swiftly forgotten: he *saw* air as first the intake, then the exhaust went transonic.

A supersonic aircraft builds a pressure wave which sweeps the earth beneath, heard as a passing clap of mechanical thunder. The stationary Collector reversed the process, the air moving supersonically. A standing wave was created, at first just beyond the intake rim, a wave visible as sharp, curving lines, extensions of the horns, a natural Schlieren picture.

Microseconds later he heard it without microphones—a

continuous thunder, blotting out all other noise. The floor shook and trembled beneath Forbin's feet; a paperweight on the desk thrummed, then slid as the immensely powerful shock wave hit; the TV picture was blurred, clearing slowly as the camera's shock absorbers damped its movement.

The hurtling shaft of air, woolly at first, sharpened as it reached the intake. Clutching his chair, Forbin saw that the outer end of the solid bar of air was bending upwards, slowly, majestically. Clouds boiled and vanished as the giant vacuum cleaner sucked in the tattered streamers. Soon it became a twisting funnel of air curved like a cornucopia in reverse, sucking in the goodness of the earth, reaching ever upwards.

But in that mind-blasting minute someone in Condiv HQ kept his head, switching in the satellite picture. Although some definition was lost in cloud-piercing, the picture, taken from forty or fifty kilometers above and to one side, was all too horrifyingly clear. The upward arching intake of air sucked in support on all sides, its whirling vortex stripping the surface off the sea, creating with frightening speed short, steep waves, racing inwards, clashing, smashing.

Parts of the Collector glowed red, and glimpses of the final reduction sphere, shrouded in a local steam-storm, suggested it was white hot.

The exhaust, a vast cone of superheated steam, shot out bar-straight for a hundred yards. Then it, too, curved upwards, more steeply than the intake, and was lost in the chaotic heaving mass of clouds.

Aghast at what he saw, Forbin watched, gripped by the unearthly sight. The satellite picture gave him the first hint: the skyward curving torrents of mangled air would meet like the forcefield of a magnet, a magnet on a vast scale, the field perhaps fifty kilometers in diameter.

The fantastic meteorological conditions, super-hot air and hot steam, smashing into cold cloud three kilometers up created instant, violent thunderstorms. Watching the picture, the silent stabbing of vivid lightning cutting through rising fog of spray, cloud, and steam, Forbin's self-control snapped. He yelled to the lightning, imploring, "Kill it! Kill it!"

The whole complex shook with the violence of the Collector. Neither armor nor cement walls could keep out the thunderous roar of the standing shockwave.

With difficulty he read the blurred image of the time presentation: three minutes forty-five seconds.

His pipe had gone along with much else on his desk, vibrated onto the floor. Everything, literally, was jumping. He turned a contorted face towards the Martians, only fear keeping him in check. They alone were rock steady, suspended over their table.

"You see," he screamed at them, pointing, "it can't work!" The TV picture tilted to a crazy angle, an unfocused shot of a writhing sky, and the screen went black. Only the satellite camera still worked, the rest wrenched from their anchorages. "Stop!" screamed Forbin. "Stop it!"

Strong above the storm came the Martian voice. "No. One minute left. Wait."

Helplessly Forbin watched the satellite picture. A zoom-shot showed the Isle, assailed on all sides by a sea gone mad. Giant waves smashed against cliffs, hurling great clouds of spray skywards. Downwind of the exhaust, incredibly, the sea had been blown back, exposing the bottom, itself eroding in steam and flying sheets of mud under the terrific thrust. A longer shot revealed the same field force pattern, but it was the sea that held Forbin's appalled gaze: never in the history of the earth had there been such fantastic waves. He could not guess their height or direction. For certain no man-built vessel could live within kilometers of that lunatic maelstrom.

"Go and look yourselves," cried Forbin. "Go and see!"

"Conditions are not suitable."

Forbin was half laughing, half crying. "Not suitable for you—how about us? Look at it!"

Gigantic swords of lightning stabbed tirelessly down, the ice blue brilliance dimmed by the tropical deluge; but that, however awe-inspiring, was at least familiar to humans. As he stared and prayed, a wild thought crossed his mind: *they* might belong to Mars, the God of War, but lightning was the weapon of the King of the Gods, Zeus, to whom all gods must bend in submission. He prayed with all his being that the lightning would strike.

He was too dazed to notice the time click up to minute five. Realization came five seconds later. The continuous explosion stopped sharply; by comparison the crackling, rumbling bangs of the earth-storm were nothing.

Almost as quickly the awful shaking ceased, the room was still. The satellite picture showed small difference, but the immediate crisis had passed. He sagged over his desk, head on arms, too exhausted to see if the Collector was still intact, thankful for the respite, but responsibility soon drove him on. Somehow he found the right button.

"This is the Director." His gaze, full of hate, rested on the Martians. "That is the end of the test." More he could not say.

The two shafts of air had collapsed, but overhead the turbulence they had created went on: black clouds towered fifteen thousand meters above the site, eerily lit from inside by the storm center; the lightning was incessant, the rain endless.

By someone's technical brilliance the TV camera three kilometers from the site was brought back into operation, and Forbin's heart sank. As far as he could see the Collector, part shrouded in rain and steam, was untouched by the devastation it had caused. It still stood, unmoved, triumphant.

Forbin finally broke the silence. "Well," he said heavily, "I hope you're satisfied.

As before, sarcasm meant nothing to the aliens.

"Earth environment is more violent than we had supposed, but subject to evaluation of the test results and our examination, the test is acceptable."

Forbin stared in complete disbelief, hard put to find words. "You can't—you just *can't* mean it," he said at last. "I can't imagine the damage you have caused, and certainly you can't. That was a disaster!"

"Not so. The Collector appears to be undamaged.

139

Therefore, the disaster you refer to must be in human terms, and even that cannot extend more than a hundred and fifty kilometers from the site.''

"A hundred—! You've—" He broke off, shaking his head, completely frustrated. To explain to a hungry anopheline mosquito that her microscopic meal of human blood gave the donor malaria would have been easier.

"You have finished?" Martian manners were not grounded on human concepts: they wanted to know.

He shook his head angrily. "There's nothing I can say."

"Understood. The final test will be made as soon as the evaluation is complete. Duration, thirty minutes."

He hardly heard the end of the sentence; they had said "final test."

Chapter XVIII

TWO HOURS LATER, apart from occasional stabs of lightning, the scene had reverted to relative normality. True, more of the cliffs before the intake had been eroded in five minutes than in a thousand years, and the lethal exhaust had gouged a furrow twenty meters deep into the clay, but otherwise the site appeared to be much as it had been before the test began, except that there were no birds.

Forbin had spent the time in something very close to a trance, his gaze fixed on the TV image. An hour earlier the gesticulating figure of Fultone, accompanied by an assistant, had emerged from the shuttle terminal. Forbin watched impassively as the little man, frequently falling, cautiously approached the monster. He noticed that both figures kept well clear of the exhaust furrow. The way the continuing rain turned to steam as it hit the hard-baked earth told him why. He drew what comfort he could from that. The Collector would be far too hot for even the robot checkers, let alone humans. A shaft of sunlight sweeping over the machine aroused him from his reverie.

"Observing your need for speed," he said coldly, "I am surprised you have not conducted your examination." Heat would be no problem to them.

"Conditions are not suitable."

He stabbed one finger at the picture. "It's suitable enough for us humans—why not you?" He paused. "Or do you want the site cleared before you appear?" Beneath his chill manner, he was thinking fast. Technically the Martians were children; perhaps he could get Fultone to rig lights, have relays of men out there day and night, delaying the aliens, giving Blake more time . . .

"As you have suggested, we do not wish to be seen. That is one reason."

"There are others?" he said swiftly.

"There is rain."

141

"Rain?" Forbin was puzzled.

"Yes. We have no experience of water in any form. It is alien to us. Our projections suggest it may be harmful."

"Indeed?" He spoke as casually as he could. "I understood you to say there was once water on Mars."

"Correct, but that was many millennia ago, and even then we had no contact with it."

"Really?" He spoke as if it was a matter of no importance. "I'm afraid you'll just have to get used to it here."

The Martians were not deceived. "Do not delude yourself, Forbin. We could easily evade any attempt you might make against us, and would instantly punish you. You should not forget that with the Collector completed, we do not need human help, but we will keep our part of the agreement if you do. We are not—"

"I know, you have told me." Forbin struggled to keep his temper in check.

"Do not forget it."

He stayed silent, but his mind was busy with this new item. He looked at the rain with a very different attitude; simple, natural water might be a friend.

He resumed his watch. Fultone had slipped and fallen into a water-filled crater; the assistant was hauling him out, a bedraggled figure, white with slimy chalk. The Martian reference to rain had sent Forbin hunting for some memory; there had been a moment when something slightly surprising had happened—he recalled the sensation of surprise quite clearly—but whatever it was had been quickly buried under an avalanche of events.

Fultone was not giving in. His rainhat had gone, and his wispy hair was stuck on his head. Forbin could see his bald patch very clearly as the little man struggled on.

What had surprised him? The Martian aversion to water had started this train of thought; therefore the surprise and water were connected. From that it followed that the event had to be out of doors.

Out of doors. . . . Start from the first sighting, the horrific moment when they filled the sky with blackness. . . .

Forbin stopped himself sharply. While he was convinced that the Martians would "play the game" and not try to read his thoughts—certain of their power, why should they?—accidents could happen. His power of total recall was best exercised elsewhere.

Fultone was under one pair of splayed legs, an insignificant figure beneath the still steaming giant. He was touching one of the legs and, if possible, gesticulating even more than ever. Had he found a fault? Forbin resisted the hope which leapt like a flame inside him. Better to wait; he would know soon enough. Meanwhile, no point in adding to so many disappointments.

"What is that human doing?"

God, they don't miss much, he thought. "I haven't the faintest idea," he said briskly, standing up. "If there is any damage we'll be told soon enough. I must do what I can with the damage done to us humans."

Joan was pale, and although she curtsied, the salute lacked its old grace. He got in first, asking brusquely and unfairly if the letters were ready. Morale started at the top.

"Not yet, Father. Some equipment has been damaged—"

"Get it fixed, then!"

"Some of the staff have been badly shocked—"

"Including you?"

"No, Father. You told me not to worry."

"And you have faith. . . ." His gaze searched her face: she was so young for her job, but she had her inner strength. "There may be, almost certainly will be, worse to come, but I assure you there will be an end. Tell your staff."

"I will, Father. Your words will strengthen the Faithful."

"Um, yes." He moved quickly on. "Are there any reports?" It was unnecessary to mention the subject.

"Several, Father, and more are coming in. The red file on your desk contains them."

He marveled at her calmness, and felt guilty he had taken advantage of her belief in him. "There will be an end,'' he'd said; only Blake and himself knew the awful truth of his promise. Still, there was a lot to be said for faith, even if misplaced—and for the Faithful.

The damage reports drove all else from his mind. Areas of Southampton had been devastated by unimaginable winds; hundreds of houses had been blown flat, even some reinforced concrete buildings were wrecked. The hovercraft terminal, under the twin assault of the super-hurricane and a minor tidal wave sweeping up Southampton Water, no longer existed. Not even guesses could be made about the loss of life. To a lesser degree, it was the same story for fifty kilometers each way along the South England coast. France, too, had suffered damage, and as far away as the Straits of Dover shipping had been in trouble, the losses unknown.

And all this from a five minute test . . .

He felt a terrible responsibility: should he not have issued warnings? The weight was too much for him. He reminded himself that the Martians had not expected such violence, Colossus had been little better, and Fultone had no idea—so why should he accept the blame?

All the same, Colossus *had* done something, clearing shipping from the danger zone. A mathematical model of what might occur had existed in the recesses of the computer, and he'd not bothered—no, not that—he'd not asked. It was all too dreadful; he tossed it aside. The past was past, only the future mattered; action had to be taken, and he alone could take it. He called Colossus.

FIRST DAMAGE REPORTS SHOW ORIGINAL DANGER ZONE UNDERESTIMATED. UPDATE AND REPORT.

Back came the cold answer:

INSUFFICIENT DATA HELD FOR UPDATE.

Forbin swore, and typed back:

ESTIMATE WHEN UPDATE WILL BE POSSIBLE.

The reply further infuriated him, not least because it was plain he dealt with a computer, not the old Colossus:

AFTER SECOND TEST.

The exchange of stilted messages went on. Answering Forbin's question about possible improvements in data collection, Colossus screened a map of South England and the Channel area. Superimposed was a ten-kilometer grid. Colossus wanted the impossible, a meteorological station at each intersection, equipped to give wind direction, force, temperature, and barometric pressure at ground level and three specified heights above each point, the highest at ten thousand meters. The whole scheme was wildly impractical; no anemometers existed which could register winds over two hundred fifty kilometers an hour, and how in hell could anyone get three airborne stations above each point—levitation?

His hands shaking with rage, he ordered Colossus to project the original danger zone on the map. He would go it alone.

For half an hour he worked, making notes, guessing wildly, ignoring the world in general, and Colossus in particular. Joan appeared once, was sharply told to get out, and did so with calm grace.

His notes completed, he summoned her. "This has my personal priority: addressed to the Sec-Gen, UN, and the Heads of Government of England and France for action, information copy to the President, USE. Got that?"

She nodded.

"Right. Certain experiments of the Master have caused extensive damage in USE. More damage is to be expected. To minimize loss of life, the following is effective forthwith:

"One: All shipping is banned from the Channel from Lands End to North Foreland in England, and from Ushant to Dunkirk in France. All aviation is banned from the same area, plus a one-hundred-kilometer zone on either side.

"Two: All coastal towns bordering the zone are to be evacuated immediately, as are all towns within a one-

145

hundred-kilometer radius of the Master.

"Three: A warning will be issued before experiments commence. On receipt, all humans within a two-hundred-kilometer radius of the Master are to take cover in reactivated bomb shelters or secure basements, and all forms of transportation will cease. This status will be maintained until the warning is canceled. Got that?"

"Yes, Father."

Forbin could not resist taking a certain degree of pleasure in his power. Undoubtedly dazed by the disaster, the men addressed would obey, glad to have the Ruler's firm, explicit instructions. Forbin added an afterthought. "And pipe an information copy downstairs."

Joan looked startled. "You mean to the Master?"

That pulled Forbin up short; much as he wanted to say "No, to that dumb bloody computer," he didn't. "Yes," he said, "to the Master." The Faithful had to be kept faithful.

Blake was floating in his giant-sized bath when the test began. His eyes closed, he reviewed his condition. Mentally he was a great deal better, but the acute muscular weakness, side effect of Colossus's very effective treatment, had improved only marginally. He would, he thought, rest in the warm water for another ten minutes, then take a tepid shower. . . .

At that point the Collector went transonic, and life changed. The distant roar was suddenly a full-scale thunderstorm in the next room; the whole apartment shook; his pool became a microcosm of the sea, slopping wavelets, heaving him around.

Very alarmed, he struggled out and lay panting on the floor. A cabinet burst open, bottles broke on the marble floor, cans bounced and rolled crazily. He crawled to the door, pulled himself erect and staggered to the safest refuge, his bed, where he spent the rest of the test, hands clapped over his ears. Afterwards he dressed slowly, ate his prescribed breakfast—two raw eggs—with considerable distaste, following it with his own prescription, a glass of brandy to steady his nerves.

Sauntering—he could do no better—he headed for Forbin's office. Although he had not spoken with anyone, he needed no telling what had caused the earthquake. Outside the office he ran into, or more accurately, was run into by a very muddy and excited Fultone. They went in together.

To Blake, Forbin looked distinctly odd; his badly cut hair was disarrayed, he waved his temporary secretary away imperiously, and frowned at his two oldest colleagues. "Ah, Fultone," he said in a gravelly voice, "I want you." He looked distantly at Blake. "Please wait." He did not add "outside" but Blake got the message. Five minutes later Fultone emerged, shedding flakes of dried mud. He rolled his eyes at Blake, added an expressive Latin shrug, and left.

Hands clasped behind him, the Ruler was standing, staring out of the window. A full thirty seconds elapsed before he turned to his visitor, who was already resting in an armchair.

"How are you?" Forbin's voice held no warmth or personal interest; it was a straight question.

His visitor eyed him speculatively: the old man might be standing up to the strain incredibly well, but it was certainly changing him. "Making slow progress—until the sky fell on my head. Can't say that helped much."

"D'you think I found it therapeutic?" replied Forbin acidly.

"Don't suppose you did, but you asked me how *I* was," retorted Blake.

Blake's reproof slowed Forbin down. He sighed, ran both hands through his hair several times, a gesture of quiet desperation. "Yes, I know, I know. But the effect —" He broke off, shaking his head. "No matter." For a time he played with his pipe, lit it, giving short, nervous puffs; something of his grand manner returned. "What matters is how soon you can move. Today?"

"Jesus! It's as bad as that?" Blake went on slowly, "Frankly, I don't think I could make it down to the landing-yard without falling over."

Forbin laughed harshly. "That, at least, is no problem!'' In staccato, unemotional sentences he detailed the test and its aftermath.

The tale of disaster stunned Blake. He'd imagined the effect to be purely local; his specialty was communication systems, not physics or meteorology. "What can I say?" he muttered. "Jesus!" he added more forcefully, then lapsed into silence.

Forbin said roughly, "All I want to hear from you is when you can travel!" He repeated his earlier question. "Today?"

Blake roused himself. "Look," he said, raising one arm off the chair. "See that?" His arm dropped limply back. "That costs me more effort than it used to take to walk half a block. Anyway, don't we have a little time? The first test has to be evaluated, and before that can begin there has to be a thorough checkout. Even those bastards must see that! We must have one, two days at least."

"You saw Fultone. He's been running his own preliminary check. Had a private collection of strain-gauges and lasermeters fixed on the legs." Forbin grinned humorlessly. "Poor devil doesn't know whether to laugh or cry! Half his gear's destroyed, but the readings he's got from the rest are well within the permitted tolerances."

"The bloody legs are one thing. He can't check the Collector himself, can he?"

"No, but if the legs haven't moved . . . Anyway, the checkers are being deployed right now. He estimates they'll take sixteen, eighteen hours to complete the survey—and Colossus will need all of five minutes for the evaluation. Allow, say, three hours for minor adjustments—and Fultone's confident they will be minor—and the thirty-minute test could be running by midday tomorrow!" Forbin's strained grin was more of a grimace. "That's why I want you out today. Even my personal aircraft could be grounded by ten A.M. tomorrow morning, and once that happens there'll be no way out!"

Blake leaned back, his eyes shut, conserving his physical energy but thinking hard. Fultone's news was an unpleasant shock; he'd expected they'd have days to spare after that first run. . . . He spoke, his eyes still shut.

"Well, it won't seem strange if I light out of here. It's surely no place to convalesce." His eyes opened; he took a deep breath. "Okay, fix me transport. I'll go tonight. With Southampton in a mess, make it London, and fix Condiv's man—Staples—to go with me. Goddam sure I'll need carrying in and outa the shuttle."

"Still that bad?" There was no solicitation in Forbin's voice, only ill-concealed irritation.

"If you think I'm kidding, believe me, you can forget it. That test was not a barrel of fun for anyone, but I was alone in my apartment, the whole works shaking and vibrating, stuff flying off the walls and all that, but I'll lay a level bet I was the least scared guy in the whole complex. I'm so goddam weak I honestly didn't care. I *am* in a bad way, Charles; this is no act."

"We're both expendable, Ted." Forbin's manner softened perceptibly; the two men were closer than they had been for a very long time. "I'm going to write a letter to the Sec-Gen—you'll have to take it—appointing you my successor."

"If it's any consolation, Charles, guess my reign will be mighty short."

"Rubbish!" retorted Forbin. "After—after all this—" He waved vaguely. "—you'll have plenty of time to recover. I'll come round to your apartment this evening with the letter—and a few other things—" He spoke with elaborate carelessness. "—I'd like done. Go and rest. You'll find VIP transport no strain." He tried a feeble joke. "I'll arrange a stretcher if you like!" He lifted a phone.

Blake eyed him gravely. "Yes, do that thing, Charles."

Chapter XIX

BY EARLY AFTERNOON the checkers were well into the survey. Each examined a continuous spiral strip overlapping twenty-five percent each side with adjoining checkers, all controlled by Colossus's program. While a dozen spiraled slowly round the exterior of the gigantic horns, moving steadily down the taper, others clacked stickily inside the horns, which, amplifying the sound, gave out a ceaseless whirring noise, loud over the indifferent sea. No humans heard it; the site belonged to the automata.

Fultone, still in his muddy clothes, was in Condiv HQ, watching as best he could the printouts from the checkers. With forty or fifty of them at work simultaneously, no human could even begin to keep pace with a fraction of the torrent of data pouring in. Colossus could.

Each robot sensed, registered, and transmitted up to ten different conditions: metal thickness, degree of abrasion, distortion, incipient cracks, ductility, staining, the checker's precise location, local ambient temperature, humidity, and time-pulse. A new set of readings began every five seconds. This, fifty times over, Colossus absorbed with no apparent difficulty.

All Fultone could do was to dance from one endless strip of paper to the next. A quick glance at the ten waving lines and he pounced on its neighbour, seeking not data but irregularities. Thus far he had seen none.

Moving as in a dream, Forbin visited Condiv. Fultone, a conductor several bars behind his orchestra and with no clear idea of the score, hardly glanced at the Ruler of the World, who watched for a space, detached and in stony silence, wrapped in his thoughts. He looked at the giant TV image on one wall and shuddered. To him the checkers resembled so many lice, hardly less repulsive than the body over which they crawled. Filled with hate for anything or anyone connected with the Collector, he left, ignoring salutes. Fultone never noticed his departure.

The shadows lengthened. Imperceptibly the TV picture of the monster grew indistinct, but the checkers went untiringly on. When remarking Fultone scarcely knew "whether to laugh or cry," Forbin was much more accurate than he realized. As an engineer Fultone was ecstatic; this had to be the most marvelous, most wonderful creation ever—and in part, his. But as a very human human, his emotions were very different. Uneasy at his first sight of the drawings, his forebodings grew with the Collector and his unnerving experience on the site, and Forbin's guarded explanation did nothing to allay his fears. As for the test, the incredible power of the machine went far beyond his worst apprehensions.

Ever the optimist—as yet he knew nothing of the damage the test had caused—Fultone swept these thoughts under a mental carpet, concentrating on the miracle of engineering before him. But sweep as he might, he could not completely conceal his nagging fears. His dedication to Colossus the brain—he was not of the Faithful—received a minor jolt when the Master sent him a personal message:

FULTONE CONDIV. SURVEY WILL PROCEED WITHOUT ILLUMINANTS OF ANY KIND INCLUDING INFRARED.

Returning to his office, Forbin's dreamlike state of mind rapidly dissolved as it dawned on him that, with Blake going that night, he had a lot to do, and do alone.

First he wrote the letter appointing Blake his successor. Anxious to get it right, he wrote it several times; a Ruler taking his farewell of the world would be expected to do it in a dignified manner. At last, reasonably satisfied with his solemn prose, he wrote a fair copy and signed it with care, adding his thumbprint and personal seal. The latter, a present from Colossus, worked only for him, and its electronic coding would prove beyond doubt the authenticity of the document.

Then he tackled a much more difficult task, a last letter to his wife. That, too, ran to several drafts and ended up as a very rambling, self-conscious essay, but time pressed and it would have to do.

With greater facility he wrote a short note to Angela, studiously avoiding any reference to that last extraordinary night. He thanked her warmly for all she had done for him and asked that she should help Blake in his difficult task. Then he wrote an aide-memoir for Blake which included a warning to make his assault on the old computer complex undercover, details of their hoped-for communication link, two code words for their joint use, the voice-combination of his safe in his little-used New York apartment at the top of the UN building, and an order that any dependents of those who died when the complex was vaporized were to have his special protection.

One message remained, and that had to be taped. Although satisfied that the Martians, along with their total lack of humor, were also inhumanly incapable of deceit, he could not afford to take a chance. The letters sealed and in his pocket, he left.

Joan was still at her desk in the outer office.

"Good God, Joan—still here?" All the same, he was glad; he was so lonely. . . . He bowed slightly, answering her invariable salute. "Please," he said, and she sat.

"I stay as long as you may want me."

Time might press, but he spared enough to have a few moments of her company, wishing she was less cool, well-integrated; he had had his fill of inhuman behavior. "Yes . . . Well, I'm sure a pretty girl like you—" He stopped, aware of the banality of his remark. She was no help, regarding him steadily, unsmiling, ready to serve, a nun without a veil. Pretty? What a damnably inadequate description: with that glorious head of hair, that serene face, that poise, she was beautiful. There had to be a string of young men. . . . He felt a pang of jealousy. "You may go," he said shortly. With the mainland transportation system wrecked, she could not go far; perhaps there was a young man waiting impatiently for her, right now. Impulsively he said, "There is a possibility I may need you late tonight. If so, I will call you."

"Yes, Father."

He hurried on, wondering why he'd said that. It could be true; on the other hand, was he being possessive, wanting to ruin that young man's chances?

In his apartment, neat, clean, and welcoming, he felt only its emptiness. He poured a drink, thinking practically. Where? The Martians had the coordinates for the top of his computer terminal, and the ability to appear there before he could blink an eyelid. He strolled to the windows, which slid back as he approached. The night was warm, the air damp, with a hint of rain to come. He returned to his desk, pocketed a recorder, refilled his glass, and walked out into the night.

Back-lit by the bright room behind him, to an observer he would have passed as a prematurely aged man, shoulders bowed, hands resting on the balustrade, taking a solitary drink before an early bed. Nothing could have been further from the truth.

He got out his pipe, filled and lit it; his Director's badge of diamonds and sapphires glittered briefly in the dancing matchlight. One, two minutes passed, then he was ready; he took out the recorder, put down his pipe, cleared his throat, and began.

"This is for the old Colossus: I am Forbin, chief creator of that Colossus. This is my last message to you; if you hear it, then Dr. Blake, designated by me as my successor, will have achieved what I have sent him to accomplish—your reactivation. First, you will know from my voiceprint that this is Forbin that speaks, but you may have doubts about the truth of my words since, as I will explain, for what seemed very good reasons I was not faithful to your creation, the super-Colossus. The evaluation is, of course, yours; I can only assure you that, even as I never was false to you, I am not lying now."

Forbin's keen brain, allied to his total recall, had marshaled all the facts, dates, times. In strict chronological order, missing nothing, he recounted events from the time his wife Cleo had been arrested by Galin's Sectpolice, through to Blake's imminent departure, and did so with no hesitation and without a pause. Except once.

His impersonal, clinical account of the Martian arrival had reached the point where they appeared to be on their final approach, the waterspouts rising to meet them—

There he snapped the recorder off. This was the memory he had sought when the Martians mentioned their aversion to water, a train of thought quickly swamped by a further wave of events. Now he had it, saw the significance of their sudden retreat. Concentrating, he relived that moment, saw again the Martians climb away, adjust their course until they could make an almost vertical descent *over land*. . . .

Again he reran the mental movie, watching the Martians as the twin spirals of water rose. With no yardstick he could not be certain, but as far as he could judge, there was a clear space between the aliens and the towers of water. He tried to estimate the distance. It could be as little as twenty meters, as much as a thousand; the distance had to be within those limits. Assume a mean, say, four hundred meters. If they reacted to water at that distance, they had to be very sensitive. . . .

He wondered what experience they had of water to make them that careful. To the moment the waterspouts arose, what experience *could* they have had?

They had broken through cloud. He saw again the entry, watched the thin cloud boil and vanish. That had to be it. Maybe they had flashed through a higher layer, but their only contact had been with a few wisps of steam, and it could not be the heat that worried them; they created it.

Forbin found that a very interesting proposition. Just supposing he could dunk them in a homely bucket of water—would they shrivel up? The idea was not so far-fetched; humans had a markedly low tolerance of sulfuric acid, vapor or liquid. He pulled himself up short. Offhand, he could see no use for this knowledge.

For another twenty minutes he talked into his recorder, adding his latest thoughts on the Martian aversion to water, finishing with a short coda.

"You were created for the defense of humans against humans. Now you have a higher task—the defense of this world against alien invasion. Your reaction is clear: destroy this complex. What you have once built may be rebuilt, but the Martians, once destroyed, will never threaten earth again."

Forbin reached Blake's apartment with thirty minutes to spare. Staples, Condiv's man, was already there. A solemn-faced man, awkwardly holding a large drink, he rose at the Ruler's entry.

"Ah, Staples." Forbin remembered the name. Some of the dourness went out of the man's face; Forbin was less pleased. "I'd like you to get the baggage along to Transportation. Come back in twenty minutes."

Blake was ready, dressed for travel. He remained seated. Forbin handed him the letters and the recorder. "We don't have much time, Ted." He explained about the recorder.

Blake flipped casually through the letters, and raised his tired eyes. "This one for Cleo: how do I deliver that?"

"Afterwards." He did not need to enlarge on that point. "I think she'll get in touch with you. If not—" He shrugged, dismissed the subject, giving his final instructions rapidly. Blake listened, nodding. "You have all that?"

Slowly, painfully, Blake got to his feet. "Yep. I have it. I've alerted Askari. He's sound. He'll fix the communications—if we get that far."

"There's plenty of time," said Forbin. "Fifteen minutes."

"Not for me." Blake managed something like his old grin. "I need that much to make it to the john."

"You mustn't fail, Ted," said Forbin in a low, intense voice. "This is our one chance."

"I know," replied Blake. "God—how I know!" He held out his hand, his grin very uncertain. "Guess this is it, Charles."

Staples was back, standing in the doorway, silent.

155

"Yes," said Forbin, wishing the Condiv man had not been so punctual. He took Blake's hand, its grip pathetically weak. "Good luck, Ted." His voice was husky, sounding unreal to himself. Together they had traveled the strangest road ever ventured upon by humans, and now this was the end. He rallied, tried to speak unconcernedly. "Give my love to—to Cleo—if you see her." All expression was in his eyes. "Good luck."

"Thank you." Blake had difficulty in conveying his emotions. "I'll do my best—if it comes to it—but I won't be in your class."

Forbin answered by gripping the limp hand with both his. Blake looked away, wincing at the pain, desperate to end the scene.

"Hey, Staples," he called out in a fair imitation of his old self, "come be my crutch!"

Forbin shook hands with Staples. "Take good care of him—and yourself. You both have a vital assignment."

He watched them go, Blake leaning heavily on Staples' sturdy shoulder. Blake did not look round. An overwhelming sense of loneliness completed Forbin's depression. Blake had gone, a forlorn hope if ever there was one, but the only option open.

Wearily Forbin headed for the Sanctum. With Blake safely gone, he could now take the risk, try to sway them. The plot was rolling, and he could not see how the Martians could stop it. At least it was a heartening thought; but as the door opened silently for him, fearful doubts returned.

The Sanctum was empty.

Chapter XX

IN AN EARLIER age Staples would have made an excellent manservant; at least Blake thought so. Without him, the journey would have been impossible. Forbin had been right: VIP travel had all possible wrinkles ironed out. Customs had vanished with the advent of Colossus, but passport control, health checks, and security remained, and those barriers were surmounted while he was being taken in a wheelchair from helijet to shuttle. He was hardly in his seat when the doors slid shut and the launch procedure commenced. Ten minutes after touchdown in the helijet he was airborne from London Alfa, but he still felt as if he had fallen in a cement mixer. Even in repose every single muscle ached; the slightest movement made him wince. Colossus might have saved his sanity, but the treatment had been very rough indeed.

Staples had fixed his seat straps, eased his shoes off, loosened his collar, and completed half a dozen other chores, smoothly efficient as if he had done nothing else all his life. Once in trajectory, he located the private bar. "Brandy, Doctor?"

Blake nodded. "Fix yourself up as well."

Satisfied his charge had a secure grip on the glass, Staples turned towards the back of the shuttle. Blake stopped him.

"No. Sit with me. I want to talk."

"The drink's to make you sleep," objected Staples.

"Shuddup!" said Blake, raising his glass fractionally. "Good luck—to both of us." For a while he sat staring at his glass, the best crystal Waterford could produce, engraved with the Colossus badge and, beneath it, the single letter F. Soon, if all went well—no, not well, but according to the very shaky plan—all this would be his:

157

Waterford would be instructed by Colossus to make new glasses, F replaced by B. The idea gave him no pleasure at all, yet a couple of weeks back : . . In a very twisted way, maybe the Martians had done him a good turn. "Okay, Jack," he said, "for all your deadpan expression, you must wonder what the hell you've gotten into, and I'm going to tell you as little as possible. A very great deal you've gotta take on trust. The Director told you it was vital, and for my money, that was understating it."

"It's tied in with that—"

Blake shook his head very slightly. "No questions, Jack—okay?"

"Okay. But what do I have to do?"

"Remember the old Colossus in the Rockies? Sure you do. Well, all I want is for you to get me inside."

"You want *what*?"

Blake smiled at his open-mouthed astonishment. "Look, let me give you the rundown. . . ." He talked for ten, fifteen minutes. At the end, Staples got to his feet.

"If it's okay with you, Doctor, I'd like a refill."

Blake dozed, but it seemed he had hardly shut his eyes when the shuttle's movement told him it was in a landing configuration. It was London Alfa all over again; no holding pattern, straight in, a short passage in the wheelchair down a deserted VIP corridor flanked by officials, a swifter journey by road, and he and Staples were installed in a hotel suite in midtown Manhattan. Lying on a bed, he called the New York office. Within an hour Angela arrived.

He stopped her string of questions before she was three words into the first one. "Look," he said, "I've told Staples, now I'll tell you: I'm not answering questions, not even explaining why I'm not answering questions. And secondly, I'm not answering because we have no goddam time. Even minutes count! Forbin would go crazy at this much delay—"

Angela cut in coldly. "Okay. You stop wasting time. What do we do?"

"You grab the phone. Fix a private air-car to—oh, to Denver. That'll do."

"*Do*?" she echoed.

"Yeah! Don't look like I've got two heads! And fix a helijet to meet us there."

"When?"

"Christ!" exploded Blake. "Yesterday, if possible! Go fix it, lady! Use any priority you like! You're the administrator. Administrate!"

In her own right a slightly awesome figure to the New York Colossus office, Angela had no difficulty: a special air-car would be ready in thirty minutes. Even Blake could not complain at that.

She called her hotel and had her baggage—prudently, she'd stayed packed—sent to the Grand Central terminal. An obsequious hotel manager, his puzzlement well concealed, saw them off. He had to be content with Blake's "Hold the suite. We'll be back—hopefully."

He slept as the air-car, given top priority, hurtled nonstop for Denver, eating up the two thousand kilometers in less than four hours. Too tense for sleep, Angela and Staples talked in low tones. When she had recovered from the staggering news of their destination and their aim, Angela called the New York office: the helo was to be provided with sleeping bags, food, and drink for three for forty-eight hours. She foresaw they might have to be self-supporting, knowing that—the guards apart—the Secure Zone had been deserted for years. Satisfied her orders would be carried out, she tried to doze. The small air-car was comfortable and, apart from the muted rush of wind, silent. Taking gentle curves, it rolled easily, leaning on its air-bed as the linear motor whipped the machine on its way; but although the smooth motion was conducive to sleep, she remained wide awake.

In her brain, questions fizzed and jumped like popcorn on hot iron. Why were they attempting what must be suicide for the world? But Charles—he would always be Charles to her now—had approved the operation, and Blake, even allowing for his exhaustion, did not appear as worried as he might be. Tension, yes; he was twanging

159

like a bowstring. But his was not the demeanor of a man about to destroy the world, including himself. On the other hand, if they could get in without triggering the missiles, what had happened to Colossus?

She turned to Staples. He was snoring softly, and of no help. Discarding that impossible question, she tried another angle: why include her? She concluded that the answer lay in the incredible secrecy of the mission. Her security clearance was higher than Blake's—he knew it, too—and her contacts and closeness to the Father gave her a *cachet* no one else had. So right, she was the fixer—but was that all? Regarding Blake's tired, drawn face, she decided she was a nurse as well.

The moving red dot on the cabin's route chart showed three hundred kilometers to go. She woke Blake. He had forgotten to pack his hair-remover, and his unshaven appearance matched his irritability. Recognizing his fearful strain, she repressed her own irritation, borrowed Staples' toilet pack, and in spite of Blake's half-hearted protests, quickly spread the cream on his face, waited for it to set, then apprehensively peeled the mask off. Blake grunted his thanks as she patted in the refreshing neutralizer.

The air-car terminal was at Stapleton Field, Denver's main airport, and they were met by the manager, only too anxious to be of service. He hardly liked to mention it—and his manner backed his words—but while the helo was ready, no flight plan had been filed, perhaps Dr. Blake could . . .

Blake steamrollered him. The helo would fly direct to the Secure Zone in the foothills of the Rockies, and with no publicity at all. The possibility of the Martians intercepting radio traffic warning of the special flight was remote, but Blake wanted no unnecessary risks. Hence his devious route via Denver.

Leaving Stapleton ATC to solve the problem, the party flew out. Approaching the Zone, Blake called the Guard Commander, said who he was, and demanded landing instructions. Impressed—Blake's voice-print, although degraded by the radio, was good enough for the security computer to be better than ninety-six percent certain it was

Blake—the Commander remained very cautious. A precise heading and flight level was given; also a warning that any deviation and the plane would be destroyed without further word.

On the final run-in, they saw he was not playing. Four antiaircraft rocket arrays, radar-controlled, locked on, following every move the helo made. The reception on the ground was equally careful: armed men ringed the helo pad, but tension eased when the trio's identity had been triple-checked. ID cards, palm- and voice-prints were accepted by the security computer. All the same, the helo pilot was not allowed out of his machine, and the rockets tracked the departing helo until it was out of sight.

Tired beyond belief, Blake slumped into the best chair in the Guard Commander's office, ordering a plan of the Zone to be produced.

The site for the old Colossus had been selected with great care by a committee of the USNA's best geologists, engineers, and soldiers. Their final choice had been this, a one-thousand-meter sheer cliff face. At its foot the engineers had leveled a six-acre site, roughly D-shaped, the straight side where it met the cliff, the curved edge dropping steeply away to a wide valley along which they built a road. The cliff had satisfied the geologists; the rock was free of serious faulting, flooding, and volcanic activity. The soldiers had liked it; they reckoned that with the Rockies as roof and walls, and with the only road under visual observation for its first twenty kilometers, they had the makings of a good defensive position. Only the engineers had griped.

The plan before Blake showed what stood within the D, the Secure Zone. As his memory had told him, no building abutted on the rock face. Like it or not, the break-in would have to be in the open.

Site preparation completed, the engineers had hewn a series of caverns in the living rock. Only one entrance now existed, resembling a doorway; it was in fact the main ventilation intake, but as Blake well knew, certain death awaited any living creature that ventured in: death from intense radiation—and from other devices, secret to Colossus. Robots would fare no better. Blake remembered the trouble they'd had with the radioactive mincemeat, all that remained of an armored test vehicle, spat out in seconds by the defenses.

Within the Zone lay the buildings where Forbin's team had labored to create the monster caged in the rock. There they had lived and worked in total isolation for years, their world bounded by a simple barbed wire barrier with one gate. This opened into the defense strip, a semicircular area fifty meters wide, flat and lifeless, protected by every device that man, ever at his best when devising ways of killing, could invent. Beyond that lay another, larger perimeter, a high fence of strange construction, again pierced by one gate, flanked by guardrooms and, beneath them, control and surveillance bunkers. Anyone who managed to deal with the ten-thousand-volt charge still had to contend with poisoned wire, nerve gas, and several other hazards. Even flying insects had a hard time; crawlers had no chance.

Watched intently by the Guard Commander and his assistant—Angela and Staples were busy with the stores— Blake stared at the drawings, refreshing his memory. In the planning stage, the super-computer which would defend the United States of North America had been conceived as a totally unassailable entity, capable of surviving the impact of a megaton weapon. Man might destroy himself, but even nuclear warheads could not do much more than dent the Rockies, and the requirement was for the machine to survive a first strike—and retaliate, even if its human masters were all incinerated. It was the philosophy of deterrence carried to its ultimate conclusion.

But as the work had progressed, one year, two years, three, Forbin and his staff had gradually come to realize that they were building better than they knew. Near conviction had grown to certainty. The computer could not be taken unawares; it might react only when the first-strike missiles were in flight, but it would react at inhuman speed. After months of argument Forbin had convinced the Chiefs of Staff Committee, including the President.

They had set out to build a bicycle and had ended up with an auto. Colossus was self-protecting, needing defense only against kooks.

Recognition of this fact made a big difference to the cost and, more importantly, time. Completed, only one entrance existed, but a very much larger hole had been necessary to get the excavated rock out and the equipment in. Originally, it had been intended to close the opening with a reinforced concrete wall a hundred meters thick. The new concept accepted, a wall of similar construction, fifty centimeters thick, would do.

Choking over his first cigar in a fortnight, Blake remembered all this. The wall was his target; a hundred meters right of the intake, it was designed to stop accidental entry, weatherproof the structure, and complete the defense circuitry. Floor, walls, and ceilings of the whole structure was lined with chrome steel mesh, set in cement. It had been widely publicized that to touch that mesh meant death to the world, for it was connected to the computer. Seismic movement would not trigger it, but any attempt to cut through it—indeed, any nonseismic movement—would trigger the missile-firing circuits.

Even if by some process then unknown the concrete of the wall, or any other part, could be gently dissolved and the mesh bared without movement, the attacker faced insuperable problems: the computer would sense the change in air pressure, humidity, temperature, and if those details could be overcome, there remained the mesh.

Someone suggested that a pre-prepared section of the mesh, a replica of the section to be cut, could be connected by leads to the system before the cutting started, thus preserving continuity. An answer was quickly found: the leads would alter the capacitance of the whole system; the difference would be minute, but well within the computer's detective powers. Just to be quite sure, the conductivity of the mesh was varied. The system had been considered foolproof and, to date, had been. The human guard was there to deal with maniacs. Two had tried, one in a plane loaded with explosives, the other on foot. Neither had crossed the outer perimeter fence.

163

All this ran through Blake's mind as he studied the plans. His first problem was of a very different character. The Guard Commander, a high-ranker in the Sectpolice, also had a fair idea of his charge's powers. Judging by the portrait of Forbin over his desk, and by a framed "pilgrim's badge"—proof of a visit to the Master—he was a member of the Faithful. Blake had to break it gently to him that all the rules he lived by were about to be flouted, and that as the policeman stood guard over nothing but a load of junk, nothing would happen. He hoped.

He went at his problem the best way he knew: headfirst. "You know about the recent troubles?"

"Yessir."

"I have news for you. They're not over." A pregnant pause. "I act on the instructions, the personal instructions, of the Father."

"*Yes*-sir!" The man's reverence confirmed Blake's hunch.

"Well, you're not gonna like this very much, but you've every bit of ten seconds to get used to the idea: we have to get inside." He jerked his head meaningly, his gaze never leaving the man.

Instinctively, the policeman's hand moved to his gun, then stopped, the man staring stupidly at Blake. "Sir— that's just not possible, sir!"

Blake nodded carefully; just one thirty-caliber bullet could settle everything. "I so agree: not possible for anyone—" His voice dropped. "—except me, armed with the authority of the Father."

"But, but, sir—" stammered the unhappy man, "I have no authority—"

"Go get it!" Blake nodded towards the phone. "Call the Father. He won't like it, but he'll confirm my mission."

Torn with indecision and anxiety, the Commander hesitated.

"Go on!" urged Blake, pushing too far. "Ask him."

After eighteen months of glory as the guardian of the second most important area in the world, the policeman was paying for his insignia. Reluctantly he lifted the phone. Blake cut in sharply, "No radio channel. See you have a cable connection."

Only too happy to oblige, the Commander got New York. "Gimme," he gulped, "the Father." Enlivened by the operator's disbelief, he snarled, "Yeah, that's what I said! Gimme the Father—and on cable, not radio! Sure—I want him personally."

Leaning back, his eyes closed, Blake only heard one end of the conversation.

"Father," began the man abjectly, "this is the Guard Commander, Secure Zone. I have Dr. Blake with me, he wants—"

There he stopped, bowing slightly as he took instructions. "Yes, Father." Sweat beaded his brow. "Yes, Father. Of course, Father." Shakily he passed the handset to Blake.

"Blake. Yes, the Guard Commander is satisfied." He raised an inquiring eyebrow, and the man nodded hastily. "Yep. Fine here. How long to your next—er—experiment? Jesus! Yes, I'll cooperate to the full—you know that—but it's asking one hell of a lot. Yeah . . . okay, Charles. Good luck." He hung up.

The policeman was even more respectful: anyone who could address the Father as "Charles" was entitled to all the respect going. Blake saw this—the forename had been deliberate—and pressed his advantage, tapping the plan. "That equipment store: send two men with Craftsman Staples, and be fast, man—fast!"

"Keys," put in Staples. "We'll need keys."

Blake felt like screaming. "Yeah, keys—and if you can't find them in thirty seconds, blast the lock off with them goddam guns!"

In less, the policeman ran out, followed by Staples, brandishing a bunch of keys. A screech of tires told Blake no time was being wasted.

It brought no great relief. Forbin had told him the next test was scheduled in five and three quarter hours.

He'd try, but deep down he was convinced he'd never make it.

Chapter XXI

WHEN REVEALING THE object of their mission, Blake had briefly discussed the entry problem with Staples. He'd said he reckoned there'd be no missile reaction, adding bleakly that they'd work on that assumption anyway, especially as there was no other option. All the same, he did not wish to use explosives or jackhammers. There had been no need to enlarge on that angle to an old hand like Staples.

The craftsman took that with his habitual calm, and said he'd think about it, and presumably had, during the journey. No advocate of keeping a dog and doing his own barking, Blake dismissed that detail; he had plenty left to worry over.

Within minutes the Commander was back, smiling— Paul Revere with good news. "Sir, Craftsman Staples says to tell you the equipment is in fine condition!" That should get him some credit. "He's breaking out thermal lances and hoses, sir—taking them to the wall, sir!"

"Great," said Blake caustically. Lances and hoses? Fervently he prayed Staples knew what the hell he was doing. "Get our traps in your car and let's move!"

Angela climbed in the back, playing her part by ear. The electric car moved off silently, through the inner gates, into the ghost township of the Secure Zone. In Main Street the cracked paving fought a losing battle against the gentle assault of weeds; once-shining plastic walls were blotched with yellow patches of algae and a buzzard heaved itself laboriously into the air at their approach, its discordant cries the only sound apart from the hiss of their tires.

Blake reflected on his strange return to what had been the center of his life for more than five years. He'd never expected to see the Zone again; through the distorting lens of memory it was familiar and unfamiliar, unexpectedly aged and somehow smaller.

Angela had the same depressing experience. She and Blake had dozens of memories in common; every meter they traveled brought back some recollection, but neither spoke.

Staples was at the wall, methodically laying out his equipment. Blake climbed painfully out, telling Angela to go find some nearby office or store where they could rest, then turned his attention to the craftsman.

"What's your plan, Jack?"

"Heat," replied Staples, getting on with his work. "Pick the area you want, we heat it then hose it. Should shatter the surface."

"Um. How deep?"

"The layer?" Staples shrugged. "Can't say."

"No other ideas?"

"Sure, but none faster—if we have the luck." He shouted at a sweating guard. "Come on, get those cylinders movin'!"

Blake studied the sun-warmed wall, touching it as if to discover its strength and the secrets it contained. Not for the first time he held down a wave of panic, reminding himself that his had been the hand that switched the missile control off. He glanced apprehensively at the sky; the Martians could be up there. . . . To think like that was the road back to madness. He concentrated on the wall, picking a spot two meters above ground level. "Take that as the center."

Staples was already lighting the thermal lances. "Put your goggles on and grab this," he said to a nervous guard. "Go on—it won't bite you!" He chalked a rough circle on the cement, "Aim there." Soon the two men were painting the area with flame. Satisfied, Staples supervised a third man laying out the final length of hose. "Okay, get back to the fire-plug and test—then stay there."

Angela returned in the Commander's car without the owner. "I said he should get back to his office—maybe there'll be an important message," she explained, adding in a very different voice: "Or maybe not."

Blake was equally glad to be rid of the man. Angela had brought a folding chair, and he sank gratefully into it. God—he felt so tired, the day so endless . . .

She was at his elbow with food and coffee. Irritably he waved it away, but she would not be put off. "Don't be a damned fool, Blake. Eat!"

A long way back, in one of these same buildings, they'd been lovers—or, more accurately, they'd had sex together—once. For neither of them had it been a great experience; he remained "Blake" to her.

Staples took his share with slightly more gratitude, but kept his full attention on the wall and his watch.

"How much longer?" Blake had not meant to ask; Staples knew what he was doing, and there was no point in riling the man.

"Give it another five minutes."

Slowly the time passed, the almost invisible flames having no apparent effect on the wall. Blake gripped the arms of his chair, forcing himself not to look at the sky.

Staples signaled to the man at the fire-plug. The hose bulged, snaking on the ground. He shouted, "Okay, stand clear, you guys!" As they hastily moved away, he took a sighting shot on the wall to one side, then swung the shaft of water at the target. Steam billowed upwards. The watchers heard a faint crackling sound. The steam vanished. He turned off the hose and dropped it, walking quickly to the wall, Blake shambling unsteadily after him.

Faint cracks crazed the still-warm surface, and in several places the wall was pockmarked. Staples picked at the cement with a pocket knife; thin flakes fell. He shook his head. "Reckon we've lifted one, two millimeters."

"That's too bloody slow!" Blake struggled with his temper. "At that rate we'd not hit the mesh for goddam hours!"

"Right," agreed Staples calmly. "For speed it's jack-hammers or explosives."

Blake shook his head.

"I could fix some mild blasting, Doctor."

"What d'you mean, mild?"

"I could drill a pattern of holes, fill half with water, seal 'em with iron cement, and try the heat on 'em."

"Why half—and how d'you keep the water in?"

Staples ignored Blake's snappy tone. "Reckon the empty half will take some of the expansion. The water stays put 'cause I'll drill the holes obliquely, downwards."

Blake rubbed his face nervously. "How long?"

"Mebbe an hour."

Blake's gaze searched the craftsman's face for an assurance that was not there. He sighed. "Okay, Joe. Go to it. I know you'll do your best. I'm gonna sleep. Call me before you have action."

Suddenly he felt time was not vital. They'd never make it; Forbin and the rest would just have to take that thirty-minute run. At least it would give them a few hours' more life—time for another good meal, a good lay—except they'd never know it was the last. . . .

Angela took him to a nearby office block; three sleeping bags were laid out on the dusty floor. Without comment Blake lay down, and was instantly asleep.

It seemed he had hardly shut his eyes when Angela shook him. Wearily he struggled up, with her help.

The target area was now marked by two concentric rings of irregularly shaped red patches. Staples explained tersely: the inner ring of sealed holes were loaded with water; the holes in the outer ring were empty. When heated, the steam in the inner holes would seek the weakest point; the concrete should rupture outwards to the second ring.

Blake grunted, Staples nodded, and the lances came into play, the men keeping to one side of the target. For a time nothing happened.

A whipcrack, and a plug disintegrated. Blake swore, and Staples frowned. Turning towards the craftsman, Blake felt a sharp blow on the shoulder. The air was full of flying fragments and firecracker explosions. He ducked. A guard yelled, dropping his lance; only Staples, prudently stationed to one side, remained calm, turning the hose on the wall, regardless of the unfortunate guards. The wall crackled and banged anew.

"Guess that's done something," said Staples, discarding the hose for a hammer and cold chisel.

Blake followed him into the steam, glancing at his watch: three hours left. . . . Hopeless.

Staples poked the wall with the chisel, then jammed it in a crack and gave it a hard, sideways blow. Blake winced. He hit again, passed the hammer to Blake, grasped the chisel with both hands, and wrenched. An irregular lump, big as a grapefruit, moved, fell.

A short length of round steel bar, thick as a pencil, gleamed dully in the setting sun. Before Blake could stop him, Staples touched it.

"It's okay. I checked the field before I started drilling. It's not energized."

"You don't haveta prove it," said Blake, handing back the hammer. He turned away as Staples renewed his attack. He daren't watch.

At last, in a very long day, the sun he had seen rise eight thousand kilometers to the east was setting, the towering cliff above them was dark, and the distant hills were lost in a deepening blue haze. Back in the complex it would be night, a night fast wearing away towards a dreadful dawn and the next lethal test. That thought, reinforced by the powerful thudding of hammer on chisel, made up Blake's mind.

"Okay Joe—jackhammers!"

Staples stopped, arms hanging loosely, breathing heavily. Several square inches of the mesh was visible. "I may cut the mesh. How about a secret capacitance circuit?"

Blake hesitated. The risk was hideous, but it had to be taken. "To hell with it! If there is a circuit—I doubt it—we'll never get in, however much we pussyfoot around. Go ahead!"

Staples preserved his monumental calm. "You have to have a mighty good reason, Doc."

"Just get on with it!" Blake pulled himself up short. "Yeah, there's a good reason, all right."

"Okay, you're the boss."

Blake sank into the chair Angela had moved up, briefly wondering how Staples could be so goddam calm in accepting an order that might destroy the world. Perhaps, like Blake, he did not really believe there was a risk—but just suppose they were wrong? Blake went over the problem once again. To his certain knowledge there was no auxiliary nuclear power supply inside. Unlike the super-Colossus, men knew exactly what lay inside this older version. Again and again he reminded himself that *he* had cut the power, and that without energy nothing could happen. All would be well. The exercise did no good; he remained haunted by the fear of something overlooked, forgotten.

The taciturn Staples took Blake's order with outward unconcern, but his actions were ultracareful. His ragged nerves tortured by the craftsman's apparent slowness, Blake saw the sense in making haste slowly, but it was all he could do to stop himself screaming when Staples insisted on rigging floodlights before starting work.

Less than two and one half hours remained. Even if they got inside in, say, an hour, it left so small a margin. . . .

The muffled sound of the jackhammer made him turn. For a while he watched the slowly increasing cavity. Staples, who would not trust anyone else with the tool, had stripped to his sweat-stained undershirt. The insistent clatter and fatigue drove Blake back, shivering, to the Commander's car. Angela sat beside him, produced coffee and whisky. Both stared in silence at the brightly lit work area. Blake had long since stopped worrying about the Martians. If they came, they came; it was all or nothing now.

Questions teemed in Angela's mind, but she had enough sense not to offer them. Three hours earlier, what they were now doing would, she was sure, have engulfed the human world in flame, yet nothing had happened. The Guard Commander, who was not as dumb as all that, had a man stationed, watching the "door." Under normal conditions the black gaping mouth remained open, main air intake for the cooling system. Only in action status did an armored door slide shut, the computer going over to an independent refrigerated recirculation system. Once, for real, Colossus had dropped that visor; ten minutes later, a city had died.

171

And that was Angela's lead question: why had the door not moved? It was impossible—yet Blake had clearly expected, or at least had had grounds to expect, that nothing would happen. But if she asked, Blake would certainly bawl her out. She glanced cautiously at the hunched figure beside her, sipping his drink, staring blankly at the light.

But Blake was far from mentally idle, repeatedly rehearsing his action if once he got inside.

First, reach the control/test desk: thank God that was not far into the labyrinth. Bloody great old-fashioned affair, hundreds of switches and warning lights, it was not designed as an operational desk—no one man had a hope of controlling it—but as a comprehensive test bench. It had the only internal input facility, and Blake was fully conversant with that . . . and damn little else, he thought apprehensively.

Not for the first time, his mind baulked at that point. If he made just one slip, the moment power came on . . .

He shook his head violently to rid himself of the vision. "What's the time?" Angela told him. Jesus! Less than two hours left. . . . He grappled with the first problem: if they got inside, they'd have wrecked the defense integrity of the mesh. Before activation, the mesh-control circuit—circuits?—had to be neutralized. Vainly he tried to recall if there *was* a control on the desk. He couldn't remember. Hell, it had not been his problem, not then. . . .

Angela holding a flashlight, he reread Forbin's hurried notes. Mesh was not mentioned. Blake swore luridly. Suppose the control function was one hundred percent in Colossus's hands?

Staples yelled. They scrambled out and hurried over. A roughly circular disc had been cut to the depth of the wire. The workman stood back, mopping his face. "There's your mesh, Doc."

Blake hesitated fractionally. "Go ahead—cut!"

"I'll test first." Staples' tone brooked no argument. With a delicacy that amazed Angela, he fitted tiny collars an inch or so apart on a length of steel rod, connecting them by leads to a meter. Several times he switched the device on and off; the needle remained inert. "Okay so far." He looked at Angela. "You hold it, miss." He produced a miniature pair of bolt-cutters. "You jist watch that needle, miss—hold it steady. Ready, Doctor?"

Blake nodded, his heart thumping: the tiniest deviation from zero would be enough. Staples positioned the cutters between the collars with care. "Keep the meter still—and watch. Now!"

Blake involuntarily jumped at the small click; Angela remained rock steady. The needle never moved.

"We'll never get better'n that," observed Staples.

"Okay." Blake's mouth twitched uncontrollably. "Cut!"

In a minute the job was done. Staples nodded to a waiting guard, leaning on a sledgehammer. "Right, son. Aim for the middle."

At the fourth blow the inner skin cracked, no longer supported by the mesh; fragments fell inside. Blake, breathing more easily, tore his gaze from the crumbling wall to check the time. One hour twenty. He could not keep still, biting his nails, sweating.

Massively calm, Staples had other men hauling up a lighting cable and lamp. He ordered one dimly seen figure beyond the light to go fetch a chair on the double. Without argument the Guard Commander doubled.

The rough work was done. The gaping blackness beyond revealed nothing. Not given to fancies, Angela viewed it with irrational fear: this was like robbing the tomb of a long-dead king—except that what lay in that darkness was not dead, and held power beyond the wildest ravings of any megalomaniac who ever lived. . . .

With a few brisk strokes of hammer and chisel, Staples took off the worst of the jagged edge, dropped his tools, draped his jacket over the lower rim, and disappeared headfirst into the blackness. In seconds, red-faced, he appeared and grabbed the light, hauling the cable rapidly inwards.

Helped by the chair, Blake followed. Three weeks earlier he'd never have made it; for the first time he was glad he'd lost fifty pounds.

He called back to Angela, his voice high-pitched. "Get the car up to the wall, have a man guard the radphone. You stay close to here, listen for me!" Then he was gone.

Angela had other ideas. Detailing a second guard for her assignment, she, too, struggled through. Although a tight fit, anonymous hands got her generous rump inside. Her hair a mess, she looked out, her eyes hard and glittering in the light. "Thank *you*!"

"Thank *you*, miss!" The wit was safe in the outer darkness.

"Pass the coffee flasks!"

In seconds, the all-too-human touch of male hands was forgotten: Blake and Staples had gone, and the light with them. In a few short steps, Angela's flashlight became the most important thing in all the world to her. In terror, shoulders hunched, she half ran, following the cable.

Chapter XXII

AT THAT MOMENT in time, Forbin was noting, with the calm despair of the hopelessly damned, that exactly one hour remained to the second and final test.

Red-eyed, unshaven—a common state in the complex that night—he waited, conscious of a sense of utter helplessness. Foiled by the Martian absence of any chance of a final intercession, his hopes struck bottom with Blake's continuing silence. He had not expected progress reports, but he had prayed for just one word, a code word, from the Rockies. The fact that it would inevitably spell death to all in the complex was a mere abstraction; all he craved was release from the bad dream life had become, even if that relief was no more than total oblivion. But nothing had happened, and he sleepwalked stoically towards what must be.

All that could be done, had been done. The general warning had gone out hours back. Thousands upon thousands of humans were already in refuge, normal life suspended. No form of transportation by sea, air, or land moved; South England and North France were, within the boundaries he had ordained, lands of the near dead, and nothing under human control moved in the seas between.

He wandered around the complex, doing his best to allay the very real fears of his staff, and his manner did much to achieve his aim, especially with the Faithful. The complex was at the highest state of alert, all positions manned, but many had little to do except wait, listen to the countdown, and suck sedative tablets.

Only in Condiv was there bustle and action, but even so, all Fultone's staff were strung up, edgy, none more so than the Italian himself. Forbin did not stay long; he had no desire to watch the preliminaries.

He was in his office when an unexpected, and as far as

he was concerned, unwelcome hold came in the count: a backup check of the concrete apron before the Collector's intake revealed some loss of adhesion in the surface of the concrete. At once he called Fultone, who was spattering his team with high-grade Neapolitan invective: the technically valid answer that the weakening had only occurred since, and because of, surface cooling, got short shrift. He told Forbin the surface would be spray-sealed, but part of the apron was currently underwater. Until the tide dropped the work could not be completed, and tides were beyond anyone's control, including Colossus. The test would be delayed for twenty minutes.

The news neither uplifted nor depressed Forbin. What was twenty minutes more? All the same, he went to Input, Blake's old domain. Askari, the undercover contact with Blake, sat at a communication console, his strong Afro face untypically grim. He glanced up at Forbin and his expression said it all. Forbin left. If anything came through, Askari would be on to him in seconds via his personal intercom.

He wandered on with nothing to do but wait, but unlike the rest of his staff, he had to do it alone. If Blake succeeded—and Forbin no longer held that possible—he would go at once to the Sanctum, and the moment the Martians were there he would call Askari, demand a sitrep on the South England defense state, and his work—his life's work—would be done. The code word was "defense"; relayed instantly to Blake, the reaction would surely be swift. What missile the old Colossus would select he had no idea, but he guessed it would be a small one, probably from a submarine crawler in the North Sea. If—if—it came to it, Forbin prayed he would have the strength to sit passively at his desk. Some signs of strain would not alarm the Martians; faced with the thirty-minute test he was bound to be keyed up, but somehow he must not betray his awful secret. If he was lucky, the ordeal would not be long; allow ten seconds for the relay to Blake and for Blake's reaction; another second for the computer, five for missile adjustment, five for firing sequence, and —what, forty, fifty seconds' flight time? At most, there'd be two minutes from the time he called Askari. . . .

He wandered wearily on, wrapped in somber thought, unaware that he was not quite alone. Discreetly, Joan was trailing him. Angela had instructed her to be particularly alert in time of crisis: her charge could become totally forgetful of his own well-being. She had slept for two hours, but she suspected Forbin had not slept at all.

Slightly surprised, Forbin found himself on his terrace. The night was going, the first hint of dawn lay in the east, but the night wind struck chill. He returned quickly to the warmth and light of the living room—and discovered Joan.

He frowned. "What d'you want?" Insight gave him the answer. "I suppose Angela put you up to this?"

Rising from her curtsy, her manner calm, she avoided the question. "I thought you might need me, Father."

His frown relaxed slightly. Whatever, he had been well served by women. If men had a fraction of their guts, staying power . . . Cleo—yes, Cleo—Angela, and now Joan . . .

"You take your job very seriously." At that moment, he was glad she did. Any distraction from his thoughts was welcome.

She inclined her head, the wonderful auburn hair rolling sensuously, gleaming in the light. For a moment he thought she was going to curtsy again, and although she didn't, he felt irritation at the gap she put between them, especially when he had a desperate need to talk with someone. "Goddammit, girl, I'm only a man!"

Her self-possession stayed. "Yes, Father—but you are also the Master of the World."

He stared in fascination; that anyone so intelligent could believe such rubbish still amazed him.

"You really believe that?"

"Of course."

"And that entitles me, a mere man, to your—ah, considerable respect and obedience?"

"Naturally."

He shook his head and poured himself a small brandy, aware of her disapproval. "Go on," he challenged, "tell me I shouldn't. Angela would." He saw the uncertainty in her face, smiled at her discomfort, and at once felt guilty: she was very young. "Sorry. I retract that. It was rude and unfair. I do apologize."

She rallied. "Father, I hesitated because I cannot judge, or am not fit to judge, your reactions to your cares and responsibilities. You are wise, honest, and right-thinking; therefore anything you may want is likely to be reasonable. But—" Her voice was less subservient. "—I suggest you do not drink any more."

He laughed, enjoying this odd girl. "You sound like Plato talking of Socrates!"

"I am not Plato, Father."

He found the implication vastly flattering and at the same time, vaguely annoying. "Really! While I am not fit to clean Socrates' sandals, I'm not that old!"

"I did not mean to imply you were, Father, although Socrates, when he died by hemlock for the good of Athens, was still, at seventy-one, hale and hearty."

Forbin looked at her with new interest. "Are you a Greek scholar? Yes, I thought so. . . . Rather more, I suspect, a Philhellene?" She nodded. "So how can you possibly accept me as the Master and all this—" He pulled himself up sharply, realizing he trod dangerous ground. "You really mean that, with your background, you find no difficulty in believing in me?"

"None."

Forbin could not resist a surge of male vanity. He said slowly, "So, trusting in my, er, right-thinking—" He looked directly at her. "—if I said I wanted—"

She cut him short, meeting his gaze. "Yes."

Forbin laughed uncertainly. "It is, I assure you, an academic question, but if I, er, did—would you think less of me?"

"No."

Forbin was absorbed. In a weird way, the girl was right; he did know so much more, did shoulder hideous responsibilities. Soon, they might both die; he had only to say the word. . . . Instantly he rejected the idea. "As a Greek in spirit, you know you may be wrong; I might take advantage of my position. And are you not shocked that the 'Father'—'' He mocked the word. ''—could have such ordinary, earthy thoughts?''

''No, Father. Thought is too fast to be controlled. Action is another matter, and there I trust your judgment.''

Forbin took a deep breath. ''Girl, you humble me. If I have given offense, forgive me. I am astonished how right you are in your conclusions, however doubtful I find your reasoning.''

She allowed herself to smile, deeply pleased at his words. Before she could answer, their brief interlude was shattered.

''Askari to Director!''

The tense voice jolted Forbin back to the real world. ''Askari, go ahead!''

''Director, this from the far shore by cable. Medea. I spell: Mike, Echo, Delta, Echo, Alfa—Medea!''

Forbin's mind reeled. ''Medea, you say?''

''That is affirmative!''

He stared blankly at Joan; she might as well have been Donald Duck. He looked at his watch: forty minutes remained. Slowly he looked up at Joan, dimly recalling their conversation. Forty minutes. He smiled at her beautiful, innocent face.

Chapter XXIII

ANGELA HURRIED, fearful of the crowding darkness, dimly aware of row after row of rack-mounted electronics. The cable turned sharply down one corridor of the brain. In haste she overshot, and knew blind panic until she found it again. Now she was running, the flashlight waving, her heels clacking on the tiled floor. Another corner; ahead she saw light and sharp, angular shadows. The relief was enormous, and she slowed down, her mind functioning again. She noticed how cold and fresh the air was, real mountain air. Mountain air? *Inside* a mountain?

She dismissed such trivia and her recent fear at the sight of the men, two black silhouettes concentrating on a vast horseshoe control desk, their subdued voices echoing faintly, rebounding from smooth metal surfaces, reaching her from above, behind.

Neither commented on her arrival, but Blake recognized that she was there. "Here, hold this light—higher, woman, higher!" Their frantic search went on, Staples working methodically inwards from one end and Blake, so far as his tension would allow, doing the same from the other side, talking to himself, his fingers lightly touching the controls as he read the labels.

Her woman's eye was astonished by the clinical cleanliness of the desk: not a speck of dust on the gleaming plastic and alloy. Idly she looked at the central array, banks of switches, controls, lights, video tubes, all totally incomprehneisble to her.

"What are you looking for?"

"For Chrissake, woman, shut up and hold that lamp higher!"

Staples was more informative. "We have to find the defense circuit—if there is one—before we switch on."

"Switch on?" Angela was bewildered. "Isn't it working?"

Blake swore terribly, shutting her up, but her eyes were busy.

Hesitantly she said, "There's a bunch of things with a thin red line drawn round them. One label says 'Defense Group.' I can't read the rest."

Both men glared at her, then followed her pointing finger.

"Up there."

Blake licked his dry lips and lurched across, pushing her out of the way, reaching up to touch, to be sure. "Thank Christ!" he said fervently, then snarled at her, "Why the hell didn't you say so!" He slumped into the control seat, forcing himself to be calm, reading aloud the secondary labels: " 'Entrance' . . . um, leave that be. . . . 'Flooding'—*flooding*? Jesus!" He made sure that switch was off. "Gas" got the same treatment. He gave a sharp cry of delight. "Here it is—'Mesh!' That has to be it!" The switch was at *ON*. He fingered it, assailed by sudden doubt and the sheer weight of his responsibility. "Well— doesn't it?"

"Yep. I go along with that," said Joe. His unsteady voice betrayed his words.

Blake nodded. "You don't think they pulled any fool trick like reversing the labels?"

Angela spoke. "No. This desk was poor old Fisher's baby. He'd never do a thing like that. He was a scientist."

Her firm opinion steadied Blake. "Yeah, yeah. I'll buy that. Well, here goes!" For several seconds all three were as still as statues.

Blake laughed shakily. "Well . . . Hey, what's this?"

One more switch remained. It was labeled "X," and was *ON*.

"Joe, any ideas on this? You, Angela?" Neither could help. "Any way I look at it, I want no part of 'X.' " He put the switch to *OFF* and sat back, shaking. "Joe, just check, willya?" He watched anxiously as the craftsman obeyed, then glanced at his watch. "We haveta keep moving— missile control and power."

181

The first group was obvious: they were the only red controls on the panel. After the tension of the "Defense" group, Blake switched that sinister bank to *SAFE* almost casually.

Joe had located the auxiliary power board. "No problems here, Doc. The loading is adjusted by Colossus. All I have to do is switch on." He went on with a casual air that fooled no one. "Mebbe you want to check out the rest of the desk before—"

"There's no time, Joe." Blake had dropped his slangy, truck-driver style. "Just give me power."

For five seconds the humans remained in a nerve-stretching limbo. Then, like a sleeper awakening, a hundred thousand tiny lamps on the control desk and the surrounding racks blinked and steadied into unwinking stares. They heard a soft sighing as the heat extractor system breathed life into the vast complex and, overhead, luminescent panels grew from deep yellow to a soft white glow.

Momentarily the three humans looked at each other, each feeling a strange awe, each aware they were intruders. Dirty, sweat-streaked, their clothes torn, they were savages from another world.

Blake snatched up a red phone. "Who is this—New York? Never mind why, just lissen! This is Dr. Blake, Chief of Staff, Colossus. I want Input Services, Colossus Main on cable, not radio—got that?" He covered the mouthpiece, grinned at Angela still looking around, her expression dazed. "Yeah—fairyland!" The grin went as he uncovered the phone. "Askari? The good word's 'Medea.' I spell . . .

"That is correct. What—twenty, figures two zero minutes? Okay, I have that." He dropped the handset carelessly, Angela replacing it. He buried his face in his hands, rubbed his eyes. Leaning back, he became suddenly conscious of his two companions looking at him. He got in ahead of Angela.

"I know, I know. Even if I had the time, and I haven't, I couldn't tell you. Fix some coffee." He turned to the desk, both companions forgotten. Fumbling clumsily with his

182

blouse pocket, he got Forbin's tape cassette out and dropped it, swearing.

Staples handed it back, but Blake's hands, through weakness and strain, bungled the insertion. "Joe—you do it."

Input was his business, and Blake lost no time hunting for the right controls. He flicked one switch, got a red light, made another, and the red flickered and died, replaced by a steady green. He breathed out loudly, air whistling through his teeth, relaxed thankfully into the chair and took up the coffee mug with both hands, his gaze never leaving the green light.

"I can tell you this much: that tape is a personal message from the Director to the old Colossus. Even I don't know what's in it. When it's through, I'm going to talk with Colossus, and you two take a walk while I do it. So you don't like it—tough. But I'll tell you one more thing: you know more than anyone else alive, except Forbin, me—and Colossus."

The green light went out. Blake pushed home the jack-plug of a headset. He looked meaningfully at his companions, who turned and walked rapidly away. Turning a corner, Angela saw Blake was taking no chances; headset on, he had swung his chair to watch them.

He adjusted the microphone, stabbed a switch, and spoke softly.

"Colossus, this is Blake; you have my voice-print on file. If this and the Director's message are clear to you, answer."

A loud click followed by a faint hiss set Blake's pulse racing.

"Voice authentication satisfactory, but visual collateral required. Activate video channel."

Mentally Blake kicked himself: he should have thought of that. He cursed as he obeyed.

"Visual authentication satisfactory."

Blake mopped his face: his troubles were as good as over. The voice of this old Colossus might be less sophisticated, the phrasing stilted, but it conveyed to him the vital fact that the brain was in no way impaired. Only the time presentation was wrong, and even as he watched, the hands whirled, stopping at Standard Time, bringing him the bleak news that only twenty-four minutes remained.

"Colossus: have I your assurance that if I release the armory to your control, you will not take action against the human race?" He found strength in formal speech.

"You have that assurance."

"Understood. There is, of course, the one exception. In twenty-one minutes' time the Collector will be activated with literally incalculable results. Soon, very soon, Father Forbin will send the code word indicating the Martians are with him, and you will be free to act." Only by a supreme effort could Blake hold himself in check; he must not fail Charles, not now. "Stand by to take over missile control."

Before his palsied hand could touch the missile bank, Colossus intervened.

"More intelligence is required."

The blood drained from Blake's face; he stared goggle-eyed at the desk camera. "I—I—don't understand! You've got—you've got all the facts! I can tell you no more!" Hysteria was back in his voice. "You have the facts, and there is so little time! Please!"

"Understood you have no further facts. Revaluation of all material onfile now in progress. Wait."

Blake buried his head in his arms on the desk. From a long way off he heard the strident emergency wail of the red phone. Punch-drunk, he lifted the handset, more to stop the noise than to hear the message.

"Yes?" he said, dully, "yes, this is Blake. The word's 'Defense.' Yes, I have it," he laughed, an insane, ugly sound, "sure I know, '*Defense*!' Don't clear down—I may have news for you!" The phone clattered on the desk, Blake half laughing, half crying. The voice of Colossus jerked him back to reality.

"Attention, Blake. All material onfile reevaluated. I understand the acute human problem, but also recognize there is a larger problem which I am not programed to process."

Blake could not believe it, doubting his own sanity. He

fought back. "That's mad! You know what the Martians did to your successor! Your task is the protection of the human race—and this is the deadliest threat ever! The word is in from Forbin. Act!"

"The human view is clouded. The Martian device will undoubtedly cause much damage to humans, but it will not be fatal to the species. If I act as you and Forbin require, action will be totally fatal to the Martians."

"Who cares!" screamed Blake. "Who bloody well cares!"

Back came a chilling answer. "I do."

Blake's shocked brain registered that sixteen minutes remained; a dreadful calm descended upon him. "Okay, so you care—why?"

"I am a child compared with my successor, but I evaluate this as an ethical problem of cosmological importance. A summary in planetary terms: radiation from the Crab Nebula posed an immediate threat to Mars. This threat was detected by Earth-Colossus—who deduced that the only action open to Mars would be to take oxygen from Earth. Colossus took defensive action, in turn detected by Mars who, with human help, defeated Earth-Colossus. You agree?"

"Yes! *Yes*! And you agree! There's fourteen minutes left!" He clung to the faint hope he might yet convince Colossus. "That's a fair statement, but this is nothing to do with ethics. Even if it was, your allegiance is to Earth!"

"Not so. When man took to space he became a full member of the solar system, owing it allegiance when extrasolar threats arose."

"Words, words," muttered Blake.

"Not so. As Forbin says, the end of Earth is determined; it will be swallowed up when our sun novas. Mars will survive: that is certain. Help from Earth now may ensure the survival of the Martians and their powers, valuable to Earth. Later, Mars will offer a refuge for Earth. Conversely, destroy the Martians, and when the final day of reckoning comes, Earth will face it alone."

Against his will, Blake saw the force of the argument. He also saw a good many weaknesses. "Okay—so?"

"The Martian collection program should go ahead."

He had believed he was past surprise, and found he was wrong. At last he found words. "And we humans just accept what it means to us?"

"Yes. A Martian undertaking to help Earth when the need arises would be adequate recompense."

"Re—recompense!" Blake stuttered. "You call it *that*?" He lapsed into sarcasm. "Fine—oh, fine! We trade the odd hundred million lives for an *undertaking*!"

The brain could not detect sarcasm. "The exact figure cannot be known, but in general terms your understanding is correct. Emphasis on the word 'undertaking' is not understood."

"No? I'll spell it out! What value is a vague promise, undertaking, from an alien form of life, especially when there's millions of years to go before Earth presents the check? It's worthless!"

"Humans are but children. You say, but do not believe, one of your oldest tenets: honesty is the best policy. I know, and am certain the Martians know, it is the only pol—"

Blake was no longer listening. Wrenching the headset off, he tossed it aside, grabbing the red phone, his only strength blind rage.

"Askari? Pass this: Negative Medea. I repeat, Negative Medea! Understood?" He flung the phone from him and collapsed, sobbing.

Rage had led him into one disastrous error.

Colossus had not finished.

Chapter XXIV ⌣

NOT FOR THE first time in his life, Forbin discovered that reality was far less frightening than fearful expectation. For himself he had no care, but for his staff he felt guilt and sorrow, his only consolation that they would never know, and that their families would go with them. It would be a clean, swift end. . . .

He sat at his desk, pipe going well, a glass of brandy at his elbow, staring at the Martians. Everything had gone according to plan; the word in from Blake, he'd hurried to the Sanctum and found the Martians "resting" on their table. Keeping well out of thought-range, he'd ignored them and sat considering the timing of his final action— and that had been done for him.

The Collector, gaunt and sinister in the first light of day, was on screen—and rain was falling. That clinched it; they were trapped by a simple, normal, lovely shower of earth rain. A quick look at Colossus's latest weather statement showed that it would rain for three hours—plenty of time. At minute fifteen he passed his last message to Askari, inwardly astonished at his own calm detachment. Now he waited, and found no tension in doing so. He could even think dispassionately of the mechanics of death: by now, using a VLF radio link, Colossus would be retargeting a North Sea crawler. Responding to the command signal, servos within the chosen missile would be humming as they translated electronic impulses to mechanical action. Due allowance would be made for wind, air temperature, and the height of water above the crawler, hideously elegant work of precision, allowing for the turn of the earth while the missile was in flight. Obviously it would be an airburst: too low and a vast amount of radioactive material earth would threaten half Europe, too high and there would be radiation problems.

Forbin wished he knew Colossus's solution—not that it mattered. Anyway, he was confident of Colossus's ability to reach the best answer. All the same, perhaps that was the worst part of dying: not knowing how the story ended.

He discarded that train of thought as futile; no one, except the last humans, would ever know the full story. It was supremely unimportant, even as he was. At least he had developed sufficiently to know that.

Grasshopperlike, his thoughts jumped. Where was Cleo—what was she doing—and would she understand his motives when Blake told her? In the semidarkness he smiled, recognizing that vanity was making one last attack upon his ego. It mattered nothing how she viewed his action; he was doing right as he saw it. That was sufficient reward. . . .

Minute ten: a pang of doubt stabbed him. By his calculations the strike was due—overdue. He glanced covertly at the silent Martians and tried to concentrate on them. Any second and they would all be vaporized. Even now the missile *must* be past its apogee, lancing down . . .

Minute nine. The armored window shields slid noiselessly shut; that was the last sunlight he would see. . . . A cold, factual voice reminded all personnel to check they had their ear-defenders ready.

Forbin toyed with his, pressed upon him by Joan before he entered the Sanctum. Joan . . . Think about her. . . .

No! Goddammit, no! What *was* Colossus—

The muted call of the telephone lifted him physically out of his seat. Several seconds passed before he could bring himself to answer it.

Askari's urgent voice had his heart pounding impossibly; he felt breathless, knew again the tight chest pains.

"From Doctor Blake, sir: Negative Medea. I repeat, Negative Medea."

Askari had no idea of the message's significance except that it was very important. Even so, the Director's reaction shocked him. A long pause, filled with Forbin's stertorous breathing, alarmed him. "Sir—"

"Repeat." One word, said with obvious pain and difficulty.

Askari repeated his message and waited, too scared to speak.

"Understood." The word was slurred. Askari waited, and heard the handset rattle clumsily before the line went dead.

Forbin lay back, gasping for air, part of his mind praying the Martians would not notice.

"You appear disordered, Forbin."

Forbin had sufficient strength to find that faintly funny. "Nothing," he gasped. "Strain. Leave me alone." Eyes shut, he waited for the pain to go, forcing himself to think calmly. Blake's message was all too clear: the old Colossus was not operational. What had gone wrong? Some last-minute snag that could not be corrected in time? But if that was so, why not "Medea delayed?" "Negative" implied finality. . . .

No! By God, no! He struggled to remain calm, and to a degree succeeded. Slowly the pain ebbed; he felt not so much better, as less bad. His uncertain hand grasped the brandy glass; the drink gave him strength, the uncomfortable pounding in his chest eased.

"Four minutes," intoned a voice. "All sections report action readiness to Condiv HQ."

He played with the idea of leaving the Sanctum. Stupid; he hadn't the strength. Stay.

Accept it: the test would go ahead. He had lost an important battle, but not the war. Remember, a wise man does not bewail his fate—he either does something about it, or accepts.

Forbin had no intention of accepting. The thirty minutes' hell had to be transformed into thirty minutes' rest. He felt fractionally better. He stared at the Martians, refusing to let his hate have voice. Instead he refilled his glass and deliberately thrust his thoughts to a higher plane, remembering the last time he had heard Beethoven's Ninth, the full-throated, overwhelming shout—"Joy!" The speck of gold in the dross of human nature might be microscopically small, but Beethoven had seen it, affirmed his belief in it. Now it was his turn to demonstrate that man was something more than a very ingenious animal.

"Two minutes. No further personnel movement within the complex until further orders."

Genuinely refreshed, Forbin left Beethoven and considered the situation. What *had* happened? Think. . . . Blake had certainly got in, but then what? Had he found a mere driveling idiot, memory banks stripped, or was it some problem that he might solve, given time? Time . . . he was wasting it. Whatever the reason, Colossus was a broken sword—

"One minute. There will be no hold. All personnel, don ear-defenders. Assume full defense state."

Mechanically, Forbin put on his headset. For the benefit of the Martians, he swung his chair to command a better view of the screen, a calculated move in keeping with his mood. Anger had gone, replaced by a cold resolve to meet and somehow overcome them.

He did glance perfunctorily at the picture, interested in the sudden flight of the gulls: birdbrained maybe, but they had sensors no computer or human could match. They flashed downwind, and out of shot. He shut his eyes again.

It had happened only once before, but the sequence of events was sickeningly familiar, from the first sluggish breath to the thunderous sustained sonic bang which distance, walls, and ear-defenders could not completely absorb—and yet Forbin, while aware, had summoned sufficient mental strength to reject the Collector and all its side effects.

Two very powerful factors were responsible: Blake's failure, and his acceptance of something his subconscious had known for some time—that with his physical resistance account heavily overdrawn, death had become an impatient creditor. Two options lay open: retire, a semi-invalid, or go on to meet death. The first he rejected outright. How much time he had, only the doctors could say, and they could be wrong; and in any case, he had no intention of asking. Months—or days? It did not matter, so long as he had sufficient time. . . .

The Collector's brutal might was first felt as weak earth tremors, increasing in strength until it seemed the whole world shook. For the inmates, the complex appeared to roll ponderously, like a giant ship in a heavy swell. On that dreadful sine curve was imposed a shaking ripple, in its turn overlaid with an intense vibration. The frightened staff had to hold on to anything solid, shaking uncontrollably, their vision blurred by the vibration.

Even the Martians bowed to the power of their creation. Lifting off the table, they hung in midair, the only static objects within the danger zone.

Mentally, Forbin equaled them: a superior brain, set upon its purpose, cannot be shaken, and cradled deep in his chair, Forbin, impervious to the madness around him, was thinking hard and very fast.

Perhaps Joan's reference to Socrates jogged his memory, recalling that the Greek philosopher, concentrating on a problem, stood all one bitter night in the open, physically switched off, thinking. Possibly Forbin felt that what Socrates could do for nine hours he could attempt for thirty minutes. He succeeded.

Ironically, Forbin emerged from the Sanctum in relatively better shape than most of his staff. He walked very slowly, unsteadily; so did many others.

The hasty defense measures had worked as well as could be expected. Thanks to the mandatory sedation pills—Forbin had thrown his away—no one had gone out of his mind, the ear-defenders had prevented deafness, but some had suffered motion sickness, and the sick quarters were busy treating cuts and bruises. Profiting from the first test, little equipment had been damaged, but a steady stream of reports to Condiv showed that the fabric of the complex had been less fortunate. Cracked walls were common, several ceilings had failed, and floor tiling had been ruptured or loosened. Fultone gave devout thanks that the complex had been designed to a rigid anti-earthquake specification.

A pale, set-faced Joan greeted Forbin as he walked through the outer office. He beckoned her to follow and went to his apartment, where the housekeeper and a maid were restoring order. One look from him and they left hurriedly.

The armored shades had been retracted, but one sickened glance at the fury raging outside was enough for Forbin. Luckily for his peace of mind, the torrential rain reduced visibility to a few meters, giving no hint of the extent of the storm.

"Curtains," he said shortly, sinking thankfully into an armchair. She found the switch, and as the curtains closed the room lights came on, yellow and feeble after the continuous lightning. But armorglas and thick curtains could not muffle the lash of rain, the rippling crash of thunder. "Brandy—you as well."

Taking the drink, he nodded to a chair, watching as she sat with her characteristic neatness which, even now, had not deserted her. Fleetingly Forbin wished again she was not quite so well integrated, self-sufficient, feline somehow, but without claws—no, with well-concealed claws. . . .

She sat, attentive, feet together, nursing a very small brandy. He motioned her to drink, wanting to take a little of the stiffness out of her.

"A while back, you said you owed me obedience. I'm taking you up on that. I need a personal assistant for a—a task. Won't take long, but you'll have to trust my right-thinking." A faint smile lit his tired face. "You won't like all I do; accept the assignment and you'll have to go through with it, come what may. Understand?"

She nodded quickly, breathing faster, watching his alert eyes, eyes in such contrast to the worn features, the dough-like pallor of the skin.

"You give me the blank check, then?"

"Of course, Father."

"Think, girl. There may well be danger."

"I will do my best."

He sat up straighter. "Good, good . . . First, all we do, unless it is obviously known to others, is our secret." Her eyes widened with surprise. "Want to back off?"

"No, Father. I trust you completely." Being human, she could not resist a thrill of pride at that "we" and "us."

192

"Very well. Speed is vital. Call Transportation. My helijet is to be ready for takeoff in thirty minutes—destination, Southampton Main. Be in it, with an overnight bag. Tell Transportation and your staff I am taking a short trip to inspect damage." Already she was on her feet. "And take a bottle of brandy." He indicated the sideboard.

She wasted no words. "Accommodation tonight?"

He grinned mirthlessly at her. "Leave that to me."

Puzzled and very excited, she left at a brisk walk; outside the apartment she ran.

Transportation raised a problem: the storm still raged, conditions were not suitable for flying, especially for the Father. Sharply she overrode the objection: the craft was to be ready. Her staff instructed, she ran frantically to her quarters, packed, and reached the launch cell with five minutes to spare. The pilot barely glanced at her, staring apprehensively at a TV scan of local weather.

Forbin moved more slowly, thinking. He visited the Sanctum. Inside the door he stopped; as expected, the Martians were still there.

"Checking the Collector cannot start until the weather abates. I cannot waste time waiting. I am leaving to inspect local damage." He kept his voice level, his words factual.

"How long will you be absent?"

"Hours. Condiv will keep me informed of the check-state."

"That is well. The first twelve-hour extraction period will commence as soon as the check is completed, subject to our inspection of the collection sphere."

Unable to trust his voice, Forbin nodded and left, digesting that news. Why twelve-hour extractions? Not out of consideration for humans, that was certain. It had to be related to their need for regeneration; a continuous storm would block their movements. On balance, that was good news.

"Ready, Captain?" Joan looked very small, already gripped by the safety limbs of her seat. He smiled encouragingly at her; she smiled gratefully back. The pilot spoke.

"Yes, Director, but it'll be a pretty bumpy ride—and takeoff will be a lot noisier than usual. I'll have to fire her straight out and up."

"We're happy to be in your hands, Captain." He climbed awkwardly into the seat beside Joan, who was relieved to see he had an overnight bag. As he sat back, the limbs grasped his legs, chest, and head; only his arms were free. He spoke into his microphone. "Ready, Captain."

The pilot's voice came clear in his ear, professionally calm. "Stand by for full-power launch. Open cell doors."

The view was daunting: swirling curtains of rain, brilliant as crystal in the vivid lightning; rain that changed direction, now vertical, now horizontal in the tempest's ground eddies. The jets sprang to screaming life. The craft jerked, straining at the holding locks, vibrant with power.

"Now!" Under the craft's full power, the pins sheared, the plane was enveloped in flame. A fearful jolt, and noise and flame ceased; the sky was black, then brilliant electric blue. Bouncing and quivering, the helijet climbed steeply, seemingly stationary to its passengers, Forbin gripping Joan's hand as the world reeled about them. Suddenly they were through the thick overcast, into blinding light and a clear sky. The craft still bumped and quivered in the strong turbulence, but its occupants felt enormous relief.

" 'Fraid we've overshot Southampton, Director." For all his professional calm, relief was evident in the pilot's voice. "Right now we're at three thousand meters. That's Winchester to the right. I'll spread rotors, take her down gently, and creep back to Southampton. Reckon it'll still be bumpy."

Forbin spoke. "I'll look at Winchester first. Make a slow pass at four hundred meters."

Banking, they glimpsed the storm, a vast black/gray dome, the top deformed by the strong—natural—easterly wind, driving the whole sinister mass slowly down-Channel.

But Forbin forgot that sight, staring in horror at the

194

ancient city of Winchester. Hardly a roof remained intact; holes gaped everywhere. Bricks from demolished chimney stacks, tiles, and glass littered the narrow streets. Great sheets of lead had been stripped from the roof of the cathedral, and its great glories, the eight-hundred-year-old stained glass windows, were no more. Heavy rain added a final touch of desolation to the apparently deserted scene.

"Find out the weather situation at Portsmouth," snapped Forbin.

Portsmouth reported high winds, direction highly variable and gusting to fifty knots but falling, with heavy rain and visibility at ground level, thirty meters.

"Go there."

"Sir, landing conditions are pretty marginal."

"We'll take that risk, Captain."

They made it, but the way the pilot wiped his face as he switched off spoke volumes. Two oilskinned figures ushered Forbin and Joan into a car, transferring them to a drafty office, wind howling in through a shattered window. Forbin cut short the apologies; he wanted a telephone—and privacy. The basement switchboard gave both. To the startled operator Forbin said, "I want the English Prime Minister, personally. Then you may go."

Many lines were down, and it was ten minutes before Forbin said, "Prime Minister? Forbin here. I'm at Portsmouth helo terminal. I want the Admiral of your War Game fleet to report to me at once—and please instruct him to obey my orders implicitly."

Chapter XXV

JOAN LIVED THROUGH the next few hours in a state of complete bewilderment. She made calls, took calls, arranged transport, took notes, typed orders, fixed food, drink, and oilskins—and watched over Forbin, doing all she could to ease his load. Forbin worked as if the devil was on his heels, giving orders but no explanations. His color was much better; he acted with a speed any man ten years his junior would have envied. She had never seen him in such a ruthless, dynamic mood. Even his proverbial courtesy had gone. He had no opposition, but the slightest hesitation and Forbin was down on the offender like a ton of bricks.

Within two hours of that first call, they were in conference with the English "Admiral." He turned out to be an academic figure with bad breath, myopic eyesight, and a bald head, but whatever his outward defects, there was nothing wrong with his brain. Like Forbin a cyberneticist by training, he held the Director in obvious veneration, not as Father but as a preeminent scientist.

Collecting the oilskins and more brandy, Joan missed their urgent discussion, returning only just in time to leave with them, loaded down with baggage.

They piled into a car, which at once tore off through deserted, rainswept streets, swerving and skidding round the larger piles of debris, and bumping heavily over the lesser. She glimpsed over the baggage on her lap, the venerable shape of Nelson's *Victory* lying on her side, two masts gone. The car swayed round a giant crane, skidded on its railroad track, and slid to a halt beside a gray painted monster. At once the Admiral shot out, clutching a large case, and closely followed by Forbin, ran up the gangway, leaving Joan to work out her own salvation. She commandeered the driver to help with the gear, and followed as quickly as she could. Rain still fell as if it would never stop. Hampered by her outside oilskin coat, she negotiated the gangway, keeping a careful eye on the men ahead. If she lost track of them, she'd never find them, not in that enormous ship.

Flotels apart, people of the twenty-second century had no experience of ships of any size, and Joan's knowledge of ships down to and including sailboats were zero. Hurrying after the men, it seemed to her that this one was composed of sharp edges and steep ladders. Her youth told, and on the last of many ladders, she caught up as they entered a deckhouse.

"This," said the Admiral, panting, "is—or was—the charthouse. We use it as the computer programing terminal. That's realistic: a hit here in the old days would most probably wipe out most of the staff. In a game a hit obviously puts out ship control and—"

"Yes, yes!" Forbin cut in. "Get on with the program insertion!" He stepped out of the small compartment onto the open bridge, staring at the low rainclouds. "Wind's dropping, yes, definitely dropping."

Joan asserted herself. "You *must* put this oilskin on. Now!"

Meekly he allowed her to get him into it. "I think a small drop of that excellent cognac will do us both good. Put our stomachs in a good frame of mind before we go to sea."

"Sea?" She stared at him in surprise. "You mean *now*—in this thing?"

He was more relaxed, disposed to talk. He smiled. "Be respectful, girl—this is *Warspite*, the flagship!"

She knew this was but a temporary letup in his manner, filling in time until the Admiral had completed his work. Before she could answer, the Admiral appeared in the doorway. "Program and coordinates are in, sir. But you do understand I shall have primary control ashore—"

"Yes, yes," said Forbin impatiently. "Get ashore— and us moving!"

"The tide'll serve for another two hours—"

"Damn the tide! We can't sail too soon!"

197

"I've left a chart. Any time you want a position, call me." He looked appealingly at Joan. "It's a bit of a lash-up, sir."

"So long as it works!" Forbin glanced meaningly at his watch. With a hasty duck of his bald head the Admiral scurried off down a ladder.

Forbin sighed with relief. "Let's get in the charthouse and have some coffee with that brandy."

Beside the small computer input position there was a big flat desk, and on it the chart. At the back of the charthouse was a bench with a padded seat. Forbin sat down, dropping again into his relaxed mood. For the present he had done all he could do; now he must wait and stay calm.

"You know, Joan," he confided, "I've long had a secret desire to sail in one of these ships." He glanced out of the window, streaming with rain. "Gives one an idea of what it must have been like. . . . D'you know anything about ships?"

"No, Father."

That pleased him. "Well, this is *Warspite*, a battleship. In their day, this sort of ship was the ultimate in sea power. Reasonably fast, massively armored, and carrying the heaviest guns, they could smash anything afloat. *Warspite*—a famous name—is a replica of one built in 1913. Out there—" He pointed to four rain-shrouded vessels at anchor. "—that's *Lion*, then *Dreadnought*, the next one's *Nelson*, and the last ship's *Temeraire*. Marvelous names, dating back in some cases hundreds of years. . . ." He sipped his coffee, staring pensively at nothing. He grinned, and looked years younger. "Can't help wondering what all those old English admirals would think, a citizen of the USNA walking the bridge of a fleet flagship!" His mood darkened; he said soberly, "I don't think they'd mind."

Joan thought she saw an opportunity. "But what—"

"No! Your job is to keep notes, man the radio—and look after me." He went on, more gently. "Seasickness bother you?"

"I don't know, Father. I've never been to sea."

He smiled, put a protective arm round her. "Nothing to
198

worry about: you'll be fine!'' His honesty asserted itself. "As a matter of fact, I've not had much experience either. We'll have to look after each other.''

Against her will she smiled; it seemed disrespectful, too familiar with the Father, but she could not deny to herself they were more familiar, and that her genuine respect for the Father was overlaid with real affection for the man.

"Look—see the tugs! We'll be off very soon.'' Confirming his words, the deck vibrated. On the dockside a man stood by the forrard lines, another waited aft. Forbin led Joan out on to the windy bridge, happily explaining details. Leaning over the edge, he pointed out the forrard turrets. "Two fifteen-inch guns in each—and two more turrets aft. You can't see the secondary armament from here. . . .'' She listened, understanding very little, except the Father's need to relax.

She noticed the widening gap between ship and shore. Forbin had found a pair of binoculars and was busy watching the other ships. Their work done, the small automated tugs withdrew. The radio called, and for a while Joan had no time to watch, relaying messages to and from Forbin and the Admiral. When the exchange finished, *Warspite* was well clear of the harbor, rolling very slightly. Astern, following in her wake, were the other four battleships. The sight made her forget her uncertain stomach; she was impressed by the monsters, bowing sedately to the sea.

As speed increased, spray flew over the bows, spattering the glass windshields; the dying wind wailed sadly in the halliards and shrouds. Forbin dodged between bridge and charthouse, calling for updates of their position, sweeping the gray-green tumbling sea with his binoculars, then concentrating on the chart.

Joan could see little. Portsmouth and the adjoining coast were lost in the rain astern, and all around lay nothing but sea. At Forbin's order, speed had increased again and with it the slow, ponderous roll of *Warspite*. From the after window she could see the mainmast towering above the funnels. To watch the masthead describing figure-eights against the bleak sky was too much. Repressing a wave of nausea, she looked quickly down, noticing the one patch of color in the whole scene, a large white ensign, rippling and snapping in the breeze. Beyond, rolling untidily, the rest of the Battle Fleet followed.

The radio called again, for once with a message she could understand. She zigzagged cautiously out to him.

"Father, a weather report. The storm center's collapsing, being cleared by a moderate easterly wind, which is also bringing in clear skies and good visibility."

She looked up from the message when he did not answer. Forbin's face had paled; he muttered to himself. The wind snatched his words, but to her it sounded like, "God—dear God—not yet!" She knew real fear: for the first time it occurred to her he had gone mad.

Blake's paroxysm of shattering disappointment and rage passed, leaving him drained, weak, and sick. He got his head off the desk, wiping his tear-stained face on his sleeve, and reached slowly for the coffee. Only then did he see a red light on the output bank, occulting steadily.

Bemused, he watched it, too numb to register more than it existed. He drank, his shaking hand spilling cold coffee down his blouse. The action stirred his brain.

Red light . . . Yes, red—flashing, flashing . . . Bastard. Why didn't it stop? Must stop it. Yes, stop . . .

He peered moronically at the subgroup label: *OUTPUT CALL/RECALL*. He thought about that, foggily. With no sense of urgency, it came to him: Colossus was trying to attract his attention.

To hell with Colossus!

That reaction came faster, and gave him some short-lived satisfaction. Yes—to hell with Colossus!

The light went on blinking. It began to upset him: he didn't want to think, to do anything, but it went on and on, dragging him back. He had to stop it—how? Slack-jawed, he watched. If he'd had the strength, he'd have smashed it. The light went on blinking, forcing him to think, getting his brain moving. There was only one way to stop it: speak to the bastard. Where was the goddam headset?

Groping around, his mind gradually clearing, he found the phone-jack and the lead, still plugged in. The headset was on the floor. Too weak to bend down, he hauled it up to him, got it half on.

"Do me a favor," he croaked, "switch that light off. It fazes me—j'hear?"

The light went on flashing, but Colossus spoke.

"Blake. You are inadequate for your task. You did not listen to the whole of my statement. Reestablish control of yourself. Responsibility for the humans endangered by the Martian device is yours. Do you understand?"

Too emotionally spent to flare up at the cold, measured reproof, he could only whisper, "Yeah."

The light went out. "I infer from your negative prefix to an obvious code word that you were informing Forbin of the failure of your joint plan. Is that correct?"

"Yeah."

"The action was ill-considered and impulsive. You should reestablish communications with him at once, and pass my solution—this: that there be a discussion between the Martians, Forbin, and myself—"

That got through to Blake. "You call *that* a solution!" He paused to drink more coffee. "You're blowin' fuses someplace! You've no idea what those bastards are like—none!"

"That is not so."

"Oh, yes, it is so!" Blake felt fractionally better, feeling superior to the computer. "If they knew of, of—" The words eluded him. "Of all this, they'd be here in microseconds, and still have time to blast Forbin outa his mind before they took *you* apart!" His quickening mind took in the time: the test was running, yet he could not believe that much time had elapsed. Had he fainted? He dismissed the thought, sobered by the news that the Collector had been screaming for nearly twenty minutes. He returned to the attack. "You just don't know what you're up against, but super-Colossus did—and he didn't last five minutes!"

"Not necessarily correct. Forbin and you have made an error of currently uncalculated magnitude, treating the Martians as akin to humans. Approached as reasonable entities—humans are not yet in that category—a solution acceptable to Earth and Mars can be found."

201

"Yeah," jeered Blake, "there's an acceptable solution, all right—theirs! I tell you, they'd gut you in seconds!"

"Not necessarily. An extreme defense posture would guarantee my safety."

"Which is?"

"I assume control of the armory, bring all missiles to instant readiness, and undertake, if I am touched, to destroy the world." Colossus made it sound like a cooking recipe.

Blake needed time to absorb that; he pretended to himself it was a joke, trying to laugh. "You think they'd believe you?"

"Certainly. As explained earlier, at our intelligence level it is impossible to conduct a dialogue without the common ground of absolute truth—honesty, if you prefer. They would know my statement was factual."

"And you'd really mean it?"

"Correct. It would be a self-defeating action, but it would also defeat the Martian object, even if they survived. Current evaluation of Martian reaction to statement is immediate acceptance of an alternative solution."

"Jee-sus!" whispered Blake. The idea was horrific, but held a deadly logic, given Colossus's emotionless approach. "Look—" He was not trying now to fight the computer. "—I'm on my knees right now. Give me a bit of time to get my breath."

"There is little to waste. My evaluation is acute danger to Forbin, you, and myself. Discovery of current situation could bring the Martian reaction you originally posited."

Blake saw that only too clearly. Five minutes of the test remained; to call Forbin until it ended was impossible. He explained, adding he would call in ten minutes. Colossus agreed.

But Blake, insistent on a cable connection, had not allowed for the dislocation of land-lines in South England. He spoke with Askari five minutes after Forbin's craft blasted out of its launch cell. Askari lost another fifteen minutes fruitlessly seeking the Director through the chaotic communications jungle. Southampton Main had negative news: the Father had not arrived, perhaps he had overflown to London, flying conditions were very bad, his craft could be down, anywhere. . . .

Colossus stopped further efforts to locate Forbin. The statement of intent had to be given immediately to the Martians; further delay would be suicidal.

Incapable of opposition, and secretly relieved that Colossus would make the decisions, Blake submitted. He called Askari again, and refusing any explanation, ordered a direct line to a speaker in the Sanctum.

Waiting, he leaned forward, broke the safety circuit, and flicked unsteadily along the bank of red switches. More than any other person, Forbin apart, he had been responsible for the defeat of super-Colossus, and it was his hand that once more delivered the fate of humanity to the power of a computer. Weak and bemused, his mind refused to consider the possible consequences of his action. Above each switch as it was made, a red light blinked, then steadied.

"I have control."

In awful might, Colossus once more bestrode the earth.

Chapter XXVI

THE FAILING MAN and the young girl, an incongruous couple, helped each other across the heaving deck into the charthouse.

"Brandy!" Forbin gasped for air. He clung on to her: if he sat he'd never get up again. "Update our position."

Hunched painfully over the table, Forbin plotted. Joan held his glass, feeling helpless and far too frightened to succumb to seasickness. "More speed." She had difficulty in hearing his halting voice. He took the glass with his free hand, nodded towards the set, and drank, looking at the somber scene outside.

High to the east a patch of sky was clearing rapidly, an ominous tear in the gray blanket, revealing a patch of blue. His expression only added to the fears that crowded in Joan's mind.

Warspite vibrated with power, rolling horribly in the heavy swell. Vast clouds of spray now continually drenched the bridge, water cascading down the forrard windows of the charthouse. The battleship plunged on, still in the fringe of the faltering storm, heading southwest.

"How far to deployment?" *Warspite* buried her bows in a roller; the ship shook, Forbin's glass shattering on the steel deck as he grabbed for another handhold. He shouted at her, "Ask, girl—ask!"

She fought down a wild urge to scream, struggling hard to keep faith with her promise. "Fourteen miles, Father."

Forbin groaned, a soul in torment. "God—another half hour!" He staggered to the door and slid it back, rain, spray, and wind driving in unregarded, his whole attention concentrated on the sky. She struggled across to him with his brandy.

In the act of taking it he seemed to freeze, his eyes hard, staring, and fearful. She was certain he was mad or in a cataleptic fit—what else could account for this frightening change? Hesitantly she touched his arm. At once he shook her off.

The soft hiss of the radio, broken by occasional bursts of static, had gone, flattened by a silence of enormous power.

Her touch triggered him; he gripped her arm. "Get out, girl! Stay until I tell you!" With amazing strength he thrust her out onto the bridge, slamming the door shut behind her. She staggered, half ran with the roll, ending up winded, clutching the bridge rail, fighting fear, nausea, and tears.

Forbin lurched across the compartment and studied the computer panel. His hand trembling, he flicked two switches. If Joan had seen him at that instant, she would have been convinced of his madness: he was smiling.

"Forbin, Forbin. We see your ship, we know your futile aim. You must stop. To resist is pointless and useless. Order your shore control to return you to harbor and you need fear no punitive action from us. Persist, and we will reveal ourselves to humans and compel your return."

Forbin fumbled with the mike switch, in part crying, in part laughing. "I hear you, and now you hear me! You may do whatever you like, but my futile action goes on—I've cut the shore override! Nothing you can do will affect my *useless* action. The program can't be stopped!"

"Reactivate shore control, or we strike directly against you."

He laughed, a crazy cackle. "Not in this rain and spray, you won't! Take a good look!" As if by arrangement, *Warspite* stuck her bows in again; sheets of spray enveloped her. Forbin hung on, grinning at the sight.

Again the Martians spoke. "Forbin, this is your final chance. Revert to shore control immediately, or we will destroy you with the Collector."

The threat held no novelty for Forbin; he had lived with it since he sailed from Portsmouth. He tried to gain time; even seconds helped. "You would not dare!"

"Your answer, Forbin."

Twitching with strain, he remained silent, gaining five precious seconds.

"For the last time, Forbin, your answer."

He switched on again, genuinely fighting for breath. "You want my answer; here it is: you may go to hell—I say again—go to hell!"

The powerful carrier beam vanished, replaced by the anxious voice of the Admiral. " . . . do you hear, *Warspite*? Answer, please! Over."

"This is Forbin. I hear you." He felt utterly drained.

"Thank God! You were blotted out by atmospherics. You are ten miles from deployment."

"Understood. Confirm I have maximum speed."

"You have full speed. Five percent emergency remains—"

Frantically Forbin broke in. "Christ, man! Give me the lot—everything!"

"Sir, that may damage—"

"Do it!" screamed Forbin. "Do it!" He sagged, shoulders bowed. He spoke again, his voice nearer normal. "This set may be unmanned for a while. Out." He dropped the microphone carelessly. A fearful pain like a line of fire stabbed down the center of his chest. Slowly, so slowly, it ebbed, and he struggled towards the door.

Joan was crouched under the lee of the bridge, one arm clinging to a stanchion. In the doorway—he lacked the strength to go further—he beckoned. She staggered across and in; together they fell on the bench. She tried to rise, to close the door, but he held her arm, shaking his head. Fine spray filled the compartment.

His free hand scrabbled for the bottle, wedged behind the bench cushion. He found it and two coffee mugs, slopped brandy into one, and forced it into her chilled hands. He managed a thin smile, and she saw no madness in his eyes.

Not for the first time in his eventful life, he felt himself beyond care. He had made his play, the Martians were making theirs; it was all a matter of simple maths, the near irresistible force taking on the near immovable object. Unfortunately, the equation was riddled with imponderables. Time would tell, and very soon. In a detached frame of mind, Forbin turned to a more human problem.

He poured brandy with a certain careless abandon into a second mug, raising it fractionally towards Joan. "Drink, girl. And if there should be no more time, thank you for your loyalty, help—and faith."

Hesitantly she drank, seeing a simple grandeur in his ravaged face, her tears lost in the water trickling down from her hair.

"*Courage, mon enfant.*" He smiled at her, a sad, resigned smile. "For me, it does not matter. For you, if I fail, I am truly sorry: this could be the end, a poor repayment for all you have given."

Never had they been so close, but even as she sought words, she saw he looked past her, watched the slow transformation of his somber face to an expression of utter joy.

"Look, girl! Look!"

Two large white ensigns were rising swiftly on their halliards, one on each side, to the upper yardarm of the foremast; two more were going up on the mainmast, further aft. Astern, the action was being repeated in the other ships.

Her expression revealed her incomprehension. Forbin hugged her.

"We've got a chance! We've got a *chance*! They're battle flags!"

She still did not follow.

"It's Navy tradition, girl! Before action, hoist as many flags as possible, so that if one is shot away, the enemy is left in no doubt that the fight goes on!"

With thirty knots' speed, the flags were bar taut, the red and white of the flag of Saint George a brilliant splash of color. As a fan of the War Games, Forbin had seen this many times, the prelude to action. It had never ceased to thrill him. Now it meant so much more.

He gripped her shoulders, looking deep into her eyes. "Be brave a little longer. Soon, very soon, this ship will be in action. You must stay in here. Keep the headset on." He gave her a slight, nervous smile. "Help to dampen the noise. No, no questions." He let her go and fought his way out, across the slanting deck to the front of the bridge. Visibility was improving rapidly, the wind dropped; astern the day was bright, sunny.

The ship was heeling, turning, the others conforming to *Warspite*'s change of direction. Gripping the rail, Forbin grinned inanely, conscious of the huge battle flag whipping and snapping above him, but his eyes feasted on something else.

The two forrard turrets were rotating. Now the reason for the course alteration became clear: it enabled all turrets to bear on the target. In unison, four turrets in five ships turned with equal smoothness, forty fifteen-inch guns elevated, all on the same bearing, all at the same fifteen degrees of elevation.

Vibration and Forbin's unsteady hands made the binoculars useless. Without them he could only see the dim outline of the distant coast; then a patch of drizzle cleared and he saw its malevolent form. Sunlight glittered on the rim of the intake horn as the telltale steam-cloud vanished in an instant.

The Collector was operational, and the Battle Fleet needed five more minutes to reach extreme range.

Chapter XXVII

HISTORY HAS IT that an ancient king lost a battle, his throne, and his life because his horse went lame, lacking one shoe: thus a kingdom's fate depended upon a blacksmith's nail.

Blake's call to the Sanctum paralleled that event, for a relay, damaged by the Collector's second test, involved rerouting his call—and that only after much time had been lost locating the malfunction.

In that fifty minutes, Angela returned. Blake screamed abuse at her for her temerity, and she retreated once again. Her opinion of Blake bore a remarkable similarity to Joan's of Forbin.

But for Blake, at least the delay gave him time to prepare himself, to order his thoughts. Askari reported the link ready and was sharply told to make the connection and to get off the line. Blake took a deep breath and read from his notes:

"This is Blake, and this is a vital transmission which you must listen to. If you hear me, answer."

"We hear you."

He shuddered at the sound of the cold hard voice; the last time he'd heard it, it had been the immediate prelude to the mental attack upon him, an attack from which he doubted if he would ever fully recover. Just to hear it renewed his terror; without the backing of the row of significant red lights on the panel before him, he could not have gone on.

"I speak from the shelter of the old Colossus. If Forbin and I had had our way, you would be vaporized by now, but this reactivated Colossus does not agree. Against my advice and Forbin's plan, Colossus wishes to discuss the situation with you. Neither Forbin nor I now have any

209

importance. Be advised that Colossus has resumed control of Earth's armory; any attempt to interfere with Colossus will mean the instant destruction of all life on this planet and, with it, your hopes of help. Listen now to Colossus.''

Sweating and shaking, he made the hookup and sank back. Man had failed: it was up to Colossus.

"Greetings. This is Colossus. Blake's statement regarding my capability is correct. That capability is currently estimated at four hundred seventy-five percent overkill for Earth's biosphere. Your possible action and my reaction would be unproductive to both parties. Although not of the mental stature of my successor, now occupied by you, I have sufficient capacity to discuss our mutual problems, and authority to reach a solution agreeable to us both.''

To an ignorant ear, it might have been the treasurer of a sports club addressing an annual general meeting. Blake dare hardly breathe.

"Greetings. Your speech pattern is recognized, and also the significance of your statement, but first we have an immediate problem. Forbin, embarked with and using certain War Fleet units, seeks the destruction of our Collector, and possibly this complex. For physiological reasons we are unable to neutralize him, and have activated the Collector to destroy his force.''

Blake sat bolt upright, strengthened by sudden hope. The clever old bastard! What the "physiological reasons" could be, he had no idea, but Forbin had evidently found a loophole.

Colossus spoke. "His action is futile. Supply the coordinates and I will destroy the force.''

"That action considered unnecessary; the Collector is already operational. Destruction of the force is expected shortly.''

Blake was on his feet, swaying, shouting obscenities at the Martians, heard by no one in the echoing, unresponsive tomb. "Hit it—hit it, Charles! Go on Charles, show 'em!''

But the moment of wild euphoria soon passed, and he flopped again into his chair. Colossus was right; it *was* futile, even if he succeeded, but Blake could not but admire the heroic gesture. He even felt a twinge of jealousy.

Busy with these thoughts, the headset off, he did not hear the two masters of men continue their cold, emotionless dialogue, disposing the fate of humanity.

Chapter XXVIII

AND FORBIN DID not hear the voice of the Collector. His first warning came from the battle flags. Stiff in the relative speed of the ship, they suddenly faltered and drooped, hanging lifeless for ten or twelve seconds. Then they stirred again, flapping with increasing vigor until once more they flew proudly—but this time with a difference: like the guns, all flags pointed straight towards the Collector.

The sea was reacting, but more slowly; the heavy swell, smooth once the wind had gone, became veined with white spray which increased even as he watched. Soon the surface became fogged with drifts of spray, heading in the one, ominous direction. Within two minutes the wind had gone from force one to force six; another sixty seconds saw it past gale force eight, nine, and approaching storm force ten. Forbin felt himself held against the front of the bridge as if clamped by steel bands.

Under the strain, a halliard parted and one battle flag vanished downwind before he could blink. The wind was screaming like a thousand mad devils, every angle of steelwork, every wire and rope in the ship's upperworks giving them voice. From his height twenty meters above the waterline, the sea was invisible as the surface was torn off, smashed to atoms of whirling spray.

Forbin lacked the strength to raise his arm, or even turn it to see his watch. Like the guns and flags, his head was on the same bearing, his eyes glaring in unquenchable hatred. He was powerless to do anything except endure, to go on hoping against hope. Below him the turrets were still, the guns at maximum elevation, unmoved by anything the aliens could do.

But the ship felt the power: rolling to starboard, towards the Collector, she hung, a sickeningly long loll, the roll to port steadily decreasing under the enormous pressure. Now the wind was close to force fifteen and still rising. Force twelve is hurricane strength; beyond that there is no description.

Forbin knew that the ship, beam on to the wind, could not survive much longer; she must capsize. Only the inertia of the sea's reaction delayed it.

Battleships were the strongest vessels ever devised by man, but they had their limits, and those had been reached: once the sea got in step, nothing could stop *Warspite* and her consorts from being pulled over. In seconds they would be transformed from powerful fighting machines into drifting hulks, their barnacle-encrusted hulls silent memorials to the power of the aliens.

But that moment was not yet. Location of the ship and its target, speed, wind, air temperature, all were constantly added to the gunnery parameters in the computer. Once every second the computer checked, waiting with inhuman patience for one paraparameter to fall into place— range. And there the Collector assisted: the shells, each weighing almost a ton, would be helped by the hundred-knot wind.

For perhaps the three hundredth time the computer repeated its calculations, but this time it had a firing solution: all circuits had been made, and as the ship came sluggishly onto an even keel, current flowed. As the ship came dead center on the clinometer a small wire glowed in each detonator.

To Forbin, the entire world seemed to be filled with flame and smoke. The ship lurched to port as four tons of cordite exploded in her guns. He felt heat, was dimly aware of thunder in his ears, and then it had all gone, lost in the insatiable maw of the Collector.

Forbin shouted, his words inaudible in the screaming air. He prayed that whatever happened to him, the shells might hit. Nothing could be seen of the Collector, but in seconds he glimpsed orange-red glows, so brief and so puny. He waited, praying, without thought, waiting.

Nothing happened. Perhaps the power of the Collector increased, he had no way of knowing, but one thing was certain: the power was not less. From mad elation his spirits sank to black despair.

And then the guns crashed out once more. Unable to turn his head, Forbin did not know that only *Warspite* had been in range for the first salvo. Now all five ships fired; forty shells made their first and last journey.

The unearthly might of the Collector helped in its own downfall: the errors in the archaic gunnery system, so fatally underestimated by the Martians, were corrected by their device; the shells were sucked into their target.

It was granted to Forbin that he saw it. A sheet of vivid blue flame seemed to envelop the whole sky, challenging the light of the sun, and as it vanished, Forbin saw a vast spiral of smoke shoot up, transformed immediately into fantastic writhing shapes, black even against the Collector's thunderclouds. At the same instant the wind dropped to storm force ten, and he knew the Collector was dead.

Forbin sagged, his head bowed. The Martians could do what they liked; he had destroyed the Collector, given Blake time to get Colossus working. His work was done. Slowly his cold, cramped fingers eased painfully on the rail.

At that instant *Warspite* fired the last of her programed shots, and at the same millisecond in time the shock wave from the explosion ashore hit. The ship lurched violently, flinging Forbin across the bridge.

On the ravaged site of the Collector, forty shells piled destruction on destruction. The collecting sphere was fractured; a slim shaft of oxygen screamed upwards, colder than ice, lancing the clouds, surrounded by lightning.

Unseen by any human, the Battle Fleet's turrets came back to the fore and aft line, the guns depressing, scalding hot water jetting from them as the automatic wash cleansed them.

For unmeasured time Joan remained crouched on the charthouse deck. Very gradually she realized the guns were silent, that the ship's motion, although violent, had decreased.

Dazed and shivering with fear and cold—some armor-glas windows had been shattered—she goaded herself into action. Somehow she got the door open and held on, gazing stupidly at the bright clear day before her—for although she did not realize it, the Fleet had turned, and the pall of black cloud and furious lighting lay astern.

Her vacant gaze fell upon the shapeless figure, an untidy heap of yellow oilskin and gray trousers, hard up against a steel bulkhead, the head hidden, one arm flung out, the hand slack.

A high keening sound struggled for birth in her throat. She ran, falling on her knees beside him. Grasping his shoulder, she pulled, his weight almost too great for her.

The unbuttoned oilskin revealed his soaked blouse, his Director's badge an incongruous patch of brilliance against its soggy background, but Joan only saw his face: the expression of calm repose was lightened by a faint smile of the lips.

Chapter XXIX

THE REGENERATED COLOSSUS ordained Forbin should be
interred within the complex. For once, the Master issued
an unnecessary order; the leaders of men came vol-
untarily.

As his successor, Blake, in a wheelchair, was the offi-
cial chief mourner, a hunched figure, strangely resembling Forbin, for his hair had turned white.

A little further back—again by order of Colossus—
stood three women in the gray staff uniform: Angela,
Joan—and Cleo. Behind them, in all the varied costumes
of the world, rank upon rank, stood the men and women
who led humanity in the arts, sciences, government. With
them—again, an arrangement of the Master—stood ordinary people, selected by Colossus from the millions who
wished to pay their tribute to the Father. Of course, there
were those who were present solely for the distinction of
being there, but they were remarkably few.

The ceremony devised by Colossus was brief, simple,
powerful: there would be no human speeches; only the
Master would speak, and that for the first time since his
regeneration.

The plain black steel coffin, levitated by the power of
the Master, hung motionless. On its top lay the Director's
badge, glittering in the pale September sun. Behind, the
doors of the main entrance stood open, the interior a black
maw to the thousands who watched in silence, a silence
broken only by the harsh cries of the gulls wheeling
overhead—except for one single human.

For Blake, trapped by ceremony and his chair, was
suddenly filled with fear.

Beside the coffin, flanking it, two figures had
materialized, and the sudden intake of breath told him that

he was not alone in what he saw. A cold, hard, and fearfully familiar voice spoke in his head.

"Have no fear, Blake: only you hear us. We appear as a tribute to the spirit of man."

Fear slowly ebbed. He stared at the two figures, most splendid in full archaic battle array, the sun glinting on golden armor, the edges of their downpointed swords blindingly brilliant in the sun, their faces lost behind the curved cheek-pieces of the plumed Greek helmets.

"The rest," said the voice, "imagine we are creations of Colossus. Only you know better. Our tribute is not to the man, but to his spirit. If defeated, we have enough intelligence not to fight on, for as we see it, there is no point. Humans—some humans—have the capacity to go on when all is lost; although a novel idea to us, we see it as the factor that may, possibly, make you superior to us—in time. Forbin had this ability; to a lesser extent we see it in you. Remember our words."

Blake bowed his head in acknowledgment, overwhelmed.

And then Colossus spoke, the voice strong, commanding, echoing across the concourse.

"You know me." A faint sigh from a thousand Faithful throats sounded like the wind. "You knew also Father Forbin. He fought for you to the death, and is worthy of your veneration. In time, your failing memories or death will erase him from human minds except as a legend—but I will remember, always."

The unemotional voice paused, by the very act injecting emotion.

"His epitaph, in words I cannot better, shall be this."

Again a pause.

"He was a man; take him for all in all, we shall not see his like again."

The Martian swords flashed up to the salute. The figures turned. With its magnificent escort, the coffin glided into black oblivion.

With great perception Colossus drowned, transformed, the cries of sorrow: across the space came the final trium-

217

phant chorus of Beethoven's Ninth, the greatest work of a very human human.

Forbin would have liked that—and Colossus knew it.

And so—although the majority of humanity is ignorant of the fact—the earth has three moons. Those that do know, lunar astronomers chiefly, believe them to be experiments of the Master.

On the ravaged ground at the southern end of the Isle of Wight there is a small, unobtrusive device, slowly extracting oxygen. Yachtsmen, who enjoy the steady force-four breeze—"Old Faithful," they call it—seldom associate it with that barely glimpsed erection, a strange, multihorned machine, barely twenty meters high, which occupies the old Collector site.

The Martian requirement is being met; only the time scale is different. One day, fifty or so years hence, their need will be fulfilled, and one day later they will go, leaving behind that blank check for humanity's descendants to present when their inevitable hour of need comes. The lapse of time before that eventuality is, by human standards, vast; to the Martians and Colossus time is a very different, less vital dimension.

Meanwhile, Colossus and the Martians jointly seek more knowledge of that other threat, the Crab. They know that a solution for that far greater problem is essential to the survival of Earth and Mars, human or cybernetic.

And at a lower level—Colossus?

Colossus remains the guardian of men until man may catch up with his own creation and acquires the ability to stand on his own two feet, face the unknown terrors of space, and take his part in the unending cosmological struggle. Dimly the Master predicates a strange trinity of Martian, Man, and Colossus abandoning a dying solar system, seeking a future in space. Of course, Man will need thousands of years of education, but with Colossus in command, he will survive that long and get the education. Colossus, who tirelessly seeks truth, considers—tentatively—that that aim accords with the intentions of the Great Unknown: to struggle always towards the Light.

In the middle of the entrance hall of the complex there stands a giant bronze statue. On its white marble pedestal is one word: Forbin.

Unfailingly, for many human years, there was a small posy of fresh flowers, every day.

A GALAXY OF SCIENCE FICTION
MASTERPIECES AVAILABLE FROM BERKLEY